NATHAN'S BIG SKY

A HENDERSON'S RANCH ROMANCE

M. L. BUCHMAN

Buchman Bookworks

SIGN UP FOR M. L. BUCHMAN'S NEWSLETTER TODAY

and receive:
Release News
Free Short Stories
a Free book

Do it today. Do it now.
www.mlbuchman.com/newsletter

To Gibson the dog, and the good friend who named him for one of my characters.
Also my thanks to my friends Pat and Donna for their guidance and stories.

CHAPTER 1

*T*he silence was deafening.

Nathan gripped the crowbar-handle of his car's jack so tightly that it hurt his hand but he couldn't ease up. It was his sole hope of survival.

The only sound for miles on the emptiness of the Montana prairie was the hot-metal pinging of his cooling Miata sports car, lurched awkwardly to the roadside by a flat tire. The chill of the cold April evening almost hurt his lungs. The sun hadn't quite set; instead it illuminated the clouds of his own breath like some horror movie with a fog machine turned on too high.

How was it that he'd come to this place to die?

Chefs were *not* supposed to die alone in the forsaken wilderness, they were supposed to have a butter-induced heart attack in the middle of a meal service. But the safety of his New York kitchen lay an impossible distance behind him. He'd bolted forty-eight hours ago, sleeping only a few fitful hours in Chicago before punching west as if all the hounds of hell were after him.

And they'd caught up with him in the form of a monster.

Two days to cross most of the country and now, like a

gunslinger fated to his doom, he was going to be murdered in the emptiness of the Montana wilderness by the largest cow ever born.

It put Paul Bunyan's mythically massive blue ox Babe to shame.

Purest black, it was an inkblot on the continuance of Nathan's life.

Horns the length of a New York cabbie's woes sprang from either side of its head, ending in points that looked sharper than his finest boning knife.

He'd hit Choteau, Montana, in the late afternoon for directions, as his little brother's instructions had turned out to be utterly useless: "Henderson Ranch, just west of Choteau." There wasn't a single app on his phone that told him where the ranch might be. There'd also been no answer on his brother's phone, but he was used to that. Apparently most of the ranch was beyond the pale of civilization and didn't have reception. His brother had always been useless about answering the phone anyway, unless you were a pretty girl—them he'd always had a sixth sense for, even on a blocked number.

Maybe Patrick's directions sucked because he was messing with his big brother. Or maybe it was because he assumed Nathan would never cross west of the Hudson River—which historically was a reasonable assumption—so it wasn't worth the effort to be more descriptive.

A Choteau (*Cho-toe* that was almost *Sho-toe*) local had known the name, however. In a town only three blocks long, it made sense that he did. "Just go down the highway apiece until you hit Anderson's farm. Can't miss it. He has the last big white cow barn this side of Augusta. Take a right on the main road and go on until you've just about hit the mountains. Out onto the dirt a ways. That'll set you in the right place."

The "highway" was a narrow two-lane called Montana 287.

By the time Choteau was two miles behind him, he'd passed two Andersons, an Andersen, and an Andreassen. This driveway had no mailbox that he could see, but it had a big white barn and a road along one side of the property. The map on his cell phone said that Augusta was fifty miles ahead. Telling him "the last big barn before Augusta" counted as a local having fun chapping his ass. He must have taken one look at Nathan's two-seater Miata and painted a little mental target on Nathan's forehead—just as the monster cow now had one painted on Nathan's life.

The turnoff road was a lane and a half wide. Nathan guessed that in its favor, it was paved and had an actual stop sign where it met the "highway." Sunlight was streaming out the backside of the sign through several bullet holes. He wondered if someone was going to shoot him for being in a sports car instead of a pickup with a gun rack.

Did upstate New York even have roads like this one—not even two lanes wide and with no painted stripes? Or was that only legal west of the Mississippi? Manhattan and Long Island certainly didn't. During his five years in Paris, he'd rarely been farther out than the Metro could carry him.

For thirty miles past the white cow barn, he drove unknowingly toward his doom as the mountains drew closer and closer. He kept assuming he'd reach them in another few miles and they insisted on teasing him just like his brother. After the unremitting flatness of the Great Plains, they had loomed tall and rough to the west as seen from Choteau. Now he was discovering that Australia wasn't the only place that had an Outback.

The peaks kept growing bigger and climbing higher but the land remained flatter than the ocean off Coney Island on a hot summer's day. The peaks' jagged flanks were shrouded in snow despite it being April. He turned on the Miata's heater as the sun settled toward the west, but he left the convertible top down because the view was so amazing. The blue sky arced forever over him until the mountains sliced it off like a kid's construction project: sharp, jagged, unreal.

Each time he'd passed a ranch, he checked the name, but none said Henderson. He even pulled out his phone to check that he'd remembered it right—and almost drove his car into the gaping ditch. Not a good idea. For all he knew, there might not be another person down this road for a week. He'd seen a few tractors—which were far bigger than he thought they would be—far out in the fields, but no one else on the road.

With a crash and thud that made him check his rearview to see if he'd left an axle on the road behind him, the pavement ended.

"Out onto the dirt a ways." Maybe the old-timer in Choteau hadn't been completely chapping his ass.

He slowed down to preserve his suspension. A cloud of brown dust obliterated his past. If he wanted to turn around, he'd have to eat his own dust. That sounded like a properly cowboy-like metaphor for the last decade of his life. Two days ago he'd cut every tie to that past. If only he could figure out how that had led him to the Montanan Outback, he wouldn't feel quite so overwhelmed at the moment. Twenty-eight years old and his life fit in a two-seater sports car—with room to spare. That might not be right, but it didn't make it any less true.

For the last ten miles he'd been hoping to meet someone on the road to ask directions again. Or maybe how to escape, little knowing it would soon be too late.

The dirt road narrowed and then he actually hoped he didn't meet anyone because he'd have to crawl to the side to get by them. Out here he wasn't threatened by ditches anymore, they'd disappeared along with the pavement, but instead by barbed wire running close down either side of the dirt track. Not a chance that his Soul Red Metallic paint job would survive the encounter.

After a few miles of dodging potholes and gritting his teeth over washboard ripples, he started looking for a place to turn around. The road wasn't wide enough to be sure he could turn even his small car without dinging it up.

He'd been climbing slowly since Choteau, and spring had turned back into winter. There was a bitter snap to the evening air that promised what looked like snow and ice up ahead...really *was* snow and ice up ahead. By this point the mountains were so high they looked as if they were going to roll over and land on him.

Manhattan didn't have places like this. Neither did Paris, where he'd done his time at Le Cordon Bleu and three years servitude for Chef Guevarre—may his brutal training and magnificent palate both be in hell by now. There was something wrong about the flatness behind and the impossible mountains ahead.

Then, topping a low rise, facing straight into the setting sun, he was confronted by the beast from hell that was going to kill him.

He'd slammed on the brakes, skidding sideways on the washboard gravel, and barely managed to avoid hitting the cow. A tire caught in a pothole where it had blown with a loud bang that scared him almost as much as the creature of his doom had.

Now he stood in the middle of the road between his crippled car, pinging the last dying notes of its hot-metal song, and the monstrous black cow that was about to charge him. The damn thing didn't so much as blink its malevolent eyes, as if it was trying to hypnotize him.

His only weapon choices were his chef's knives, which would be very useful if the cow was already dead and butchered but not until then, and his car's jack handle. Retreating into his car and pulling up the convertible's roof would be pointless—this monster was so big it could practically step over the Miata. And the tips of its horns were actually wider than the car itself.

His ears rang with the silence, now broken only by a scuffing of one New York metro bus-sized hoof as the cow prepared to charge. Nathan had served a thousand roasts, ten thousand steaks, and this meal-still-on-the-hoof knew it. It had come to exact revenge for all of its spiritual forebears...fore-steaks?

The last thing Nathan was going to smell was the crackling dry grass of the prairie, the biting chill of the fast-approaching night, and the hot breath of the demon cow so big it seemed to block out even the vast expanse of the Montana sky. There had been fourteen hundred miles of flat since Chicago, but here, with his back up against the mountains, the vast horizon seemed far bigger than should be possible. His last-ever vision would be to actually see the curvature of the earth.

Then, impossibly, as if it wasn't bad enough that his epitaph was going to read: *Here a once-decent chef was trampled to death by a cow*—trampled sounded like a marginally more pleasant way to go than gored—he heard a clip-clop sound coming from behind him.

He didn't dare turn, because he knew the beast-cow would charge the moment he looked aside.

Still, the sound behind him grew.

Unable to stand it any longer—the sound was so close—he spun and raised his foot-long jack handle in one last desperate bid for life.

Backed by the sun, a silhouetted cowboy sat up on a horse even taller than the cow and looked down at Nathan from under the brim of his cowboy hat.

"What are you doing out in the road?"

Not cowboy, cowgirl. A soft voice, but no less disgusted for all that. Against the dazzling sun he could see that she wore cowboy boots, a heavy leather jacket, and had a rifle tucked close to hand.

Hope?

Maybe she could shoot the demon cow before it trampled, trompled, gored, or whatever demon cows did.

He tried to speak, but his throat was clogged dry with fear and road dust. The air was so dry it seemed to suck the moisture right out of him.

She rode around him and his car as if he wasn't even there. "Go on now, Lucy. Scoot!"

A hell-beast named Lucy?

He'd had a great Aunt Lucy, but she hadn't been very fierce— more the quiet and retiring type, which was perhaps inevitable beside her husband's garrulous stockbroker charisma.

The woman rode her black-and-white patterned horse up to the "monster cow from hell" before he could warn her off.

Yet, in a startlingly sudden surrender, the gigantic animal turned and ambled back through a broken gap in the barbed wire fence that Nathan hadn't noticed. As it walked, he recognized the scuffing sound that he'd thought proceeded a deadly charge—it was just the sound the cow made by walking.

After riding her horse through the gap as well, she then swung a long leg over the back of the saddle and came down out of the sky. Paying no more attention to him than if he was a bump in the road, she pulled out some tools and walked up to the fence.

He could only watch—numb with his unexpected last-second stay of execution and the biting cold—as she repaired the fence. It was only the work of minutes before she had three fine strands of barbed wire strung back up between the posts; her and the cow on one side and he and his broken car on the other. The flimsy wires had no chance of stopping a baby cow, never mind the hell cow Lucy, currently tearing at the low dead grass.

The woman had been towering in the saddle; on the ground she was still tall. Perhaps slender beneath the heavy leather jacket. Straight, light blond hair fell past her shoulders. Her cheeks were rosy with the cold, which he'd always thought was just a saying.

When she finished, he finally found his voice before she could disappear back into the landscape as eerily as she'd arrived.

"Excuse me, can you tell me how to get to Henderson Ranch?"

"I can," he could just see her eyes beneath the wide brim of her cowboy hat. They were as brilliant blue as the sky and seemed to be laughing at him, though her mouth wasn't. What was it with locals chapping his ass today?

"Would you mind telling me?"

"Not a bit," and she let it hang long enough to make him sigh. The failing sun caught the cloud of his breath in the chill air.

"You're standing on Henderson land."

"I am?" he looked down at the road, but it was keeping its secrets to itself. "This doesn't look like a ranch, it looks like a whole bunch of nothing."

"It's two *ranches*," she sounded miffed by his description, which, he decided on review, hadn't been the most tactful thing he'd ever said. "You're standing on Henderson's, but your passenger seat is on mine—property line runs up the middle of the lane. You've been on Mac and Ama's land for the last five miles or so. If you'd like, I can chop your car in two and then you'll be off *my* family's land."

"That's okay. I like my car the way it is."

"Even with the flat?"

"Okay, except for the flat." Was this what passed for a sense of humor out here, or was she about to pull the rifle hanging on her horse's saddle and make good on her offer—maybe shooting his poor car for trespassing before skinning it? Perhaps it would be safer if he kept her talking. "What are you doing way out here?"

"Riding the fence."

He assumed that meant something to someone other than him, but he couldn't figure out how to ask what. Her horse stepped up to her and rested its chin over her shoulder. She reached up a gloved hand and patted it on the cheek a couple of times.

"I was looking for different," and it didn't get more different than the woman in front of him.

"Thought you were looking for Henderson's."

"I was. I am," and he was on the verge of being turned into a babbling idiot. He'd left New York looking for a change. For something he'd never done, someone he'd never been. Couldn't get more different than a burned-out New York chef and a tall, blond cowgirl out "riding a fence" who had a horse for a pet.

"Their drive is another mile yet, on the left. Can't miss it," she tipped her head toward farther down the road. Then, in a move so smooth she might have been doing it since birth, she stepped one foot up into a high stirrup and swung atop the tall horse. He'd briefly dated an American Ballet Theater dancer—sleeping through her performance had not earned him many bonus points —who didn't have the grace or posture of this cowgirl. Cow-woman. Was that a real phrase? She stepped once more into line with the low sun and he lost her in the glare.

"Thanks," he called out. One of his more charming lines.

"Need help with the tire?"

"I can change a flat."

Her blinding silhouette nodded as if that might be a miracle worth witnessing, then tipped her hat and turned to ride away. He couldn't argue with that conclusion, but it would be too embar-rassing to admit his gross incompetence.

"Will I see you again?"

"It depends," she spoke over her shoulder without fully turning.

"On what?" Nathan had to call more loudly as she headed away perpendicular to the road.

"On how long I can avoid you."

UNWILLING TO TURN, Julie Larson kept an ear out. It took a bit, but then she heard a soft laugh.

A minute later, the rattling sound of someone jacking a car—a sound far enough away to be no louder than the ticking of a lone cricket. Anything else was lost beneath the sound of the last of the dry winter grass swishing against Clarence's hocks, but that laugh intrigued her. She didn't know why the man made her more prickly than a stinging nettle.

This had been the last stretch of the fence line. There were a half dozen places where the winter had snapped a post and occasional runs where wood rot had finally taken down a whole stretch of wire, but nothing bad in the entire run. In the morning she'd grab one of the hands and a truck; they'd have the spring pasture put together before the cattle were ready for it. Old Lucy had somehow slipped in early, but she'd been a certified escape artist since her third day afoot.

Will I see you again?

"Not a chance, city boy. I've already got my big strong man. Don't I?" she leaned forward to scrub at the side of Clarence's neck as his ears pricked back to listen to her. What was it with city boys and a woman on a horse? For that matter, what was it with cowboys and a woman on a horse?

Number One question: *You aren't married?* (delivered with an astonished gasp). Twenty-six and single was definitely a crime. Or at least a freak of nature.

Number Two question: *Wa'll how about me, darlin'?* (as if a lame Texas accent worked wonders in the Montana Front Range).

I was looking for different.

What had he meant by that? Didn't matter—he was Mac and Ama's problem now.

She leaned in just enough for Clarence to lift up to a quick trot. It was still comfortably above freezing, but there wasn't a cloud in sight so it would chill down fast once the sun hit the horizon. Even now the long shadows of Old Baldy and Rocky Mountain stretched across the prairie leaving her in a narrow slash of red-gold sunlight across the still-brown prairie.

Julie resisted Clarence's urge to gallop. She didn't want him to get all heated before a cold night in the barn.

Different. The city boy had that right. A sports car in the land of pickup trucks. A convertible in a place where rocketing winds and plunging temperatures defined seven months of the year. He had tousled dark hair, warm eyes, and an easy smile that seemed to be aimed first of all at himself.

Different. She looked at the sweep of land around her, the Larson barn, house, and sheds coming into view, and wondered at it. There were so many things to love here, but different wasn't one of them.

Clarence asked again with a shift in his stride. She eased off and let him slip into a canter. Even big, handsome boys like him deserved to have some fun. She tugged down on the brim of her hat to make sure she didn't lose it and decided that she deserved some fun, too. She gave Clarence his head and between one stride and the next he took her to the pure exhilaration of a full gallop over the rolling pastureland.

Why anyone would want *different* when they could have this, she didn't know.

~

IN NEW YORK, turning onto someone's driveway said that you were close to the house. Out here it apparently meant only that you were in the same time zone.

At the turnoff, the first one in miles, a big arch of wood weathering to gray crossed above the dirt drive—no smaller than the road he'd been on. The headlights barely caught the carved "Henderson Ranch" in big letters with a horseshoe nailed in at either end.

It had taken forever to change the tire, thank goodness the manual had pictures or he'd still be out there wondering what a lug nut was. Though a flashlight certainly would have helped. He'd been able to see the manual in the dome light, but he'd finished hanging the wheel in darkness by feel alone. Even with the top up and the heater on high for the last stretch, he wondered if his fingers would ever recover.

A mile or more up the lane and around a low hill he spotted a porch light and had never so felt like he was coming home. To his left were several big barns and sheds. A few small houses lay beyond them. The main house, the one with the ever-so-welcoming porch light, was a big, two-story, log cabin structure. The foundation was stonework and the roof disappeared steeply into the night. There was a real elegance to the place—no less than a Long Island mansion, but in a style all its own.

When he'd finished changing the tire, he had stood up—and was utterly alone. The only sound was the chattering of his teeth. He'd swear he could hear the starlight puncturing brilliant holes through the ice-cold air.

Where was the stunning blonde now? Had she ridden off into the dazzling sunset and gone back to some Montana fairyland in the sky? He could almost believe it. She'd galloped away so fast into the orange sun that it was as if she'd sucked the light out of the sky with her slipstream.

He'd never had a pet and the women he'd dated never anything bigger than a cat, but the cowgirl made a horse seem like such a natural companion that it was hard to imagine her with anything less.

"Not going to find a welcome there," he told the night.

She'd ridden away from him without a name or a backward glance.

Had her driveway been around the next bend, or was her family ranch so big that he'd need to set his watch ahead an hour in order to find her?

Well, he was here. Finally. Unsure where else to go, he climbed out of the car and stumbled up the ranch house's broad wooden steps onto the deep porch that ran off either direction into the darkness. The door was a warm red with a semicircular arch of glass above that glowed with a soft light.

He knocked. Waited. Knocked again harder. If he had to camp in his car on this Arctic night, he was in deep trouble.

The door creaked open and a tall woman with dark, Native American features and waist-long straight hair—black and shot with steely gray—looked at him eye to eye. She wore jeans and a simple flannel shirt. She was positively majestic, except for her pink bunny slippers.

She noticed the direction of his attention, "A Christmas gift from my daughter-in-law. She has a curious sense of humor." The first words spoken between them. She had a warm, steady voice, as if nothing in the world could ever surprise her.

Then she looked right at him for a long moment as he shivered on the threshold.

"You are lost," she said simply and stepped aside, then waved him in.

"No," Nathan stepped into the firelit warmth chaffing his hands together. "If this is Henderson Ranch, I think I'm found."

If the woman smiled, it wasn't on the outside.

"Sorry, best line I've got after the crazy evening I've had."

She turned and walked away without another word, but he had the impression that he should follow.

He almost lost track of her when he stepped forward. The entryway gave way to a massive great room. Cedar finish, gigantic beams, shining hardwood floor, and a towering stone fireplace: it was an absolute showpiece. But it was also much more than that. Red and brown leather couches were gathered in comfortable groupings. Geometric throws of strong colors were draped over the backs of the couches.

"This is like a cliché out of Montanan Architectural Digest." His tact-o-meter had never been high but tonight he seemed to be hitting new lows.

"Yes," her voice echoed from somewhere back to the left.

He tracked her through an arch into a large dining room, with a rough wooden table that could seat thirty or more family style, and into a kitchen.

"It is what most guests expect when they come to vacation on a working ranch. It makes them happy when they find it just as they'd expect. It has been three generations since my family wove Cheyenne rugs. But I researched and studied the techniques and now teach classes for guests because they expect it from someone like me."

"I suppose that's irony at its finest." A weaving class taught by such a striking and regal Cheyenne woman, he'd sign up for that class in a heartbeat. "Do you at least enjoy it?"

"Very much, or what would be the purpose?" This must be the Ama of "Mac and Ama's" that the blond cowgirl had referred to.

He meant to ask some polite question next, perhaps even introduce himself, but that thought was gone the moment he looked about the kitchen. The chef in him almost drooled with envy.

It wasn't a commercial kitchen, not really, but neither was it a residential one. There was a large prep island with a wide array of cast iron and copper pans hanging on iron hooks above. Below were sheet pans, cutting boards, and a dozen other handy containers for large-scale meal preparation. The gas range had a dozen burners, and there was a broad griddle plus three ovens. A pair of big Sub-Zero side-by-side refrigerators dominated one end of the room. And it wasn't merely the space: it had the best of everything from its borderland between residential and commercial. The pair of the largest residential KitchenAid stand mixers, a big Cuisinart, a Vitamix blender and juicer: everything a chef could need to have unlimited options. The cabinets were bright oak and the counters dark granite. It screamed cozy efficiency.

At the other end of the room was another dining table, this one for a dozen at most. The family dining room. There was also a single gathering of chairs and couches around another stone fireplace. So, not just the family dining room, this was the part of the house used by the family, whether or not there were guests.

"Can I stay forever?" He meant it as a joke but the woman, who had yet to introduce herself, simply put on the teakettle and pulled out a drawer with a dozen flavors of tea for him to choose from. He selected chamomile because his nerves definitely didn't need caffeine at this point.

As he watched the kettle not boiling, Ama set about other tasks. By the time he had his tea, a steaming bowl of vegetable beef stew and a slab of homemade bread were waiting for him on the big table. He dipped the first slice and tasted the stew. Carrot, sweet parsnip, chunks of potato, and long-cooked beef in a thick gravy that was so good it was dribbling down his chin as he tried to eat it too fast. Thyme and bay, salt and pepper, and a dash of... not hot sauce...Worcestershire Sauce. The beef was tender and rich—definitely grass fed to get that degree of flavor with a moderate Burgundy red wine.

"Now I'm definitely found!" If this was farm cooking, he was all over it.

The woman tipped her head as if to say maybe.

"I'm Nathan Gallagher, Patrick's brother."

She nodded as if that much was obvious, even though he and Patrick looked nothing alike. Sons of different fathers—his own hadn't stuck much past conception. Patrick's had arrived before Nathan's birth and raised them both as his own.

"Is my little brother around?"

"He is in Great Falls, then Bozeman, making deliveries and getting a load of supplies. He should be back tomorrow night, maybe the next. Your bedroom is through there," she pointed to a door off the kitchen. She couldn't have known he was coming, he barely knew he was coming himself until he arrived here. Yet she'd said *your bedroom* not as if he was a visitor or guest, but as if he somehow belonged here.

Though it would only be for a few days, Nathan welcomed the *suggestion* of stability. The world's rug had been yanked out from under his feet in the last few days and even a moment's respite was welcome.

He really was in heaven. Another taste of the stew. It was

simple, rich, but there was one flavor more that he couldn't quite identify. "What's—"

But he was alone in the kitchen as if it had always been that way. He never heard her leave on her bunny slippers and now he wondered if he'd dreamed her, just like the cowgirl and her two-toned horse.

CHAPTER 2

*J*ulie dreamt of clowns.

Small ones. Tall ones. Wide and narrow. All driving teeny, tiny cars and brandishing teeny, tiny steel bars at one of the gentlest cows on the range.

And all making her want to smile. Not at their ludicrous gestures and overblown reactions, but because they all smiled at her as if she was something special.

The only clowns she was used to were the ones at the county rodeos to distract the bulls after the rider was thrown. On this cold April morning, the summer rodeos were still too far off for even dreaming. She hadn't decided if she'd sign up this year or just go and watch from the stands.

She rolled out of bed in time to help Ma with the cooking. Dad and her three older brothers came in from the barn as they were finishing up, with Dad handing out orders like usual.

"Matthew, get that bale stacker greased and going by noon. The cows aren't going to feed themselves for another month yet. Mark and Luke, check the Poplar Creek pasture. They're dropping their calves like hotcakes right now; bound to be a couple in trouble out that way. Julie—"

She always wondered how much it irritated her father that he'd had a girl instead of a boy that he could name John, but he was such a stern man that she'd never dared ask. At least he'd resisted naming her Johanna. That would have made it even more of a slap in the face.

"—finish riding the spring pasture fence line today."

"Already done. I fixed a lot of little things yesterday. I'll take the F-150 and some posts. I'll have the whole spring pasture clean and tight by midday."

"Good girl."

"Then I'm switching over."

That just earned her a grunt.

She had her own business to run, no matter how busy the spring season was on a cattle ranch. Frankly, if she never saw a birthing cow again, it would be too soon. It was freezing April and they were as likely to drop their newborns on a wind-torn snowbank as a soft bed of winter grass in a sheltered hollow. Cows started out dumber than most sheep, but the more trouble they were having, the dumber they became. The twins, Mark and Luke, were likely to find a hard birth in the middle of a stream where the cow could also fight the battle of hypothermia and drowning, as if giving birth weren't a challenge enough for a woman.

"Don't forget we've got a party tonight. I expect you all to be clean and presentable," her father rode over her reminder that J. L. Building was launching its second year tomorrow—its first full year if she could find the contracts.

Wait. "What party?"

Her father's scowl said she should have kept her mouth shut and asked Ma.

But May Larson saved her only daughter, something she didn't do much for the boys. "Hendersons. Mark and your friend Emily are moving back to the ranch."

"Oh, that's tonight?" She barely remembered it as news at all. She didn't know Mac and Ama's son particularly except that he was ex-military of some sort. Julie had met him a few times, but the guys tended to cluster around the "military man" so she'd had little contact with him.

She knew Emily a little better and liked her well enough. She was a stern, taciturn blonde—an incredibly striking one. On the rare occasions they were together, they drew puzzled looks. Other than her white blond to Emily's golden, folks who didn't know them seemed split on asking if they were mother-daughter or sisters. Probably because she was an Easterner, it was impossible to tell what Emily was thinking and Julie had always been a little uncomfortable around her. Julie would never label her as a friend.

Dad's scowl said exactly what he thought of Julie not keeping up on such things. And probably a hundred other things wrong with her, like her still being single rather than bringing another man into the family to work the ranch. Oh! Which was exactly why her father wanted her to be excited about tonight's party. It would be the first gathering after the hard winter snows and hands would be coming from all the ranches around. The place would be packed with eligible bachelors.

Someone please shoot her now. She'd rather spend the night with Lucy out in a cold camp.

Then the last piece connected.

J. L. Building's one contract for work was at Henderson's, enough to last her through the first month or more. And that's where that guy in the tiny clown car had been headed. With the way her luck ran with men, he'd be on the ranch the whole time she was working there, underfoot and in the way.

The local boys had learned not to mess with her. A hand on her ass was likely to earn a slicing swing with the short end of a hard lariat rope across theirs. That settled most of them quick enough.

But city boys were like puppy dogs—she never quite had the

heart to shoo them away so harshly that they'd actually remember it.

She suspected that she'd have to make it extra clear this time.

∾

NATHAN HADN'T THOUGHT to close the curtains so he woke when the sunrise pounded into his face. He could have slept a dozen more hours. He'd barely slept in his final week in New York—being a chef at a high-end restaurant like Vite, sleep wasn't a big part of his life. Then the two-day mad dash across the country.

He tried pulling the covers over his head, but the room was freezing. He peeked out and saw a thermostat on the wall. He hadn't noticed it last night. With the bowl of warm stew inside him and twenty-two hundred miles behind him, he hadn't noticed much of anything. The thermostat's little handle was slid all the way to the left.

He bolted from the barely warm covers and into icy clothes that had him rushing into the kitchen praying for a cup of hot coffee. At sunrise he expected to be alone. It was an hour he was wholly unfamiliar with except as the time of day for that brief excursion to do the day's shopping for the restaurant at the fresh markets.

His normal day started in late afternoon, ran through dinner service, a couple of bars, half a night's sleep, a few hours of shopping if he couldn't palm it off on some other chef, more sleep, and waking in time for a late lunch before prep began for the next dinner service.

He stepped into the gorgeous farm kitchen now flooded with early morning sunlight. The dark granite warmed. The rich oak glowed and the burnished steel did some other welcoming adjective that he'd think up after he had some caffeine flowing through his system.

Ama Henderson was at one of the counters greasing up a pair of big waffle irons.

Nathan found a mug, filled it from the round glass pot on the commercial dual-bay coffee maker. A brief search turned up cream and sugar.

He didn't see any batter going yet.

She made no comment as he pulled out a steel bowl and a basket of eggs. They were dirty, like they'd been rolled in mud. He carried the basket to one of the sinks and began to wash them off. "Do your store your eggs in mud puddles?"

"Chicken shit," she didn't look up.

For a moment he wondered why they would do that. When the obvious reason registered—because that was the other thing besides eggs that was under chickens—he lost control of the egg he'd been washing and it hit the bottom of the sink with a sickening splat. In his world eggs came from clean little cardboard cartons, not from...chickens.

Ama might have been smiling as she passed him carrying a large plastic container filled with sausage meat. It didn't look as if her sausage meat came from neat little Styrofoam trays covered in plastic wrap either.

Once the rest of the eggs were clean, he began cracking them into the bowl. "How many?"

"A dozen eggs should do."

From that scant clue as to how many they were feeding, he began building a waffle mix. She didn't tell him where things were, leaving him to discover that milk was in the steel jug in the dairy fridge, and which cupboard held the baking powder and flour. When he didn't have enough flour, she pointed him toward another door.

"Oh. My. God." This time he could feel her smiling at his back, though he didn't turn to see.

The door led to a pantry that could feed an army. There were walls of staples. Lidded plastic buckets on the floor were labeled:

21

rice, lentils, red beans, black beans, and more. There was an entire wall of shelves dedicated to canned goods. Not canned like from a store, but canned like the glass jars that cost him ten or fifteen dollars apiece at Dean and DeLuca's in SoHo. Asparagus, beans, corn…the whole alphabet of vegetables was represented. Jam jars nudged up against quarts of cherries and tomatoes—maybe he'd died and gone to heaven. A massive chest freezer was packed solid with bags of frozen fruit. Another with cuts of meat wrapped in brown butcher paper.

It was so overwhelming that he had to look at the empty container in his hands to remember what he'd come in to find. Flour. Right. He dipped a couple of scoops from a fifty-pound bag into the container and wandered back into the kitchen completely dazed.

Ama had taken over the waffle mixing. His delay would have put the meal out of sync if she hadn't.

Rather than switching back, he handed off the flour and took over the sausage. She'd made patties and dropped them on the griddle. He knocked off a cooked bit and tasted it. Pork, heavy on the salt and light on the pepper.

Nathan ducked back into the pantry and grabbed an onion and a jar of roasted red peppers in oil. He diced both down quickly and got them running on the griddle. Thyme and a shot of Tabasco. More pepper, but no more salt. Soon the kitchen was thick with the smell of good sausage, fresh butter sizzling on the griddle, and hot waffles.

People started coming into the kitchen through the back door. They brought a wash of cold air and the smell of dry grass and sunshine in with them. Wow. He wasn't first up, he was last. Minutes past sunrise and they'd all been outside working. That explained the two pots of coffee that had been going.

As each person came in, Nathan dropped an extra egg on the hot grill. Another taste of pepper-onion mix, then he added a touch more hot sauce and a pinch of tarragon.

No one spoke to him—they'd all know who he was by this point—but he could hear them chatting about the morning's work. Horses, farm equipment he'd never heard of, and cabins under construction—a lot of discussion on that last point. But he was too busy cooking to let it be more than a wash over him.

Ama began handing him plates with a trio of giant waffles on each. Big appetites here.

With a broad spatula, he dropped a sausage patty beside the waffles, smothered it with the onion-pepper mix, slipped an over-easy egg on top of it, then handed off the plate. Finally, no one arrived to take the next plate.

In confusion he slipped out of the zone and discovered that he had no more eggs to serve either—the last one was crowned over the sausage on the plate he was holding.

He turned and everyone was sitting at the kitchen table. They all had plates before them and were busy dressing the waffles with butter and syrup.

The transition was always hard, but this one was stranger than most. He generally made a point of cooking the staff meal himself. Before the day's dinner service began, he would serve everyone a plate, and himself last. They always ate together before the night's mayhem began. Even Chef Guevarre, despite all of his control freak madness, always sat and ate with the crew—though he'd never cooked for them as that would be a "waste of his time and talent."

But this was no table with hungover chefs, predatory sous chefs, and waitresses dressed far more to please with their bodies than their personalities.

Mac and Ama sat at either end. Six others sat scattered along the length. A striking redhead was leaning in to tease a guy with brown hair down to his collar. There was a huge guy with a buzz cut and paired steel hooks sticking out of one cuff, a sharp contrast to his other big powerful hand of flesh and blood. Two of the men, both sandy blond and rancher solid—and alike enough to be twins—rounded out the crowd.

Ama patted the spot by her side and he slid into it gratefully.

He picked up a fork, then set it back down when he noticed no one else was eating. They were all looking at Mac.

Mac's glance traveled around the table, stopping on each of them. Nathan found that his own was doing the same. The big hard guy with the hooks to his right, Ama to his left.

No one spoke. No one closed their eyes or mumbled prayers. There were looks and smiles and nods around the table.

It lasted only a second or so, a few moments of acknowledging that these were the people whom they were breaking bread with. Before it could get weird or uncomfortable, Mac declared "Hooyah!" from the other end of the table with some kind of military call. It rippled like a wave around the table and then they began eating and talking all at once.

Nathan sat a moment longer appreciating the feel of the moment. He wished he'd thought to do something like that at his restaurant. If he ever spoke to his buddy Estevan again, he'd have to suggest it.

Nathan was the last to pick up his fork.

"Wow!" the redhead exclaimed. "That's some seriously good sausage. You can cook for me anytime. I'm Chelsea, by the way. I married-in last spring," she hooked a thumb at the man beside her. "Doug was just too good a package to leave on the shelf. He can even kinda cook, which is good because I'm totally hopeless despite my mom being a cook for a whole bunch of Oregon firefighters ever since before I can remember. Doug is the ranch foreman and never speaks."

"Sure I do. I just can't ever seem to get a word in edgewise. It's Stan who never speaks."

"Give me a reason to," the big guy with the hooks for a hand grunted out. He looked rough, but not angry. More like the guy you wanted on your side in a brawl.

"He only talks to his dogs," Chelsea explained.

"At least they listen," Stan shot back.

"You know Mac and Ama, of course," she continued the introductions as if Stan hadn't spoken at all. Maybe he spoke plenty and she just never heard him. Or maybe she was teasing him.

As to Mac and Ama, not at all and barely. But as it was obvious there was no stopping the speeding train of Chelsea, he simply nodded. The big guy at the head of the table offered him a wink as she turned to the last occupants of the table.

"These two we call Tweedledee and Tweedledum. They aren't twins, they only look that way."

"I'm Dee. He's Dum," the not-twins said in practiced unison, aiming a forkful of waffle at each other.

"Actually I'm Fred and he's George," one said.

"Can't be," Nathan was getting the hang of their conversation.

"Why not?" the other asked.

"First, are either of you magical?"

"Like a fairy? Sure, Dum is. Magical like a giant? You're talking to the main man." Even though he was slightly the shorter of the two.

"Your hair isn't red."

"Depends on the day of the week."

Nathan couldn't help but laugh. He'd wager that the two of them never gave a straight answer to anything.

"Maybe you're the twins from *The Parent Trap*. Then you could both be impersonated by a young Lindsay Lohan." His suggestion started them off on using little-girl voices.

The rest of the meal carried on the same way. They teased him some about his sports car. Dee and Dum, whose actual names he still wasn't sure of, wanted to take it for a spin.

"Found these still in the ignition," Doug reached into a pocket and tossed him the keys.

Nathan must have been even more out of it than he'd thought to do that. Very *not city* of him.

"I moved it into one of the garages, what with the storm

coming in tonight. Stacked your gear inside the front door." His smile said he might have taken it for a quick spin on the way. Chelsea's smile confirmed that he had and she'd been along to enjoy the ride.

If this was New York, he'd be pissed that someone had taken liberties with his Miata. Here it didn't seem such a big deal. "Careful, there's no spare. I had a flat about a mile from here last night when I nearly plowed into a sky-tall cow from the underworld named Lucy. I thought I was a goner until an angel on a horse rescued me. Where's the nearest station to get that fixed?"

"Choteau."

Thirty miles to the nearest gas station? Where the hell was he?

"But I can patch the tire for you if it's just a puncture. Not a chance I have a spare of the right size lying around for something that small."

Nathan didn't know how to answer that. Full or flat he knew. Puncture vs…what? He hoped for the former and just nodded his thanks to Doug.

"Lucy spooked you off the road?" Chelsea had a bright, merry laugh so he played it up. The saga of the mighty horns and the nostrils streaming with fire in the evening light. When he got to the part about the angel on the black-and-white horse, they all nodded.

"That'd be Julie up on her Clarence," Dee said.

"She loves that painted horse," Dum replied with a sad sigh that said he'd found no luck with its rider.

"*Really* loves that horse," Dee's sigh said that he too had failed there.

At least he now had her first name.

Thankfully no one pushed him about why he was here. There were some things he wasn't ready to explain to anyone, not even himself. Or how long he'd be staying, which was awfully polite of them—especially as he had nowhere else to go.

Instead the talk turned to the plans for the spring.

Apparently the cowgirl's ranch had cows, thousands of head of them. Mac and Ama had a horse ranch. They were a guest ranch, so fixing up and expanding the cabins before "the season" started really was a big priority.

"You have any carpentry skills?" Mac asked, then sighed when Nathan merely shook his head. "This spread lay dormant for years. Been a load of work knocking it into shape. Last year was the first we actually turned a profit. A whole lot of it is in hay. Still lease about a third of it as grazing land to Nils Larson across the road."

Larson. Julie Larson. Now he had both her names—though Nathan wasn't sure why he cared or what good it would do him.

There was also talk about a celebration dinner tonight. Before he even finished helping with the cleanup, Ama began cooking. She made it easy for him to pitch in.

"How many are you expecting?" Nathan asked as she hauled a gigantic roast out of the meat fridge.

Ama shrugged, "Most of the ranches hereabouts. It's coming up spring. People are tired of staying in." And that was pretty much all she had to say as they worked through the morning.

JULIE HAD BEEN on a winning streak all afternoon, no sign of city boy. Not even his car. As a bonus, the two cousins who looked like twins, Devin and Drake, were nowhere about, though she almost had them trained into treating her like a person. And Patrick—who she couldn't seem to train at all—was off on a supply run.

It had just been her and Mac all afternoon. He'd named the five cabins for the local trees: Douglas, Lodgepole, Larch, Ponderosa, and Aspen. They went through each one making notes. Douglas would just be a matter of fixing some blown shingles, and Larch had a cracked window. A fresh coat of paint on all of the doors and trim would make them feel well maintained, but the wood siding was left weathered to give the rustic, Montana Ranch experience. Ponderosa was a much bigger job; it was the oldest cabin and the bathroom predated the dinosaur bones that Jack Horner became famous for unearthing at nearby Egg Mountain.

Aspen was a little sweetheart of a cottage and had always been her favorite. It was off by itself a bit and sheltered by a small copse of aspen. It didn't need much work to merely be ready for guests, but with a little attention it could be a real showpiece. If it was hers she'd— There was a pointless train of thought. If she didn't get her business going she was going to be living on the Larson spread for the rest of her natural-born days.

The first guest wasn't booked for a month, so she had plenty of time to finish all this work herself. She'd fix up the easy ones right away so that Mac could take advantage if someone called in.

"It's the delay on the new cabins that worries me, Julie. I had twice the calls last season than I had the guest housing for."

Last fall they'd sited-in the plumbing and electrics, burying them deeply underground—well below the freeze and frost heave line. Mac had loved the excuse to give his backhoe a workout, but an early and hard storm had frozen the ground and stopped them before they could dig in the basements. That was a problem of a different scale. Their plans to start building atop the basements while the ground was still hard hadn't been possible.

"We need to get down deep and I don't have time for that now," Mac sat down in the clearing for the first cabin. They could probably dig now, there'd been enough warm weather. But even if they started today, it was too late. It would take a month of hard work to even get ready for the foundation pour; the cabins wouldn't be done until the fall. And that was only if she could find enough crew to hire on during the busy summer season. While she'd welcome the steady work, it wasn't going to help Mac at all.

Julie sat beside him, the grass crunching slightly after the chilly night—the remainder of last night's snow hadn't melted yet—and looked out at the land. It was an ideal setting. The main house was perched on the south side of a broad rise, sheltered from the hard northerlies that slammed down off the Arctic and the Canadian plains in the winters. Below, in a protected swale: horse barns, shops, lodging for the hands, and the foreman's house.

The guest cabins were upslope from the main ranch house, circling the crest of the rise. They had commanding views in every direction, yet were close by the main house for meals and evening activities. This new cluster was to be on the next rise, another hundred yards away from the others. They'd be for those guests who wanted the extra feel of privacy.

For a while they talked ideas back and forth.

Forget the frost heave and let the cabins "float" on heavy footings with adjustable jacks? It meant more maintenance every year. Cut in just two basements this year? That would leave those two cabins feeling remote and lonely, rather than adventurous in a group. Nowadays, with instant reviews up on travel websites, the experience had to be perfect, right from the beginning.

But for all his worry, Mac was easy with taking the time to just sit and chat about it. Her father would have mandated "get it done" and stomped down the slope, the same way he stomped down every obstacle that rose in his way. She didn't like how much she was like him in that respect, but no matter how she looked at this problem, she couldn't seem to bludgeon it into submission.

"Something will come to us. We don't have to solve this today."

"But—"

"No, Julie," Mac waved to encompass the landscape lying before them. "This isn't some battle scenario. Nobody dies if we don't solve it until tomorrow."

"Maybe not, but it feels that way. I've been thinking about this all winter. If we don't solve it today, it could be next winter before we do."

"No, it doesn't feel that way. Not really."

That's when she remembered his background. He'd been a Navy SEAL for twenty years.

And his son and daughter-in-law had spent nearly as long in the Army, a lot of it in Special Operations.

"You're looking forward to them coming here to live, aren't you?"

He nodded. "A father worries. Can't tell his wife or kid, because it's up to him to be the strong one. But trust me, he worries."

Julie wasn't so sure about that. Her father might worry some, but it would be about his cows first, his male children second, or maybe third after his standing in the community. Her mother next, and then she was somewhere far down on the list of things Nils Larson worried about.

"Yes, it will be good to have them home. Miss the grandkids, too. Having Mark and Emily fighting wildfires was bad. When they were in the Army before that, it was worse. I lost count of how many times they were shot down. Twice on national TV for Emily; once for Mark. Damned hard to watch, I don't mind admitting. At least to you. They will probably never tell me all the times it happened."

Julie looked out again at the view. The house and ranch buildings tucked safely below. The massive Front Range of the Rocky Mountains sweeping up out of the Great Plains in a grand gesture of towering rock. The fierce snow-covered mountains soared to the west and the limitless horizon of the grasslands to the east. Big cumulus were moving south out of Canada, one last snow or else a freezing rain. There wasn't a rancher who wouldn't prefer the snow—a chill rain killed animals far more quickly.

"It's such a beautiful place. I hope they love it here," Mac's voice was barely a whisper on the soft breeze.

Julie heard the new worry in his voice and felt foolish for her own petty concerns. Mac and his family had risked everything for their country. Risked and made it through to the other side.

What in the world had she ever done? Lived her entire life on a cattle ranch, scrabbling for the thin line that meant success each year and hating the struggle.

Off in the far distance, she saw a tiny plume of dust out near the horizon. Someone on the road.

"When are you expecting Mark and Emily?"

"Any time now."

"Then I think you'd better head on down to greet them," she pointed out the far-off blemish. A small cloud of dust rose way out along the line of the road in from Choteau.

Mac looked for a long moment. "You've good eyes, Julie. Notice detail. That's important. No wonder Emily likes you so much."

"Emily doesn't like me."

Mac simply smiled without quite facing her.

"You'd better get a move on, old man, if you're going to meet your son."

He nodded and rose to his feet, brushed himself off. Rather than teasing her back, he reached down and scrubbed the top of her hair to mess it up. "You'll find him, Julie."

"Find who?" She flipped her hair back into place with a shake of her head. She'd thought they were talking about Emily.

"*Him.* Trust me. You're too good a girl not to."

He started down the path.

"But I'm not looking for anyone," she finally told the big sky long after Mac passed the lower cabins.

Maybe his years in the Navy and then worrying about his son had made him some kind of a romantic.

She was a practical kind of woman. Had a business to get going and that required solving the problem of Mac Henderson's cabins. It was her company's first big job. If it didn't happen, then her company probably wasn't going to happen. Slinking back into the cattle ranch life was *not* an option. Landing once more in the role of the daughter who should marry another strong farm hand into the family was *absolutely not* going to happen.

But sometimes she would just watch Henderson Ranch like she was now, or ride Clarence to the remote corner of her family's property where she could just see the main compound. She would sit and watch the comings and goings, or just listen to the meadowlarks as the cloud shadows slipped over the waving fields of hay. She never thought much about it, but just liked the way it looked.

Stan working with training his dogs.

Chelsea and the other three men tending the horses. Late in most afternoons of the spring through fall, Mac and Ama would take off riding. Their property ran almost twenty thousand acres and backed up against two million acres of the Flathead National Forest. They could ride a half dozen miles in a straight line west or south and not leave their property. Or plunge into the primitive area and not see a soul for weeks in any direction.

Soon they'd hire in the summer help. The horses were foaling and the tourists were coming, the ranch would be more than this crew could handle alone. Mark and Emily would be welcome assistance, even if it was only sitting around evening campfires and telling stories. Though they were such active people, it was hard to imagine them coming to any sort of a stop.

Julie looked at the storm rolling out of the north. It wouldn't be here until evening, but she'd best take Clarence back before then. It would be hammering across Larson land before it reached the Hendersons.

As she stood and began heading down the trail, someone came out of the back door of the main house. The kitchen was the closest part of the house to the barn buildings and the guest cabins—the working entrance to the big house.

In a second she knew who it was—clown-car boy. He looked about him as if he'd never seen the sky before. Montana's Big Sky did that to newcomers. Did it to her often enough and she'd grown up here.

Then he looked down from the heavens and spotted her. He gave a cheery wave. She wasn't close enough to see his easy smile, but knew it was there.

She raised her notebook in a "Howdy" gesture. Then she cut off the path and over the meadow, down toward the horse barn where she'd left Clarence napping in a stall.

His hand lowered uncertainly, making her feel bad.

"How hard would it be to be polite?" she asked an early crocus shoot that had fought its way through the hard soil.

She held her focus straight ahead.

Apparently too hard.

CHAPTER 3

*T*he crowd was so thick that Nathan retreated to the kitchen. Actually he hadn't left it except for the occasional run at the sideboard groaning with food. The families and hands of all the ranches for miles around had come by. In addition to the monster roasts and dozen pies he and Ama had made, everyone brought a dish big enough to feed ten or more. They'd have excess food for days. Maybe that was the plan. Though his brief foray for seconds revealed that the crowd was able to inflict a serious amount of damage on the spread.

He had no reference for this. New York wasn't big on potlucks. Sometimes a group of chefs would go out together to try a new restaurant, then spend the evening confirming that it was no threat to any of their own, no matter how good it was. Other times they'd all gather in one chef or another's kitchen where they'd cook outrageous creations and old favorites, and drink until they could no longer stand up.

That was his circle of friends.

Friends?

Most of them would barely note that he was gone. "Did you hear about Nathan? Another one bites the dust." The only message on his phone during the whole drive out was from Estevan, and Nathan hadn't returned it because he had no idea what he'd say. When the nights were quiet and all that was left was the drinking, the two of them would talk about opening their own place together. Their menu, their way. Always a dream, never quite coming together.

Didn't seem to matter now.

This Montana potluck was so completely different from any of that. It was busy with talk of weather and cattle. Some women wore nice dresses, but others were dressed in jeans and denim or flannel shirts like most of the men. No one seemed to care one way or the other. Cowboy boots outnumbered everything else combined, by a fair margin—enough that he was actually self-conscious of his sneakers whenever he ventured out of the kitchen.

He hadn't even met the guests of honor yet, though he'd seen their arrival...at the same time Julie Larson had given him the polite version of "Go to hell and do it quickly." He'd known it was her the first instant—too far for any details, but he'd known.

Normally he could gear up and be gregarious enough to join any crowd, but when out filling his first plate, he'd seen Julie Larson. Her back had been to him, but he'd known it was her in the first instant—and not only because the setting sun was dazzling through the window behind her. She glowed. It was as if she had made a special deal with Mother Nature to always have a solar backdrop.

Apparently her idea of dressing up was changing her scuffed brown cowgirl boots to ones with pretty stitching around leather of red and gold. Her jeans were as worn as any high-fashion boutique could provide, a blue flannel shirt made her ramrod posture look soft, and her straight blond hair fell to the middle of her back like the smoothest fall of sunshine.

A whole cluster of cowboys were gathered close about her.

A glance around the room revealed that the redheaded

Chelsea, just by her very nature, was also charming a whole circle of big ranch-hand types even as she was sitting beside her husband. Stan was nowhere to be found. Ama must be with her son...

The kitchen was his exclusive domain and his retreat.

It wasn't like him to hide away, but the quiet was comfortable. And there wouldn't be any uncomfortable questions about what he did for a living...nothing at the moment. Or what he was doing in Montana...he didn't have a clue. He could hear the buzz of the crowd beyond the door and pretend that it was a crowded dining room—a world separate from the kitchen. All he lacked were a sous chef, a grillardin, and the half dozen others necessary to make a dinner service. Mix in a clattering dishwasher and a small flock of waiters and he'd feel right at home.

Except he didn't feel at home there anymore—one of the many reasons he'd bolted from the city.

The echoing silence of the ranch kitchen was wrong as well. He shifted from the kitchen to the family dining table. And from there to one of the big wing-backed armchairs by the fire where he settled deep into the soft dark leather. Not being able to see the kitchen helped some. He wasn't all that far from retreating right out the back door to freeze in yet another Montana night.

Then he heard the door swing open and shut again followed by a deep sigh.

"Dear Lord above. Spare me from such men."

Julie Larson. It was a voice that had ingrained itself in his soul the minute she'd rescued him from the demon beast.

He should reveal himself, the wings of the big armchair blocked his view of the door, but after her brush-off of a simple friendly wave this afternoon, he remained hidden, hoping she'd leave quickly.

Nathan traced the track of her footsteps as her boot heels paced over to one fridge, then the other. After a long pause, they tromped toward him.

She plummeted into the next chair with a loud exclamation of, "Refuge. At long last."

"Perhaps I should go," he said softly to not startle her.

By Julie's squawk of surprise, he'd totally failed. She nearly lost the plate that held a big sandwich apparently scavenged from the refrigerator. And if she hadn't plunked the beer bottle down on the coffee table before she sat, she'd be wearing it.

"Sorry," he started to rise.

"City boy! You scared half a life out of me."

"Where's the other half?"

"I'm like a cat. Nine lives, and I'm trying to conserve them." It was a good thing she didn't smile, she was already far too pretty without it. The blue flannel accented her blue eyes. Seeing her without a horse, a monstrous cow, or a barbed wire fence, he could appreciate why she might need refuge. Up close she was even more stunning than his memory of her.

"I'm Nathan," he had to do something to break his own desire to stare at her. She was like a breath of fresh air. Chilly Montana air, but still incredible.

"Hi, Nathan. I'm Julie. You can stay as long as you promise not to act like you're a white knight, a shining prince, or a rutting cowhand."

"So I can *be* one as long as I don't act like it?"

She eyed him as she took a sip out of her beer bottle. "Let's see. I don't think that a white knight or a shining prince would be so scared of a cow as gentle as Lucy that he'd wave his little jack handle in the air."

"Which leaves me the category of 'rutting cowhand.' I'll pass."

"Good," she bit deeply into her sandwich. "Or I'd whack you with something a lot bigger than a car jack," she spoke around the mouthful.

"No food out there?"

"I couldn't get near it without some hoot-n-hollerer saying,

'Let me help you with that, Julie. I'll set you up a plate just the way you'd like it.' As you said—"

"You'll pass." Nathan slouched deeper in his chair and considered the fire while trying to think of the next thing to say. "Only cows I've met before have already been butchered. Those I know what to do with."

She managed a garbled exclamation around her next bite, but it sounded disbelieving.

"Very few unbutchered cows in Manhattan."

"Manhattan, like New York City? Why would you want to live there?"

Nathan decided that if he slouched any lower he'd be on the floor and his feet would be in the fire, but he couldn't find the energy to prop himself back up either. "Can we skip that question for now?"

"Okay," he could feel her looking at him. "I already know why you're here, so that shoots down the next question."

"You do?" He turned back to her and she was studying him with those impossibly blue eyes. Even at night by firelight they spoke of the sky. "I sure as hell don't."

"You're looking for something different. You told me so yourself, so I figure it must be true."

"I suppose." He had said that. He returned to his former slouch.

"New York and the Montana Front Range, couldn't get much more different than that."

"The Arctic," he mumbled just to be contrary.

"Sure, though in winter the temperature here is about the same. Make sure you're gone by September if you don't like the cold."

He shrugged. He didn't really expect to be here more than a few days to see Patrick. Though he didn't care much one way or the other about the weather. If the city scorched in a heat wave or bogged down under a foot of chill slush, it never affected him one way or the other.

"You've really never seen a cow?"

"At a distance out of a car window, but never up close and personal. Their horns don't look so big and dangerous when you're doing seventy down the interstate."

"Lucy's breed is called longhorns for a reason."

"Sure, for scaring the crap out of chefs. I think you bolted extra-large horns on her when you saw me coming."

∼

"RIGHT," that detail had slipped her mind. "I forgot Ama said you were a chef. You sure made a hit with your roast."

"Did you like it?"

"Couldn't get near the thing." She'd grown up on a farm and could skin a cow or butcher a hog as well as the next man, but wielding a knife on a roast was clearly beyond her. It had been a close thing, not taking her own knife to the Olsson brothers.

When he didn't offer to go get her some, Julie actually appreciated it. "You're not acting much like a city slicker."

"I'm not a city slicker. I'm a chef."

"You drive a fancy sports car."

"Not very. It's Japanese, not a Porsche or a Ferrari or anything. It's cheaper than a truck."

"Not mine." Her business couldn't afford a decent truck and there wasn't a chance that she'd ask Dad for the use of one of the farm's vehicles to get her business going. She'd scraped up enough for a 1959 Ford F-250, which was a whole lot of rust from being a classic. But it was all hers right down to the last worn ring and gasket leak. If she could just solve Henderson's cabin problem, maybe she'd have enough cash to rebuild the engine. She only needed a couple hundred bucks in parts and a week of peace and quiet—though not a chance that was going to happen this side of winter.

He shrugged again.

"Why are you hiding in here?"

"Tired I guess. I practically drove straight through to get here."

There was something more than that. Julie had no idea why she wanted to pry—she'd spent her whole evening trying to avoid men—but she was curious. Drove straight through? As if something had been after him.

"Why—"

"Sanctuary!" Someone cried out as she entered the kitchen.

Julie leaned out of the chair far enough to see Emily Beale leaning with her back against the door as if she could bar anyone else from following. She had her newborn cradled in one arm, though there was no sign of her three-year-old girl.

"Hey, Emily." The woman unnerved her, but not enough to deny her an escape. "You're safe enough in here. What are *you* escaping from?"

Emily hit the fridge. "I would kill for a beer, but I don't need a drunk newborn." She came over carrying a ginger ale, but didn't seem to know what to do with Belle. As if even her own child was too much to handle at the moment.

Julie reached out and took her; she was fast asleep and too cute for words. Just a few months old, it was easy to see that she'd gotten her mother's delicate features. Only time would tell if she'd take on her mother's incredible strength of character as well.

"Thanks," Emily sighed as she dropped down on a couch.

"Too many people! I know five and there must be a hundred out there. They all think that my sole value is that I've made two babies. And conversations! I haven't had to talk that much in a year. Is he safe?" She nodded toward Nathan.

"Not sure yet. Are you safe?" Julie couldn't resist prodding him. She enjoyed babies, and this one was a sweetheart—at least while she was asleep. It would be a long time before she had any but if she did, she'd gladly take one like this.

"Me?" Nathan looked back and forth between them. "Do you think I'm dumb enough to take on two dangerous blondes? Is the kid blond? That makes three. Ama told me you're a warrior," he nodded to Emily, then turned to her. "And I've already seen you ride down a *longhorn* hell-beast—"

"He met Lucy on the road last night," Julie filled in with a mock-panicked look that stung even more than an eye roll.

"Not a chance I'm going to tangle with any of you," Nathan concluded. "The kid could probably throw me down already since she's yours."

"I've met Lucy," Emily shuddered. "Never seen anything look so big in my life. Mark had taken me out to a fishing stream one of my first times on the ranch. I was sitting there not hurting a fly, just reading a book. Then this huge cow came out of nowhere and tried to eat my straw hat while I was still wearing it. My scream spooked Mark face-first into the stream—didn't seem to bother Lucy a bit."

Julie laughed. "Hard to imagine anything scaring you."

"I'm not some superwoman. Just an Army pilot now retired. I grew up in Washington, DC. Very few giant cows except in the Capitol Building."

"Ask her what she hasn't done," Julie prompted him. "Go on. Ask her."

NATHAN BLINKED AT JULIE, feeling no sharper than a cow. He was still trying to get over the two women sitting with him. Both were tall, blond, fit, and couldn't be more different if they tried.

Emily Beale looked the warrior. Narrow face, jewel-blue eyes, and her hair sliced sharply at her jawline. She wore a black turtleneck, a fleece vest, and khakis with sneakers. Julie's hair was a lighter shade that fell well past her shoulders in a soft flow emphasizing her open face. The blue flannel shirt accented her sky-blue eyes and the worn jeans that he'd admired earlier were no less admirable up close. Her fancy-stitched cowboy boots really were nice work. It was the first time he'd ever seen cowboy boots that made sense—in New York they'd always looked incongruously ridiculous worn with skin-tight leggings by the city's trenders.

He didn't know what to make of Julie cradling a baby. She made it look like the most natural thing, whereas he'd never really seen one from so close before. Patrons of high-end restaurants hired babysitters. A few of his staff had reproduced over the years, a very few, and the babies were rarely more than a briefly flashed photo on a phone's screen that always seemed to blank to black the moment it reached him.

Again he was staring as he tried to puzzle her out. Had to stop that, at least the staring part, no matter how pretty she was.

"Okay," Nathan forced himself up straighter and faced Emily. "What haven't you done?"

Emily rolled her eyes as Julie answered for her.

"She was a military helicopter pilot for some secret Special Operation types—the first woman ever. And a major, too, which is awfully high up. Then she led a fleet of the best heli-aviation firefighting helicopter pilots around. I know they're the best because they stopped a monster wildfire from escaping the primitive area and overrunning all the ranches hereabouts. She has a gorgeous husband—"

"I do," Emily admitted finally.

"—and two of the cutest girls you can imagine," Julie actually cooed at the one sleeping in her arms. "She makes me feel inadequate just by walking into the room."

"I do?" That had Emily sitting up. "No I don't."

Nathan didn't know whether to mediate or to egg them on and see where it led.

"You sure do," Julie insisted.

"This from a woman who can herd cattle, has won a string of state rodeo ribbons, drives a combine, and rebuilds tractors when they act up."

43

"That's just ranch stuff," Julie protested around the last of her sandwich.

"Can't do a one of them," Emily tipped her soda in a salute.

"I can cook," Nathan put in his grand bid for fame, but couldn't think of anything else to add.

"That roast was you? What did you do to it?" Emily redirected her bottle toward the dining room.

"Nothing fancy, just lending a hand."

He saw Julie eyeing the door, but he understood the issue. "I could use some more. Anyone else want something from the spread?"

Julie eyed him now like she didn't trust his motivations, which was a good bet. He didn't want someone else snagging her attention. In addition to her beauty, she was also skilled and dryly funny. He had a weak spot for funny.

He took her indifferent shrug as a yes.

Most everyone had migrated out to the great room, leaving the dining room empty except for a couple of hands obviously going for fourths. No one paid him any mind as he loaded a platter with several slices of roast and a nice-looking beet salad. He filled another with three different slices of pie: rhubarb, apple, and one he wasn't sure of, but the crust looked golden and flaky.

The three of them ruled their corner of the kitchen until well into the night.

It was the first thing in Nathan's life that had made sense in months.

JULIE STOOD out on the porch, surveyed the empty driveway, and wondered who she needed to kill: Dad or her three brothers? Marooned.

By the time the Henderson's hands began bringing plates back into the kitchen, she'd learned a lot more about Emily and decided that maybe she could like her even though she became more daunting rather than less with each story.

Nathan had continued to be surprisingly tolerable as a fireside companion. His depth of cluelessness about Montana was so awesome that she wondered how he'd survived the trip from the barn, never mind Choteau. It was like he'd found the fourth largest state in the nation by stubbing his toe on Wyoming and landing in Montana face-first.

Beyond that he'd spoken plenty but said little. He was the one who had teased stories out of Emily and, now that she thought about it, out of her.

It was only as she had followed Nathan to lend a hand with the cleanup that she realized she still knew little more than he was a New York chef and his little brother Patrick was a pain in the ass. She knew that herself. Patrick was a nice enough guy, but he was *so* full of himself—even more than most locals. And he was always trying to find a line on her.

A New Yorker turned ranch hand was not what she wanted, no matter how painfully persistent. What did she want? *That* was a mystery that eluded her with even more skill than Lucy.

Now, she was out on the porch. It was pitch dark. Well below freezing. And *both* of the family trucks were gone. The storm that had threatened this afternoon had passed through quickly and left a veneer of white snow on everything. Already the clouds were shredding enough to reveal the starry sky—the temperature would still be headed down. It would be a very slippery walk in leather soles unless she cut across the rough pastures in the dark.

"Something wrong?" Nathan stepped out onto the porch behind her. He wore only a light turtleneck. He hadn't lied about not caring about the cold; he didn't even ram his hands into his pockets.

He wasn't startlingly handsome; she kept expecting that from him, but he wasn't. He was average height and build, his brown hair seemed tousled by its very nature. His face would have been plain without the easy smile that reached his eyes most every time. The only really exceptional thing about him was his hands. She could see the chef in them whether he was offering her a choice of pie or picking up a beer bottle. They weren't rancher weather-beaten, but they were strong and callused—even if it was in ways she didn't recognize. They implied that he worked long and hard at his cooking.

She'd never seen that before. Ma cooked. Ama did too. But that roast had been different somehow, as if she'd never really tasted beef before. There were cowhands and there were real, honest, born-to-the-saddle cowboys. There were cooks and there were...whatever Nathan was.

"Thinking mighty hard on something, Julie," Nathan's comment brought her back to the present and the complete lack of any vehicles parked in the Henderson's driveway.

"I'm going to jail tomorrow for killing a family member. Nothing new," she turned back to the night in order to not think about how nice Nathan looked. He looked...normal, in a way no ranch hand ever did. Not with some "get the gal" agenda. Not with an ego saying "look at how impressive I am." He was just...Nathan.

He looked out at the empty driveway, "No car." He also wasn't slow.

"No truck actually, but same result. Going to be a long cold walk, and then I'm going to kill someone with my bare hands." She flipping up the collar of her sheepskin jacket.

"How far?"

"Three miles by the road, two by the pasture."

He held up a finger telling her to wait and went inside. He was back a moment later in a heavy jacket and a woolen hat. "Ride or walk?" He held up both car keys and a flashlight.

She almost called his bluff, then decided maybe it wasn't. "Do you even know how to drive on snow, city boy?"

"Sure, you take the subway. Easy-peasy." He appeared to be serious, but his eyes gave him away.

If she had her work boots, she'd walk and see if he was for real. Instead she looked around, "Don't see a car either."

"It's in the garage..." he tapered off as he looked about the farm. "At least that's what Doug said. Any guesses on which building that is?"

"That thing you said about not being a shining knight..."

"Tell me about it," Nathan sighed a big plume of cold air. "Actually don't. I've known it for years." He made it easy to share a smile.

"The Hendersons have a couple of garages," she led the way off the porch and into the darkness.

The family garage had a couple of pickups, including Mark and Emily's, which was robin's egg blue. According to Emily, Mark had mounted a major campaign to repaint it black and, for that reason alone, Emily had said she was having none of it. "He thinks he's still Mr. Macho Military, not the guy who agreed to be the fishing guide for his dad. I have to retrain him on that. Not much hope, but I do what I can."

When Nathan had asked why he wasn't leading hunting parties, she'd said that they'd both seen enough blood to last a life-time, which had silenced their conversation long enough for the fire to need tending. Julie had had to tell him how to do that as Belle was still asleep in her lap and Emily had no more of a clue than he did.

Nathan's sports car wasn't in the equipment bay either. It was funny to watch his eyes bug out. The Hendersons weren't farmers, except for a big kitchen garden, so mostly it was just a hay mower and rake, a baler, and several work trucks. He looked at them as if they were alien spacecraft. The ranch's helicopter and a small cluster of ATVs were parked down at the end.

She knew that Doug's garage didn't have space except for his own truck, which left her wondering if she was going to be walking home after all.

"It seems unlikely, but let's check," she led him through a door into the main horse barn. "God but I love this smell." It was hay and horse and leather. The Hendersons were doing some horse breeding, but most of it was lessons and guest rides.

"Really?" Nathan rubbed at his nose with the back of a glove. "It smells...horsey."

"You thought pretty horses were going to stink like cattle?"

"Cattle stink?"

"You have no idea." Actually, he probably didn't. Most of the horses were asleep, but a few stuck their heads out over stall doors to inspect them as they walked by.

Parked in the last stall at the end, complete with a rope halter fashioned around one of the tires, sat his little car.

WHEN JULIE STOPPED LAUGHING, she helped him get it out of the barn. Not wanting to pump exhaust into the horse's faces, they pushed it out of the stall and back up the long central aisle of the barn. Now all of the horses were awake. They looked out of the stalls, nickering and snorting between themselves as if his car was the funniest thing they'd seen in a month of Sundays.

"I'm guessing that my next move would be to pay Doug back somehow," Nathan tapped on the brake when they reached the main door.

"Absolutely pay him back," Julie started laughing again.

"Any suggestions?"

"Pepper in his shorts? I'm sure Chelsea would be glad to help you out there."

"I'll have to remember that you have a low sense of humor, Julie Larson."

"I'll take that as a compliment." She slid the main barn door sideways and he gave the car a final nudge out into the chill darkness of the barnyard.

With the top up, they were suddenly very close together. The smell of horse lingered until the heater finally kicked in. Then a richer but gentler scent filled the car.

"You smell like Montana." Nathan knew that he should have kept his mouth shut, but he hadn't been this close to her before. Practically shoulder to shoulder in the car, she seemed to fill the space.

"I what?"

"Fresh and, I don't know, spring-like?"

"Keep your nose to yourself, buster."

"Not much choice. It came attached as standard equipment at birth."

Julie glared at him for a moment—which seemed to be her standard expression for covering a laugh—then pointed down the driveway. "Left at the end."

Nathan eased down the driveway. There were a dozen sets of tire tracks through the snow. He'd heard the secret to driving on snow was no sudden moves, so he stayed in first gear.

"Walking would be faster."

"I put the car in a ditch and you'll get that option." He'd been half hoping that she'd opt for the walk. It would be worth facing the cold to walk with her. Emily had led a fascinating life, but it was Julie's stories that had really captivated him. She'd slowly painted a picture of a day-to-day life like none he'd ever imagined. She almost made him want to learn to ride a horse just by the way she described it.

She didn't say anything during the short drive. He gained enough confidence to shift up to second, which had him arriving at her front gate far too soon.

"Double-L?" Nathan looked at the big arch over the driveway.

"Founded by Lars Larson a hundred and fifty years ago. Thanks, Nathan. Here's fine. I'll just hop the gate and walk up to the house. Besides, it looks like Lucy escaped again and I don't want to force you to face the 'demon beast'."

In the glow of the headlights, he could see the cow watching him through the gate. She didn't look one bit smaller than she had last night. He could only see the house beyond as a vague, dark outline against the starry sky.

"Do you have your keys?"

"My keys?"

"To unlock the door?"

Julie gave him a puzzled look. "Why would we lock the door out here?"

Nathan didn't have a good answer to that one. His apartment door in New York had had three locks—deadbolt, door handle, and jammer—and that was inside a secure building.

"So you're okay from here?"

Julie looked at him for a long moment. He really could smell her, like the promise of spring.

Then, without any words, she leaned toward him and kissed him lightly. "Don't read anything into that. You're just a good guy." Then she was gone.

He watched as she climbed over the gate rather than swing it open. Her long legs and fine physique were caught for only a moment in his headlights before she crossed over.

Through the slats, he saw her pat Lucy the death cow on the flat spot between her eyes before heading toward the house. The last he saw of her was a quick wave and his headlights catching a flash of her bright blond hair.

He drove back to the ranch just as slowly, not because of the snow, but because he wanted to imagine Julie still sitting beside him.

CHAPTER 4

*J*ulie had the Douglas cabin fixed up by midday. The winter had been kind to this one and it would have to be a little warmer before she could paint. It was warm enough that last night's snow had melted and she was able to work in a light jacket, but not a chance that paint would set up properly.

She had the measurements for the new window for Larch called into town, which she would pick up over the weekend. Harvey promised to throw it in his pickup on Sunday, and she'd transfer it over at church.

Aspen would be the last one she'd work on. It didn't really need much, but she didn't think that Mac would complain if she spent a day or two sprucing it up. She wanted to hold off on it as a treat to herself.

Ponderosa. Just like the tree, this one was going to be a *big* problem. She spent a grim hour pulling out bathroom fixtures. The sink had a bad crack. The toilet definitely had to go. Yanking that revealed rotten flooring. The monstrous clawfoot tub had punched one leg down through another board because a hundred years ago no one had thought to place a support under where the heavy iron feet landed. It was not one of those charming old tubs that leant character. It was a big, ugly, heavy lump. Even in summer, no amount of hot water would make the cast iron comfortable to sit against.

Mac had taken very little convincing to replace it, but now she had to get it out of here. She could either cut out the side wall, cut down a couple of trees that were in the way, leverage it onto her pickup, and turn it into a water trough somewhere, or she could bust it up in place and haul it to the landfill.

"Sledgehammer, definitely."

In a minute she was back with a sledge, dust mask, goggles, and kitted up in heavy leather chaps and jacket. Busting up cast iron was nasty work.

Julie raised her big twelve pounder and gave it a hard swing. It bounced off the side of the thick tub. On the fourth swing, it finally did what cast iron does—it didn't crack, it shattered. A one-by-two-foot chunk broke free and slammed into the open door, missing her shins by inches and making a deep gouge in the doorframe she'd now have to fix as well. That would have hurt despite the leather.

There was a yelp of surprise close behind her.

She spun around to see Nathan Gallagher standing in the doorway, his eyes wide with shock as he inspected the chunk of tub mere inches from his toes.

"What in the world are you doing?" He eyed the sledge that she'd swung up to rest on her shoulder.

"Breaking up a bathtub."

"You look dangerous as all get out."

"Normally I only pummel on something that ticks me off."

"Remind me to never do that."

"Deal. What are you doing here?"

He held up a cloth sack. "Lunch. When you didn't come down to the main house, Ama worried."

"I was supposed to...?" Of course she was. On a ranch you fed everyone working on the property.

Nathan looked past her at the mess of the Ponderosa bathroom. "This looks ugly. You need a break. It's sunny and almost pretending to be warm on the front porch."

She really wanted to keep moving on the project, but it was hard to resist Nathan when he was in one of his coaxing modes, as she'd learned last night. Actually, he was quite charming about it. A shining prince was supposed to be tall, strapping, and blond. Nathan was her height, comfortably built, and had medium brown hair with eyes to match. But giving her the ride home, asking after her keys instead of just dropping her off or making a grab for her, and now bringing her lunch, he was definitely delivering on the charming.

Before she knew quite what was happening, they were out on the porch swing, looking down over the ranch. The chains creaked annoyingly at the first rock. She eyed them and saw that one of the eyebolts was wearing out. She made a mental note to replace that.

"I wasn't sure what you wanted, but you opted for a sandwich yesterday, so I went with that. Did you get inside okay?"

Julie opened the cloth bag he handed her, but had to take off her goggles and mask to look down into it. After shedding her leather gloves, she pulled out a monstrous sandwich. Not a bit of *a woman should only eat a dainty amount* from Nathan. This was a feast on a bun for someone who'd been burning calories all morning. Still in the bag was a can of pop and a plastic bag of—

"What's wrong with the potato chips?"

"Nothing. They're homemade."

"You know how to make potato chips?"

He shrugged as if such magic was nothing.

She tried one. Thick, crunchy, and heavy on the salt with just a hint of something spicy. Several more followed the first before she recalled the sandwich in her hand. Julie bit in and sighed: last night's roast, thick brown mustard, winter spinach, and pepper jack cheese.

"This is so good," she took a second bite before answering his question. "I got home fine, but you were right, I needed my keys."

"You did? Now I feel awful for leaving." He actually sounded upset, as if he could have helped.

"My brothers aren't the smartest cattle on the ranch. They locked the doors to prank me, but Mark and Luke left their window unlocked. They're both sound sleepers...until I dumped a five-gallon bucket of snow all over them." Their shouts had woken the entire household, but she'd slipped back out the window before they found the light switch and climbed up the outside of the porch into her own second-story room without anyone else the wiser. She'd locked both her window and the door to prevent retaliation.

Nathan's easy laugh had her smiling back at him. "Promise you'll never teach your vengeful tricks to Patrick. I'm the only brother he's got and I'd rather not wake up with snow in my bed."

"You make me another meal or two like this and you have a deal." Julie wondered just what he did like in his bed and then was aghast at her own thought. She went back to eating her wonderful sandwich.

"Done. You say when and I'll gladly cook for you."

NATHAN COULDN'T STOP SMILING as he watched Julie eating his food with such obvious pleasure. He couldn't remember the last time he'd simply watched someone eat his food. He liked the kind of deals he was making with Julie. They were easy, comfortable. They didn't feel like the *quid pro quo* of the infinite tally sheet of the city. *Sure I can lend you an extra eight lobsters, but you'll owe me ten back.* He always knew who he'd borrowed what from and what favors were outstanding when— Nathan wasn't missing that at all.

He also liked that she made no affectations about who she was. There wasn't a woman in Manhattan that wouldn't have checked her hair or brushed at her jeans if caught in mid-project the way he'd caught Julie—as if the city women he'd met would ever tackle such a thing. Instead, she'd been completely unapologetic about the mess she was. She sat there like a leather-clad warrior and not the sexy, Xena Warrior Princess kind. Julie looked impossibly real in her working gear.

This is who I am, deal with it.

And he was good with that. She had such a refreshing honesty.

"I like that you don't play games."

"Sure I do. Wait. What kind of games?"

"Passive aggressive-ego manipulating kind of games."

"What would those be?"

At first he thought she was joking, but maybe not. "Saying one thing. Meaning another."

"Give me an example."

"Last night when you kissed me," and then he wished he'd started anywhere else. It had been a means-nothing kiss of thanks that had cost him half a night's sleep.

"I told you not to read anything into it. I just..." and then she shrugged as if she wasn't sure what she just...

"I'm not. That's my point. I mean, sure I'd like to kiss you again and do it like we meant it. But you meant it as a thanks and then you made sure that I knew that's all it was and that it wasn't a come-on or a tease or any kind of a future promise, it was just a friendly kiss and Christ but I'm babbling. Shutting up now."

She ate a couple more of the potato chips he'd made specially for her. "No. I don't play those kinds of games. Half the ranch sons around here think I do, but I don't. The other half think I'm a stuck up witch just because if I say no, I mean it."

"Same thing when you say yes?"

She nodded.

"Damn, I could really get to like you, lady."

"Don't!"

"Why not?"

"Because at some point you're going to go back to your big city. I'm not a country-girl-for-a-fling sort."

"Never thought you were," Nathan couldn't imagine anything further from who she was. But she was right about him going... even if he didn't know where. "You strike me more as the one with the club."

"The club?"

"Conk the man over the head and drag him back to your cave?" He could imagine her very easily in the role—right down to the leopard skin dress that she'd killed and cut herself.

"Might be," she nodded as she finished her sandwich, then chips, then soda in methodical order.

"Well, there's an image for me."

"If you're picturing me in animal skins—" she left the threat hanging.

"Bet you'd look good in them," but he was unable to avoid the blush at being caught.

"Be glad the snow already melted or you just might find a bucketful down your shorts. Cool down, city boy."

"Yes, ma'am," Nathan offered his soberest tone, then decided his libido needed a subject change. "What are you working on?"

"Fixing up these cabins for guests. First ones will be here end of month. Mac hired my company to fix windows, replace a bathroom, things like that."

"You own a construction company? Emily was right, you *can* do anything."

She was shaking her head. "I can't fix the problem with the cabins we started construction on last fall."

"What problem?"

In minutes, she'd shed most of her leather protection and was leading him past the cabins and up the hill in a light jacket and worn jeans that he was starting to think of as one of her trademarks. It was a trademark that, on her fine figure, he wholly approved of.

He looked around for a distraction just as they were passing the last older cabin in the row.

"Hey, I like this one."

"It's my favorite. Its name is Aspen."

He didn't know exactly why he liked it. There was just something about it. It looked...cozier than the others. It was two stories, set into the side of the hill. The only one with a porch on both floors.

"It's solidly enough built to ride out the winter without trouble and it's tucked in a nice little shelter of its namesake trees. I also like the proportions. Come inside, it gets even better." She looked a little surprised at her own suggestion, but he followed.

The cabin was a single room deep. Either side of the main door was a living room and kitchen/dining room. Up the heavy-tread stairs was a pair of snug bedrooms and a small office, all facing the southern view. It was done in the same style as the ranch house: heavy timber beams and hardwood floors. But that was where the similarities stopped. It was cozy rather than majestic. The layout was for three or four people (plus a few sleeper couches for extra guests), but not forty.

After the tour, he gravitated back to the kitchen. It would take very little to make it an ideal space for testing new dishes or cooking for a family. He'd add an island with an extra sink and maybe a wok burner. Enough width for a couple of stools at the island so that stormy-day meals could be eaten at the counter while looking out the big windows.

"I love this place," Julie's voice was unexpectedly soft.

"It's easy to imagine you here." And it was. Her beloved Montana out the front door, but safe and warm within. Horse barns only a few hundred yards below.

"What about you? Can you imagine yourself here?"

≈

JULIE WAS AGHAST at her own question.

She could picture Nathan here. Right here. Beside her.

That simply wasn't possible.

He leaned on the sink counter and stared out the window for a long time.

Unable to retract her question, her only choice was to wait.

"I don't know what I want anymore," his voice was rough; harsh in a way she wouldn't have thought him capable of.

"Something different?" Julie prompted him when he again fell silent.

"All I know is that I don't want what I had. I'm almost thirty. I had an executive chef position at a top restaurant called Vite. It means 'breeze' in French—not like a wind, but like an easy motion. Could have had my own restaurant in another year or two. Guess that I could have a couple years ago, but for some reason never got around to it." Then he looked down at the sink and appeared to be holding onto the edge with both hands as hard as he could.

She wanted to apologize for asking. For breaking whatever shield of lightness that he'd been projecting. She had the sudden suspicion that his problems were far worse than her own.

"I've done nothing but been a chef for over a dozen years. And then one day, I was making my eight millionth *steak au poivre* with a side of tiger prawn-stuffed mushrooms and it was all so meaningless. I finished the dinner service, packed my knives and my car, left a note for my landlord, and hit the road by two a.m. Slept a night outside Chicago in a goddamn yurt in some screwed-up kind of hippie motel along the interstate. Now I'm here and I'll be damned if I know why."

Something tugged at Julie, made her want to go to him, but she didn't know what she'd do if she went. Consoling a horse was one thing. Consoling a man? She didn't have a clue.

"Sorry," he stood up and wiped a hand down his face as if brushing off his past. "My shit. Shouldn't be making you wallow in it. Let's go see your new cabins." And he was out the door before she could think what to say.

He was well up the trail by the time she caught up with him.

"Nathan, I—"

"No. Don't say anything. You're right. I'm probably going back to the city someday. I don't know why I would, but it's where I've always been. And I sure as hell can't imagine myself anywhere else, though I keep trying." Then he stopped so suddenly that she almost ran into him, and he took a deep breath. "I *can* see why you might love this though. There's nothing here and it goes on forever. It's like there's no pressure."

"No pressure?" Julie practically screamed at him in her own shock. "My entire company, getting out of my psychotic house, depends on this working. Do you think I want to live with my father and three brothers the rest of my life?"

He turned and blinked at her in surprise.

Julie wanted to pound a fist into his smug face.

Except it wasn't smug.

Instead it had that worried look again, like when he was asking if she'd be okay getting home fifty paces from the house she'd grown up in.

"You're right," he said in a tone of apology. "I don't know anything about living out here or what you're dealing with. I'm just a lost city boy. Sorry."

And he looked doubly sad.

Julie searched for some calm and wasn't having much luck. This *had* to work. She'd never had so much riding on a single problem. If she could beat the basements into the ground with her fists, she'd do it.

"Sorry," he shrugged an uncomfortable apology. "Maybe we'll get together and have a mutual whining session about it some time."

59

She felt the bile knot up in her stomach at even the thought of failure.

"Or maybe not."

Her expression must have been dire for him to be backpedaling so fast.

"For now, tell me about your cabins."

Julie managed to rein in her fears and worries. This must be how Nathan felt only moments ago, holding on to that sink for dear life.

He retreated a step and she felt bad for it.

"I get it now. My shit. Shouldn't be making you wallow in it." Her simple repetition of what he'd said brought a soft smile of understanding to his face.

He brushed a warm finger down her cold cheek as if signing a pact between them to set all that aside for the moment. The gesture was both surprisingly intimate and infinitely kind.

The combination took her breath away for a moment.

"Where are these cabins?"

"You're standing in one."

He looked down at his feet in puzzlement and then back at her.

"Snowberry, Ninebark, Wood's Rose, Beargrass, and Meadowrue," she pointed as she named them. "The downslope cabins are the trees. This cluster are to be named for the bushes and grasses."

"Still not really seeing it, Julie."

She sighed and looked at the grassy slope. "Neither am I. That's the problem. An early freeze last fall meant that we didn't get the basements cut into the soil before the ground froze too hard."

"The ground freezes basement deep here? Patrick said it got cold, but I never thought he meant that cold."

"It can freeze down a couple of feet. We have to go down to

five or six to avoid frost heave. But if I build the basements starting now..." she struggled against the ill feeling.

"There won't be any way to get the cabins built by summer for them to pay for themselves," Nathan finished with deep insight. "Don't look so surprised. I've run a number of different restaurants. I know how to run a business."

Julie sighed and sat down on the grass—and regretted it immediately. The snow had melted, but the ground was still too frozen for the water to go very far. Her butt was instantly soaked.

"Don't!" But Nathan had already landed beside her.

"Thanks for the too-late warning, cowgirl."

"Anything for a friend, city boy."

"So, since neither of us is smart enough to stand back up..."

"Yep."

"What if you didn't dig the basements?"

"The buildings would tend to shift around. Buildings don't like that."

"Big pilings?"

Julie tried to picture it. Pilings would probably take more concrete than a basement, but there would be savings in the digging. Could run the utilities up in an insulated box. And the cabins had no use for a basement except as a support. "Maybe..."

"Can you do that and still have time to build the cabins?"

"Not even with a crew." So much for hope.

"What about those temporary things?"

"Tents?"

"No, yurts. It didn't look as if there was much to those."

"Yurts?"

"Sure. Like that one I stayed in outside Chicago. They were mighty proud of it; told me that state parks are using them all over the place. Little ones, big ones. It was kind of nice, once I got over the strangeness of it. I liked the domed skylight and all of the wood lattice work inside. I don't know anything about yurts or building, but it looked like the only built structure was a circular deck for a floor."

"Would they survive a winter?" Julie was liking this idea. Liking the glimmer of hope even more. A cluster of yurts could really be attractive here. She'd put down some extra pilings for outside decks to open up the view of the ranch. From up here she could even see Larson's Double-L Ranch and was surprised that at enough distance, even it looked picturesque. Far more importantly, pilings and yurts could be fast.

"Do you need them for guests in the winter?"

"Winter guests are rare, but—" And then she saw it. If they went up fast, it meant they'd also go down fast. Up in the spring, down in the fall. Drain the utilities and leave the decks in place. Maybe with a protective cover.

～

JULIE GRABBED ONTO HIS ARM. Hard. She was far stronger even than she appeared.

Nathan could see her thoughts were churning. "More adventurous than the cabins. 'Stay in a yurt on the Montana Front Range.' It even sounds adventurous."

"And you could upgrade them to cabins later, then shift the yurts into another section as the place grows. Could even do a communal bath and showers like a campground so there's only one set of utilities to put in this spring. Microwaves and water coolers in the cabins."

She began shaking him back and forth by her grasp on his arm.

"I take it you like the idea."

"Like it? Like it! That could actually work. You're brilliant."

"No, I just passed out in one near Chicago is all."

"Cut it out," she shook him again. "This is good. I've got to go run some numbers. I have to find Mac. This could really do it."

Nathan liked how she looked when she was excited. There was more than beauty, there was joy, and it looked really good on her. He hoped that it worked out.

"You're a lifesaver!"

"Great!" Her change in mood was incredible. It was easy to feel swept up in it. "Do I get a prize?"

"Sure!" She let go of his arm, grabbed him by the lapels of his jacket, and pulled him into a hard kiss.

His thigh squished into the cold mud as he rocked toward her. She didn't just make it a short, hard smack. In moments she was leaning into it as hard as he was. He got a hand around her back, though he wasn't sure which of them he was steadying, and gave back as good as he was getting. As with everything else she did, when Julie Larson kissed him, he knew that, by god, he was being kissed.

Then between one instant and the next, she leapt from his arms up onto her feet.

He was far too dazed to follow.

"I've got to go," she started off, displaying a perfect muddy imprint on her butt.

"Hey, cowgirl!"

"What?" She stopped ten feet away and turned back to him. Her dazzling blue eyes, her blond hair caught in the light breeze, her unthinking stance of grace and power: she looked like a miracle.

"I just want you to know," he'd meant to make it a question, but that wasn't how it was coming out. "I am absolutely going to be reading something into that kiss."

"Why?" A look of uncertainty slid across her face.

"Because it was absolutely lethal. That's why."

"Lethal, huh?" Her smile lit her up brighter than the sun playing across her hair. "I like the sound of that."

And then she was gone, practically skipping down the hill.

CHAPTER 5

*N*athan sat in the chill mud with the taste of spring and brown mustard on his tongue.

He'd had his share of lovers over the years.

The ones who weren't chefs never lasted through the maddening hours that consumed his life.

The ones who were chefs never lasted through the maddening hours that consumed *both* their lives. Or the job would tear them apart: competition, opportunity elsewhere, there was always something. For a while he'd been screwing a sous chef fast and hard in the walk-in refrigerator. There was a fantastic synergy when they cooked together and it was the only bit of privacy where they could burn off the mid-dinner-service heat that consumed them in a flambé-towering burst. There was a hostess-floor manager who he'd had every night for months, but only in the back booth of Vite after everyone else had gone home. Then Nathan had learned that she had a husband—when he came to the restaurant with some business partners and wanted to meet the chef he'd heard so much about. That was the end of that lifestyle.

For the last year since then, he had cooked. He had just put his head down and worked.

And now he had a wet butt and had been kissed in a Montana field by the poster girl for wholesome blonde.

What the hell?

As Julie hurried down the trail, Nathan spotted a big truck that had just pulled up into the main yard by the barn. The driver climbed down and tried to slow Julie's passage, but she blew right by him.

Despite the cowboy hat, Nathan knew his walk as well as he knew his own.

"Patrick!" His shout must have carried down the slope because the big tall cowboy turned to look and then waved both arms.

Nathan hurried down across the meadow, following far less nimbly in Julie's path.

They slammed into each other and pounded one another on the back.

"Is it the apocalypse?"

Nathan looked up at his brother. He himself wasn't short, but Patrick took after their dad, both of them hitting six-three. "Apocalypse?"

"It must be for you to just up and leave New York. I was bettin' on that happening this side of never." Patrick had picked up a cowboy twang that sounded unnatural compared with the other people Nathan had met here, even more unnatural considering his Suffolk County, Long Island upbringing.

"Maybe it was." A personal apocalypse would explain a lot. "Honestly I still don't know what happened. One moment I was cooking in a top Manhattan restaurant and forty-eight hours later I was eating Ama's stew."

"And kissing granite lady."

"Who?"

"Granite lady. Julie Larson: stone hard, stone cold."

Nathan would never apply any of those adjectives to her.

Patrick sat back on the big truck's bumper and leaned back

against the front grill. "You sayin' that you wasn't just kissin' Julie?"

"I'm thinking that's between the lady and me."

"Crap, Nathan. You're such a stick in the mud. Is that what it takes to get to her? She won't give me the goddamn time of day, though the lord knows I try some fair bit. I'm gone for a couple days and you're all over her."

"I'm not all over her." He sat down on the bumper beside his brother.

"I just can't believe you'd cut me out like that."

"Cut you out? I'm not cutting anybody out."

"You kissin' Julie Larson is gonna piss off a whole lot of boys around here. You're my brother so I'll give you a pass. But it's a close thing, I can tell you."

~

JULIE STOOD close by the truck's door, just out of sight of the two brothers.

She'd caught up with Mac in the barn and he had loved the idea of the yurts. Now she'd doubled back to tell Nathan before hurrying off to do more research.

And he and his brother were talking about her as if it was up to anybody other than her who she kissed. As if she was a commodity for exchange like a side of beef.

Anger built in her until she was shaking with it; it wasn't an emotion she was used to. Just moments ago life had been so good. The solution of replacing the cabins with yurts. The bone-melting kiss Nathan had delivered almost made her think something good could happen with a man, no matter how little time he was going to be in Montana.

And now—

She turned and was stalking away, she didn't know where, when Emily stepped out of the barn and flagged her down.

"I had a question for you..." Emily trailed off. "But I'm guessing this is the wrong moment."

Julie swallowed down her fury, blinked away the burning sensation in her eyes. "No, now is fine." Her throat felt as if she'd been chewing glass.

Emily's eyes called *Bullshit!*

"I'm fine. What's up?"

Emily scanned around, caught the two voices at the front of the pickup. Julie couldn't hear what they were saying at this distance, but she could still hear the bantering tone they'd been using to talk about her. Emily's sigh was sufficient. It *was* nice to have another woman around.

Ama was so reserved that she rarely spoke, and Chelsea was so young that she did little else.

Emily looped her arm through Julie's and guided her away toward the barn.

She braced herself for some conciliatory talk or empty reassurances that she had every right to be mad. Instead, Emily was quiet as she led Julie into the warm, horsey air of the barn.

She would *not* remember the easy fun of finding Nathan's car corralled down at the end of the row, or the consideration he'd shown for not wanted to start the engine inside the barn. Last night he'd been intriguingly different. Now he was just like all the other cowhands, though he'd gotten further than most with that kiss. He could read anything he wanted into it now, she was a closed book as far as he was concerned.

At the center of the building was a built-out set of rooms. To one side, two large tack rooms were filled with neatly arranged saddles, blankets, and halters. On the other side was a room filled with brushes, hoof picks, and a locked cabinet with all of the medical supplies necessary when the nearest vet was thirty miles away, and an office. Chelsea was there keeping up the paperwork on all of the horses.

"Hey, girlfriends. What are you two up to? Ooo, sad face," she scrambled out from behind the desk and gave Julie a surprising hug. "I saw that kiss," she pointed toward the window in her office. "You're not supposed to be wearing 'sad face' after a whopper like that. Was Nathan a bad kisser? I thought he was kinda cute. I had hopes for him. Or is he leaving already?"

Julie couldn't even catch her breath under the barrage. Any thoughts that her private life was somehow...private died fast deaths.

"What's up with him anyway? Is he—"

"Chelsea," Emily sad softly, which ground Chelsea to halt.

"Oops! Running off at the mouth. I've really got to watch that."

Chelsea's preferred mount, a big dapple gray named Snowflake, stuck her head out the first stall by the office at the sound of Chelsea's voice. Without hesitation, Chelsea shifted over to scratch Snowflake's cheek and straighten her forelock. Julie could forgive her a lot for that thoughtless bit of care for her horse.

Julie stepped over to greet Snowflake and to let Chelsea know it was okay. But she definitely needed a subject change. "Emily, you had a question?"

Chelsea jumped right back in, "She wants an office out here in the barn, but I need mine. We could convert one of the stalls, but I'd hate to lose the horse space, that's already at a premium. How much space do you need, Emily?"

"It's not a question of space really. A couple of chairs, a few computers. It's a question of security."

"Security?" Chelsea seemed glad to carry Julie's half of the conversation as well.

"Sound and electronic. I want to run a small but secure communications center."

Julie resisted the urge to ask why and looked about the barn.

For once Chelsea was stymied as well. Emily shared a smile with Julie at that.

Julie nodded and looked around again. "What about up there?"

A narrow stairway led up between the two tack rooms across the main aisle from Chelsea's office. On top of the rooms was the big open loft close under the barn's roof. It was filled with the normal detritus that accumulated around horses: worn leather that might still be useful someday, ropes in need of splicing, old saddles that someone hadn't wanted to throw out, buckets of rusted horseshoes and nails. Once the three of them had climbed up to survey the space, it was clear that most of it was crap that simply hadn't been dealt with.

"Really?" Chelsea held up a rusty pitchfork missing a tine and a shovel with a broken handle. She tossed them back down in disgust. "I can clear all this in an afternoon. Well, most of it." There were some things worth keeping.

Julie paced out the space atop one of the tack rooms as well as she could, threading her way through the debris. "What if you boxed in an office on top of this room? On top of the other one, you could build a couple sets of shelving and hooks to organize the rest of this."

"Works for me," Chelsea shrugged.

Emily stepped over as if entering her new office.

"It's close under the slope of the roof, but you'd have full height for most of the space," Julie could see it taking shape. "Insulate the roof here. Maybe punch through a skylight down here on the slope so you'd get sunlight as well as a view out over the property. And if you want a more open feel, a couple of windows inside overlooking the barn as well."

Julie liked the view from here. She could look down into a dozen or so of the horse stalls. Some were sleeping, some tugging at the hay in their feeders, one or two watching what the three women were up to so high in the air.

Emily followed her gaze. "You really love the horses."

"Born to them," Julie shrugged. "Never was much of a one for the cows. That's my dad and brothers. They'd just as soon use an

ATV as a horse—they see them both as just tools. I'll take Clarence any day of the week."

"Yet you've never come here, to a horse ranch, to work."

"Sure I have. In fact, I should be working now. I've got to do some research and then get back up to Ponderosa. That bathroom won't fix itself."

"I meant to work with the horses."

Julie shrugged. Mac was a great rider and Ama rode like a dream as well. Doug had been born to horses as much as she had and Chelsea was a natural athlete at anything having to do with the outdoors. "The ranch has always had all of the horse people it needed."

Emily kept whatever her next thought was to herself, which was just as well. Instead she took one more tour through the junk, then nodded her head.

"So, you like the idea?"

"Yes," Emily nodded. "When can you have it finished?"

"Excuse me, what?"

"I don't have the skills to build it."

"Me neither," Chelsea agreed. "Though I'd be glad to help if you need an apprentice. Always cool to learn how to do something new."

"I was just helping you figure out what you needed," Julie wasn't sure why she was protesting. She didn't have any other work lined up after the cabins for Mac. She'd rather hoped that the work and his recommendation would generate some more business at other ranches around.

Time to change her tune if she was going to make a go of it as a contractor.

"Building a space is easy. I can build you a space. Sound insulation is no problem; good ventilation and heating isn't hard. I can run in any power you need, but I don't know anything about electronic security."

"I have some friends who can help us there. Let's worry about physical security. A stout door, with a good locking mechanism. Your job if you want it," Emily finished.

It was a simple structure. A couple of walls. Windows and a skylight. A subpanel for the electrical, maybe with a battery backup of some sort or a small generator. Better yet, solar on the roof. She'd been dying for a chance to tinker with solar. And with Chelsea's help she could knock out the shelving on the other side in a couple of afternoons.

"Okay," Julie took a deep breath. "How fast do you want it built?"

Emily's smile was as close to a laugh as Julie had ever seen on her. "Imagine me, retired, leading people on fishing trips."

Chelsea actually snorted out her laughter.

Julie smiled back at Emily, "So, that would be soon?"

OVER THE NEXT couple of days, Nathan couldn't get near Julie.

She was in some kind of a whirling dervish mode that was worthy of a New Yorker. One minute she'd be ripping the floor out of the Ponderosa cabin's bathroom. The next she'd be loading a dumpster in the barn. When he tracked her to the equipment shed, she and Mac were so involved in hooking up a nasty piece of spiral-shaped steel auger, two-feet across and a person tall, to a backhoe that she didn't even notice him there. Then they were up on the hill punching holes into the ground with it. After that she was back to ripping out the broken window on Larch. She was working sunrise to sunset and often as not Mac or Emily took her a lunch. Mark was soon involved as well.

And Nathan could feel his welcome growing thin.

His few attempts to get near Julie had been met with a reaction he couldn't quite understand.

She mostly appeared to be too busy to stop when he was

around, but every now and then he'd catch her *getting* busy the moment she spotted him.

The longer it went on, the more sure of it he became.

Patrick was no goddamn help. "Granite lady. Like I told you. She's as hard as those hills," he pointed at the snow-shrouded peaks of the Front Range.

It was almost a stumbling shock when one day she simply wasn't there. He was on his twentieth foray from the kitchen to see if she'd arrived, when Emily came walking along the path from the barn to the house.

"Have you seen Julie?"

"Not today."

Nathan sighed. "I'm starting to think she's avoiding me."

"Starting to?" Something in Emily's tone confirmed the worst of his fears.

He'd spent most of the week trying to figure out if he'd done something wrong. It wouldn't surprise him, but he had no idea what it could be. They'd kissed, and then she'd gone invisible with no apparent transition in between. The word "flighty" had fit other women in his past, but not Julie. Moody too didn't seem to be her style, based on what little he knew of her. The only option that was really left was pissed—but he couldn't think of why.

"She's not avoiding you today, if that makes you feel any better."

"How do you know that?"

"It's Sunday."

"Oh," he'd lost complete track of time here. He'd arrived... Monday, Tuesday...he wasn't sure. It wasn't like when he was a chef with every night blending one into the next until there was no difference. Out here each day was so distinct it could have been sliced from the sky in discrete chunks. But which day it *was* seemed to have little meaning. Horses and ranch hands had to be fed. Today there was less of the frenetic pace that seemed to fill the rest of the week, but not enough to really stand out. So this was Sunday on a ranch.

"I expect she's at church with her family."

"Where's the nearest—" but he knew, it was the same as everything else out here.

"Choteau," he and Emily said in unison.

"Do you have any idea...no, sorry. I told her I didn't want to drag her down with my own worries. I'm guessing that you don't want to be dragged into this either."

"Can't say that I do," but Emily waved for him to follow her into the barn.

He hadn't been out here since the night he and Julie had found his car together. He wished he could find some way to rewind to that night.

Emily led him up a flight of stairs to a set of framed walls covered in bright plywood. He didn't remember this being here.

"Her work?" He didn't know enough to tell if it was good or bad, but it looked solid.

"She's building me an office," Emily sat down on a saw horse in the middle of the space.

Nathan sat on one opposite her.

"I can't tell you what, but I can tell you when."

He really didn't want to put Emily in the middle of it all, but was helpless on what else to do.

"She was standing beside the truck when you were talking with your brother shortly after his return. I've seen warriors in combat who looked less furious."

Nathan tried to recall the conversation.

Patrick had been talking about Julie like she was a side order dish on the menu.

And if she'd thought he was doing the same...that would explain a lot.

"But I wasn't," he said it aloud without meaning to.

"But she thinks you were, whatever it is. And right after you kissed her."

"She kissed *me*," not that it made any difference.

Emily glanced out one of the windows at a horse's nicker. "So she likes you?"

"I like her, too. For all the good it's going to do me."

"Do you want some advice?"

Nathan shrugged, "Couldn't hurt anything at this point."

Emily smile was brief as a New York cabbie's as she rose to her feet, "Remind her of that."

~

JULIE LIKED SEEING EMILY UP in her office. She'd been pushing hard to keep all three projects moving, which is why she was back after church. That and she had a fresh load of supplies from town. In addition to the window for Larch, she had all of the glass and skylight for Emily's office.

As she came up the center aisle of the barn, Emily descended and nodded a good afternoon. Then she nodded up towards the office as if warning her there was someone else up there. As if—

Oh no!

Emily's third nod confirmed her guess.

Nathan.

Julie was not ready to deal with him yet. But Emily repeated her signal with a commiserating shrug of her shoulders. How did she communicate so much without speaking? Julie would almost swear that there was another implied level saying, *give him a chance.*

She'd come here to work, not to... But Emily was gone before she could protest.

Fine. She'd fix this fast and then get to work on things that really mattered.

She tromped up the stairs, the treads creaking badly. They

were stout enough and served their purpose well enough for a storage loft, but for an office space, she needed to pop them up, then glue and screw to kill the squeaks. Another task on her already overwhelming list. Maybe she should just pop off all the treads and maroon Nathan up here by himself.

He was sitting on a sawhorse facing her when she walked in.

"What is it with you, Nathan?" Not the nicest of greetings.

"I like you, Julie."

It took her a moment to shift gears. She wasn't expecting such a simple statement from a guy. "You've got a damn weird way of showing it."

"Wasn't me. Just my brother. I never could beat decent manners into him."

"He wasn't the one bragging about kissing me."

"Neither was I. *He* was complaining that he hadn't and I had."

"But I heard—" What had she heard?

"He saw us. And I couldn't get him to shut up. Has he really been coming on to you like you were a side dish?"

"More like a slab of female first course."

"I should pound the shit out of him," the look of anger that suffused his face only fit Nathan if he really was the white knight. She'd never met one. Didn't even believe in them since she'd been groped at ten by an eleven-year-old Danny Andersen. Julie had thrown every single one of her cherished princess and fairy tale books in the manure pit that day. It didn't seem likely that a New York chef could actually be a white knight, but he was doing a fair imitation. Either he was better at it than most others—because at least he was trying—or maybe it was one of those sneaky games he'd mentioned.

"If you do decide to beat him up, I'll be glad to help. I've tried most everything else to get him to back off."

"There won't be anything left after I strangle the little shit." Nathan was still angry enough that he looked ready to spit out horseshoe nails.

"Are you now doing some macho, she's-mine, kind of crap?"

"No! It's just not the way you're supposed to treat a woman," then about half his fury dissipated when he looked up from the hole he'd been trying to glare through the floor. "You mean like some hound dog pissing on his turf?"

"Exactly like that."

Nathan actually looked puzzled as he inspected her, the floor, the ceiling, and then her again. "No, I don't think so."

"You don't *think* so?" She finally sat on the other sawhorse.

"Never thought about it really. But I don't strike me as the guy who does that kind of thing."

"All guys do that kind of thing." At least all of the guys she'd ever met.

Nathan just shrugged.

He was silent long enough for her to become aware of the dust motes in the air and the occasional huffing sighs of horses perfectly content to be inside on a chilly day.

"As I said, I like you. But I'm not stupid enough to think that a kiss, no matter how spectacular, makes you *mine* in any way. The only claim I can make on you is that I like you. I seem to keep saying that. I guess because Emily said I should."

"Emily said you should keep saying that you like me? You asked her for relationship advice after a single kiss?" Julie didn't know whether to go back to being furious or to laugh.

"Not exactly. She said that I should remind you that you like me. And no, I didn't ask for advice. I just asked if she knew where you were."

"She thinks that I was so angry because I'd forgotten I liked you?"

Nathan shrugged a yes.

That tipped her over into laughter.

"What?"

"So much for the infallible Emily Beale."

Nathan tentatively matched her smile, but he didn't get the joke yet.

"I got so angry because I *do* like you. Now get out of here, I have work to do."

He nodded and rose. He didn't go for a kiss. Didn't even hesitate to see if she'd offer one. He just took her at her word, rose, and left.

If he wasn't the strangest thing in the history of Teton County, she didn't know what was.

CHAPTER 6

*A*s soon as Nathan knew what was going on, he had a plan. It couldn't be sneaky, instead it had to be utterly blatant or it might just irritate her again and there'd be no predicting the end result.

The plan was so clear in his head that he hadn't even thought to kiss her when leaving Emily's loft office until he was out of the barn and most of the way back to the house. It was just as well, he didn't want anything messing up his plan.

He couldn't do anything about it that night, except a bit of prep. Sunday dinners were apparently a big deal on a Montana ranch. Emily helped him and Ama with the cooking, others chatted from the fireside or were recruited to peel or chop.

Julie was her usual all-over-the-place on Monday, which worked well for him. Unexpectedly she came down to the house for lunch—which he still couldn't get straight in his head was supposed to be called dinner. Her arrival almost screwed up his preparations, but he managed to hide the ingredients he'd been assembling without having her any the wiser.

Only Ama knew what he was up to and she didn't say a word.

Patrick and the not-twins were merely *moderately* obnoxious to their unexpected lunch guest—at least they weren't downright offensive. He didn't dare jump to her defense because that would just egg on different rumors. Emily shut that down hard when she joined them, though. Hard enough to earn his appreciation of her, even if no one else at the table appeared to notice. Maybe it had been just normal teasing. Julie had certainly handled it as such, but he still didn't like it.

After lunch (dinner), she headed up onto the hill.

Perfect.

He carried his first load of supplies up to the Aspen cabin as soon as he and Ama had lunch put away. Julie was right, of course. If he had to choose any cabin of the five, now that he'd toured them all, it would be this one. The others stood together on the grassy hillside. Aspen's treed cloister cut down on the vista to either side, but it made it private and cozy. Once inside, he fired up the cabin's heat and the oven.

Julie answered his casual wave with a nod from where she, Mac, Doug, and Mark were auguring piling holes up at the new cabin sites. They had giant cardboard tubes that they slipped down into each hole as soon as it was dug out.

His hands were full on the next trip as he brought up most of the rest of the cooking supplies. She was driving her truck down for more of the tubes as he walked up the trail from the house, so this time it was his nod to her wave.

Last night he'd set a pair of steaks in marinade made mostly of red wine. The wine pre-digested the meat just enough that it would be fork tender by the time he cooked it. He started in on German scalloped potatoes, done in a vinegar-bacon sauce rather than a cream one.

As he worked through the warm afternoon, he was pleased to discover that he still enjoyed cooking. He hadn't been sure if that was something else he'd left in New York. Helping Ama prepare the meals for the family and the ranch hands had been pleasant, but it wasn't *real* cooking. This was, and it was fun.

He used a cookie cutter to make sure that each circle of puff pastry was exactly the same size for the tiny puff pizzas which he would garnish with roasted pepper, a sauce he'd spent all morning building on jarred tomato, and identical slivers of caramelized onion cut on the bias to make each piece a curling arc around tiny cubes of roasted winter squash and Ama's sausage.

He'd had to discard a dozen different dessert ideas due to lack of ingredients before he'd decided that simpler was better. Fresh vanilla bean ice cream on individual-sized huckleberry and candied ginger pies.

The sun was headed down when he made his last trip to the house for a bottle of wine and a couple of glasses. He'd purposely left it behind because he wanted to pique her curiosity with another back-and-forth.

The work crew knocked off about the time he returned to Aspen cabin. His timing was perfect.

He checked on everything that was cooking, poured two glasses, and headed out to sit on the porch swing.

By the time Julie rolled her truck to stop on the dirt track below the cabin, he was relaxed and enjoying the last of the sun's warmth before it ducked down behind the mountains.

"What have you been up to all afternoon, city boy?" she called from her open truck window.

"Come see for yourself, cowgirl." He picked up the second wine glass and held it aloft as an offer.

She cut the engine and eased out of the cab with the care of someone who'd been working hard all day. "All I want is a hot shower and a beer."

"Damn! I didn't think to turn on the water heater." She looked just fine to him in dirt-spattered boots and jeans. Her fleece-lined denim jacket, a yellow bill hat with a blue Ford logo on the front, and her hair pulled into a ponytail through the back loop were also just what he'd expect of a woman like her. Utterly practical.

"Do you even know how to turn on a water heater?" She came up on the porch. "Are you trying to seduce me?"

"Probably not."

She eyed him strangely.

"I mean the water heater."

"So, you probably *are* trying to seduce me? Fair warning, it's not going to work."

"No, I know. I just wanted to cook for you. We had some bargain about me having to cook for you."

"So that I don't teach my evil ways to Patrick."

"That was it. I think he has enough of his own already. He *is* a good kid, you know. Even if sometimes he doesn't show it so well."

"Sure," Julie agreed as she finally unwound enough to sit down beside him and take the glass of wine. "Or maybe he will be if he ever grows up."

Nathan decided that both parts of that statement bore a lot of truth.

"So what did you cook for me?"

"Dinner. Or I guess you call it supper."

"I'VE NEVER in my life had a meal like that." But it seemed that she certainly should have. Food was normally just something to be eaten, but not Nathan's supper.

Through each course he'd explained how, when there was time to make it properly, a meal should unfold in layers of flavor. The tiny shredded pork ravioli were swimming in a broth that she could gladly have bathed in it was so tasty. He'd explained how the meal would have shifted if he'd followed with a fish course rather than a winter greens salad with walnuts and a mustard vinaigrette.

The night of the party, when he'd said he could cook, she'd foolishly thought that meant he could "cook." Maybe at one of the fancy hotels in Great Falls, which served scallops and fancy fish from Alaska. She'd had king-crab-stuffed sirloin once and it had been...good. She'd thought it had been great, prior to this moment.

Now all she cared about was how glorious she felt. The flavors, the preparations, she'd never cut a two-inch steak with just the edge of her fork before. And it had practically melted on her tongue.

The company had been shockingly pleasant as well. The warm fire, which Nathan had built tolerably well, made Aspen even more welcoming than she'd ever imagined. There was no candle on the table, which she realized was *not* an oversight. Nathan really didn't seem to be running a seduction here. Instead they ate by the light of a single lamp—the table so friendly that there was no motivation to leave it for the living room. The meal itself seemed to have wandered forever, meandering down odd conversational lanes into strange and dusty corners that were always interesting.

"How can you know so little about the world? You live in New York."

Nathan shook his head as he nursed a cup of tea and took a final scrape of melted ice cream. "I live, lived, in a kitchen. My world is ingredients, not..." he flapped his hand outward, "...all that noise."

"Sherlock Holmes," she said, wondering if he'd get a literary reference.

"Right. The case of the... I can't remember... *A Study in Scarlet.* Sherlock complains when Watson tells him that the planets orbit around the sun. That fact was irrelevant and useless to his purpose of solving crimes. He didn't wish to have it cluttering his thoughts. Works for me."

Julie tipped her head back and forth studying him. "You're a very strange person, Mr. Gallagher."

"I could have told you that much. Why this time?"

"As far as I can tell, you haven't done a single thing to try and impress me."

He laughed, "I told you that I only had one skill. I know how to cook. If that didn't impress you, I've played the only card I've got. Shot my full quiver."

"Impress me? *That* was not cooking—I'd call it delirium, it was so good. Not what I meant anyway. I mean, you aren't trying to show off your knowledge, or how good you are at something. Not how many cattle you can brand in a single hour, or your epic ride on the latest rodeo bronc, or even how many prize belt buckles you've won."

"There's such a thing as a prize belt buckle?" He sat forward shoving aside some plates and dishes so that he could lean on the table. But it wasn't as if he was leaning in to get closer to her. He was just being comfortable.

She laughed because she couldn't help herself. She was very proud of the ones that adorned her bedroom wall.

"There are even things called Buckle Bunnies. They're women who wear cowboy boots and painfully short shorts."

"Let me guess. They go to rodeos and try to trip cowboys."

"Bingo."

"Any boy buckle bunnies trying to trip cowgirls?"

"Nah. Just—"

"Rutting cowboys," they said in unison and she laughed again. She could feel the attraction across the table—a very nice bit of sizzle. But Nathan had none of the aggressiveness necessary to be a rutting cowboy. Overall, though, he was still climbing on both the prince charming and white knight scales.

Nathan sobered, "As to how many of those things I can brag about? That's easy. Does zero count as an answer?"

"It does. I'm not particularly sure what to do with it. But it counts. I think."

"I can't wrangle a cow. I can't build a cabin. I can't train a dog or ride a horse. I'm—"

"Wait a second. Back up there, city boy."

"A dog? I was watching Stan out there working with those military dogs he's training. I see why he doesn't talk to people; his main language is dog. And he's good at it."

"Not that. You can't *ride a horse?*" Julie didn't know if she'd ever actually met someone who couldn't ride a horse. Even the most incompetent city guests who came to Henderson Ranch were coming to ride horses. "Tessa is three years old and can ride a pony just fine. Though it spooks Emily every time she does. Belle will be three months in a little bit. Definitely time to get her up on a horse."

Nathan looked aghast, exactly as Julie had planned.

"In someone's arms. She can't even sit up yet. You let go and she just tips back over and giggles. Cutest kid you ever saw." And how she'd ended talking babies with Nathan Gallagher, she had no idea. She gunned back for the prior topic. "Really, really never ridden?"

Nathan just shrugged. "They rent horses up in Central Park. At least I think they do, but I never hired one."

"You can't ride a horse."

Nathan looked around the room. "Strange echo in here. Never heard a delay like that one before. Never pet a horse either. Don't think I've so much as touched a horse. Or a cow. Well, you know, not before it was butchered. No interested in petting Lucy, just so you know."

"Oh, city boy. We really are gonna have to fix that. Soon."

He squirmed uncomfortably in his seat.

"Not an option, city boy. It's just too sad for words."

"Yeah, that's me." The way he said it stopped her.

There was something more behind that, something she'd caught a glimpse of earlier in the week—sad and painful. But it was clear he didn't want her prying. And after the amazing meal, she decided that kindness was something she could give him, tonight anyway. But it was the second time she'd caught something wrong and she was going to have to dig it out; it was bugging her like a stone in Clarence's shoe.

She went searching for a different topic—and spewed out pure stupid.

"So what's the course after dessert? Is this when you try to seduce me?" Talk about giving him an vast opening. Bad move. Very bad move.

Nathan smacked his forehead with his open palm. "I knew there was something I was supposed to be doing next. I've got to run down to the main house and get some bedding. Could you check upstairs and see if the mattresses are musty? Probably should have scattered rose petals up the stairs and into the bedroom. You don't have any rose petals handy do you? Crap!" He started patting his pockets as if he'd find them. For half a second she thought he was going to actually rush out for sheets and blankets and, god help her, rose petals.

Then the joke caught up with her. "You run a crappy seduction, city boy."

"Special for you, cowgirl," he dropped back in his chair as if exhausted by all of his momentary flurry. "Actually, I thought that maybe just getting to know you a bit might be fun. That, and find out if I can still cook."

"Put a big check in that last box, Nathan. It was truly amazing."

He was nodding to himself as if he wasn't so sure.

"Okay. Spit it out. Enough of this sad dog act."

"Spit what out?"

But he didn't deny the sad dog part of it.

After a moment he raised both hands in resignation. "Not tonight, okay? Not over my food. Maybe over someone else's."

"Well, don't be looking at me. I can cook on a grill or a campfire well enough to not poison most folks, but I'm all thumbs in a kitchen."

"I'll keep that in mind for the future. What are my survival odds? Fifty-fifty? Sixty-forty? Still might be worth the risk."

"Might end up accidentally knocking your cowboy hat into the fire," she made it a threat.

"Don't have one of those either."

"Oh, city boy," she sighed.

SHE'D HELPED him clean up, which wasn't much. Nathan always ran a clean kitchen: washing up as he went, reusing what he could. But they'd fallen into an easy synchronicity even over that simple task. With him washing and Julie drying and putting away, they'd cleaned up the Aspen kitchen in record time.

He closed up the cabin and walked her to her truck by the moonlight shivering down out of the crystalline dark sky.

"You really weren't running a seduction on me, were you?" Julie hesitated with one hand on her truck's door.

"Seems to me, way too many guys have been trying to run that game on you just because you're nice and you're pretty."

"Most of them don't care about the nice part," the chagrin sounded as if it came from deep experience.

"So, here's my deal with you—seem to be making a lot of those. No games. I cooked for you because I wanted to. As a bonus, I enjoyed this evening even more than I expected to, which is saying something. You make a great dinner companion."

It was only a quarter moon, but it seemed so close here, much closer than in the city. There were more stars in the sky than at the Hayden Planetarium on the Upper West Side. The light caught her hair, though not her expression. Her breath into the chill air sparkled for a moment before dissipating.

"Also, there's a lot to like about you. The fact that you're gorgeous is definitely on the list. But so is your competence, your quiet sense of humor, and your incredibly positive attitude." He knew he was getting too serious. "Though your misplaced belief that you can teach me to ride a horse definitely makes your common sense suspect."

She looked up at him from under the brim of her hat for a long moment. "That's a kinda long list from someone who claims he isn't trying to seduce me."

"No games. No lies. I've had enough of both to last a lifetime."

"You're walking a thin line there, Nathan."

"What line?"

"You cook like a dream. You're thoughtful. You think your brother is a better man than he is, and you just might prove you're right and he's wrong someday. You've got this sort of sad little corner that makes a girl think about taking you home and feeding you a bottle of warm milk like a sick calf."

"I could have done without that last image." Being pitiable wasn't exactly the trait he wanted to be known for by a beautiful woman.

"It works on you." Then she took her hand off the truck's door handle and instead slipped her chilled fingers around his neck and kissed him. It wasn't the hard smack of their last kiss. It was soft, warm, and slowly eased into full body contact.

Even on this cold winter night in early April, she tasted of spring. Warm, lush, and welcoming. Neither of them hurried through it, nor did they cling afterward.

Just as he'd thought of her since the first moment they'd met, Julie's kiss was exactly what it was—a really amazing kiss. No promises of tomorrow. No offer to share her body. No teasing rub together hinting that there might be more if he did everything "just right." It was simply and thoroughly a kiss.

He managed not to ask if all Montana women kissed that way after she climbed into her truck and slammed the door shut herself.

"'Night," was all she said through her open window as she started the engine.

"Goodnight," was all he managed before she rolled away into the night.

CHAPTER 7

"*R*ise and shine, city boy." Nathan jolted awake when Julie kicked his bed.

Damn but he'd looked cute all curled asleep in his bed. Cute, hell, she was more than half tempted to wake him with a kiss and see if last night's had been as real as she was remembering. While they'd kissed, he'd just held her. Not groped or even gone for a quick "accidental" feel. He'd just snugged his arms around her waist and held her tight. It had felt mighty good.

He blinked at her in sleepy surprise and pulled the covers up tightly around his neck. By the neatly folded clothes on his chair, she could see that he didn't even wear underwear to bed, unless he was a pajama man. He didn't strike her as a pajama man.

"Wha'?" he mumbled as he twisted to look toward the window —it was still pitch dark. Then his clock—the hour on it seemed to surprise him some.

"Enough of you sleeping in 'til all East Coast kind of hours," she gave it a good country drawl. "If you're gonna be on a ranch, it's about time you shift over to ranch time. Besides, now is the only time I've got. I'm busy the rest of the day. You've got five minutes. Meet me in the main barn. Dress warm and wear boots, if you've got any."

"I have boots."

"Wear 'em."

He nodded, but made no move to get out from under the covers while she was still in the room. Definitely not a pajama man.

Julie turned on her heel and, after a brief stop for coffee, headed out to the barn.

Nathan was there in close enough to five minutes, but he'd clearly skipped a lot of things to make it. His softly curling hair was more uncombed than usual and his night's beard showed a stronger chin that one would expect of him at first glance. There was a little toothpaste caught at the corner of his mouth that she didn't comment on but he eventually licked away. His boots looked like they'd come out of some New Yorker-in-the-snow movie—soft rubber with a furry lining. Something else they'd have to fix if he was going to stay in Montana for any length of time.

She wasn't going to think about her own reaction to that thought. Why should she care if he stayed or went? They'd shared a great meal and a spectacular kiss. That was all.

"Let's start with the basics," she walked up to the stall Chelsea had set aside for Clarence. He popped his head out over the half-height door when she approached. "This is a horse." She scrubbed a gloved hand between Clarence's eyes.

"Ha. Ha. Ha."

"Well, you thought Lucy was a savage animal. I figured I should start simple."

He didn't bother to repeat himself, just stood there looking grumpy. He had his fists jammed into his jacket pockets and his head still hung with being only partially awake.

Julie took pity on him and handed over her half-finished coffee.

"That helps some. Thanks."

She handed him a couple of sugar cubes.

"No thanks, I don't use it. Though some cream next time would be nice."

Julie sighed. "Starting with *this is a horse* maybe was the right place. The sugar isn't for you, it's for him."

Clarence was watching it with great interest.

Julie showed Nathan how to hold palm and fingers flat so that Clarence didn't accidentally chomp down on them.

"That tickles," Nathan smiled as Clarence lipped the cubes eagerly off his hand, then crunched them loudly. She wasn't sure how she felt about her horse receiving Nathan's first smile of the day rather than her. He finished her coffee and set the mug aside.

Step by step she led him through all of the beginner stuff that she didn't remember learning. There was more than she'd thought and it took some effort to unravel it for him. His instincts around animals were nonexistent—maybe Lucy had spooked him for real.

No sudden moves, keep your toes well clear of the horse's hooves, speak to him as you move, and so on.

He laughed at how Clarence's skin rippled wherever Nathan's hand traveled. Julie had been trying to teach him how to let the horse always know where he was by trailing a hand over him, but Nathan's touch was so tentative that Clarence's nerves treated it like a fly and kept trying to flick it off.

"No," she clamped her hand down over his, pinning it against the warm, bristly surface of Clarence's shoulder. "If you're going to touch a horse, really touch them. Make your presence and confidence clear."

"I'm guessing just the opposite works with you," he brushed a finger of his free hand so lightly down her cheek that it utterly took her breath away. She was suddenly aware that pinning his hand to Clarence's shoulder also had them holding hands—at least hers holding his.

"Don't do that," she managed on a whisper. She didn't have the ability to twitch her skin like a horse to shoo him away. Julie also didn't like what his gentle touch was doing to her knees. Her knees and her heartrate were *not* supposed to be connected to her cheek.

"I've been thinking about last night's kiss."

It had been an amazing kiss, though she kept that thought to herself. Nathan was a man who looked like a comfortable, average man, but under the surface had a startling intensity. She saw that now in the way he cooked, had felt it in the way he'd kissed. Now, he seemed to be trying to hypnotize her.

It was working.

She couldn't shift a muscle as he leaned down to kiss her again. Just a brush of the lips. Just a taste of the possible. Just—

∾

NATHAN JOLTED and yelped right in Julie's face. He yanked his hand free and slapped it on the sharp pain in his ass as he turned to see who had attacked him.

Clarence snorted in something that sounded very like a laugh.

A sound that Julie clearly echoed from close behind him.

"Well done, Clarence!" Chelsea was leaning on the stall's half door. "High five, buddy." She held up her hand and Clarence nosed forward enough to accept her affectionate pat.

"What the hell just happened?"

"Clarence doesn't like you kissing his girl," Chelsea explained. "Pity. It looked like it was gonna be a really good one."

"But—he's a horse!"

"Doesn't mean you didn't deserve a nip on the ass for manhandling Julie."

"I wasn't—" he didn't even know why he was trying. He checked his butt. No tear in his jeans and he didn't feel any blood. "Do I need a shot or something?"

"For what?"

Julie was still laughing, her amusement sliding into a giggle that would have been charming under any other circumstances.

"I've just been bitten. Am I going to get rabies or something?"

"Hey," Julie shoved against his shoulder to get between him and her horse, which was fine with him. "Clarence is a clean, healthy horse. Don't you malign him."

"Malign him? Malign him!"

Clarence eyed him warily.

"He bit me!" The next biggest thing that had ever bitten him had been a mosquito. And his brother had then read aloud a whole website entry on the different diseases that a mosquito could carry and all the symptoms that Nathan now had to watch for. If a mosquito had all that, he couldn't begin to imagine what something as big as a horse had.

"It was just a nip," Chelsea and Julie said together in a unified defense of the perpetrator.

"Just a nip? Why I oughta—"

Clarence raised one hoof and stomped it down hard. The stall's floor was just dirt, but Nathan swore he could feel the ground-shock up through his boots.

How low did a man have to go to have a horse get impatient with him?

Pretty low he supposed. He rubbed his butt once more and decided that maybe—just maybe—it was merely a nip; the pain had mostly faded while he was busy ranting.

"Pretty damn pleased with yourself, aren't you?" he asked the horse.

Clarence jerked his head up and down through a three-foot arc that was disconcertingly similar to a human nod.

"He's my guardian angel," Julie confirmed as she leaned back against the horse's shoulder and the perpetrator turned to snuffle at her. A great blast blew her hair aside. He'd been left the option of "rutting cowhand" and her damned horse got "guardian angel."

"Yeah," Chelsea still leaned on the stall. "Next time you want to manhandle your woman like that, I wouldn't do it near this horse."

"I wasn't—" What was the point? Arguing with a redhead, a blonde, and her horse struck him as a losing proposition.

"His *what?*" Julie's shout had even Clarence stepping aside as much as the stall would allow. Without his shoulder supporting her, Julie almost went down on the straw bedding. "I'm *nobody's* woman except Clarence's."

"No secrets up in the big house, Julie," Chelsea was enjoying this more than any of them. "Fancy dinner—at least the list of ingredients sounded fancy to me. Do you have any idea how long it takes to make puff pastry? I didn't, but Emily filled me in. Then lights on up in the Aspen cabin until mighty late with your truck out front. Was it sweet or romantic? Did it get steamy? Oh, I really hope it got steamy; I love steamy. Give me the details, girlfriend."

"I'm not *his woman,*" Julie ground out the words.

"Why not? A cute man who cooks and owns a hot sports car? That would be more than enough for me."

"Chelsea! You married a ranch foreman who owns a pickup and can barely fry an egg."

She nodded, "But there are other things he does so...very... well." Her smile said exactly what some of those things were.

"Enough!" Julie cried in defeat, pushed out of the stall, and she and Chelsea were gone in a moment.

It took Nathan several heartbeats to realize that it was just him and Clarence alone in the horse stall. The horse was eyeing him suspiciously.

"Her guardian angel, huh?" The horse did a headshake that flopped its mane neatly into place. It might have been a yes or a no...or maybe a "look out, bub."

"I guess if I'm going to go after your girl, I better be nice to you." Was that what he was doing? To what end? Wasn't he leaving soon?

Clarence had no comment.

There was only so long he could freeload off Mac and Ama. She'd ignored him when he tried to pay for the ingredients for last night's dinner. Yes, he helped in the kitchen, but she didn't really need him.

"Well, there comes a time in every man's life when he must..." but Nathan couldn't remember the rest of the quote. "I guess... when he must take his life in his own hands and suck up to a horse."

Make your presence and confidence clear, he reminded himself silently. That's what Julie said was the secret to handling a horse.

He stepped up to Clarence, gave him the best imitation Nathan could conjure of a manly thump on the shoulder, then stepped confidently—and quickly—out the stall door.

There was a sharp clack of horse teeth close behind him, followed by a whinny that he was simply going to pretend he hadn't heard.

∾

JULIE'S PROTEST that she "didn't want to hear it" was about as effective on Chelsea as could be expected. Finally resigned to her fate, she followed Chelsea into the barn's working office and closed the door.

It was a good space. She'd helped Chelsea rearrange it last fall and Chelsea had made it her own since then. Like everything else in the barn, it was clad—floor, walls, and ceiling—with heavy lumber gone dark brown with age. A big roll-top desk sat up against one side wall. Out a big window in the back one, Chelsea had a sweeping view of the property up toward the ranch house and the cabins.

All around the desk and on the other side walls were photos of happy families and couples up on their horses or camping up by the waterfalls on the far side of the Henderson property. There was also a big monitor hanging on the wall, which at the moment was showing the information on her laptop's screen: every horse broken down into...

Julie hadn't seen a rating like this before, but once she figured it out, she couldn't help but laugh.

"I know, right?" Chelsea looked pleased.

The columns headings weren't: OK for beginner, intermediate, advanced rider only... They were: easy-going, opinionated, *really* opinionated, and downright ornery. There were only a couple of names in the last column, and Doug—the best rider on the ranch —was working with those. Julie wouldn't mind doing some of that work herself, though it wasn't as if she had the time.

"I'd always thought Clarence was, like," Chelsea tipped back in her chair and stared at the chart, "—easy-going. Something about Nathan really sets him off, right up into *really, really* opinionated."

Julie had to grant that. She'd never seen Clarence act up so around a man. Not even when she lost her virginity right out by Henderson's waterfalls. He'd just munched away on the high summer grass as if nothing of interest was going on. Regrettably, Clarence's sense of what was happening had been more accurate than her own.

With her desk to the side, Chelsea could swivel her chair to face a small couch and a couple of other chairs so the big desk wouldn't sit between her and the clients. Julie sat on the couch and thumbed through the magazines sprinkled across the coffee table: *Western Horseman, American Cowboy, The Trail Rider, Young Rider,* and a couple of rodeo and barrel racing titles she hadn't read in far too long. She had to remember to hang out in Chelsea's office more often. *American Farrier's Journal* and *Equine Wellness* were lined up on a shelf above her desk—of less interest to a ranch guest but still looking well thumbed, probably by Chelsea, who inhaled knowledge about horses.

"You've really settled in well here."

Chelsea shrugged. "What's not to like? I was always an outdoors kinda gal. Thought I might spend my days out trekking.

I loved the Himalayas. Decided I was going to do all the long trails. I was most of the way up the Pacific Crest Trail, my first one, when I stumbled on Mark and Emily's firefighting outfit in Oregon. Kinda needed a break and they took me on as Tessa's nanny. Didn't last long 'cause they brought me here. Met Doug a year ago Christmas and now can't recall what I was walking so hard and fast to get away from. Pure bonus, I get all of these sweetie pies to take care of," she waved a hand at the wall of photos.

Julie wasn't sure if she meant the horses or the guests. With Chelsea's big heart, she probably meant both. Julie flipped through the magazines again.

Chelsea's laugh stopped her.

"What?"

"You know that you're gonna have to spill at some point."

"What are you talking about?"

"Duh! Me or Emily. At some point you're gonna have to talk about it or it'll just build up in you until you don't know what to do with it. I guess you could talk to Ama, but she still spooks me what with her see-into-your-soul bit and then pointing out the shit you didn't want to see with, like, one word or a well-timed shrug."

Julie had always rather liked Ama—a woman of few words. Though talking to her about relationships did sound a bit danger-ous; Ama would be sure to point out something Julie didn't want to hear.

She didn't exactly like getting advice from a twenty-two year old either—no matter how ideal Chelsea's and Doug's relationship appeared to be.

"Everything's fine. There's nothing going on."

"Sure," Chelsea leaned back in her chair and propped her cowboy boots on a copy of *Barrel Horse News*. "I believe you. Even if neither Clarence nor a blind man would."

Julie made a show of lying sideways on the short couch, propping her head on one arm and her calves on the other. "Go ahead, Dr. Chelsea. Try me. I dare you."

Chelsea made a show of tugging her long red hair back into a tight ponytail and trying to look severe, then gave it up as a lost cause.

"Nah! I'm gonna leave you to Emily. She's way better at this kinda shit. Besides, it's time for breakfast...if Clarence let Nathan out of the stall alive so he could go cook it."

Julie found it easy to laugh with Chelsea as they double-checked that there was no body on the floor of Clarence's stall before heading up to the house together.

NATHAN DIDN'T GO BACK to the house.

Instead he tracked down his car.

It had become a game and locking it up didn't help.

One day it had been put out to pasture along with the horses, along with its own burlap feedbag. The time that he'd finally tracked it down in the hay loft, he'd simply turned away—no idea how they got it up there and no idea how to get it down. Waiting out the jokers seemed to be his best strategy at that point.

Sure enough, yesterday it had been an element of Stan's dog training obstacle course. The memory still made Nathan smile.

"Unarmed explosives," Stan had explained when Nathan had asked why the dogs were sniffing his car so intently. "Stashed some for them to find in door panels, the trunk, and so on."

For over an hour he'd watched Stan working the dogs. It was a small litter, just six animals, but his patience with them was remarkable.

"They're really too young for this work," Stan came over to the fence after telling the dogs to go play.

He leaned against one side while Nathan leaned against the

other. The way the dogs collapsed to the turf convinced Nathan that Stan wasn't the one who needed the break.

"This is more about me practicing my training methods. Lackland Air Force Base trains all of your standard military war dogs. But the ones for the Special Operations teams—SEALs, Delta, even Rangers—they're trained up by contractors to different standards. This litter needs another year of aging and then we can start their real training. Mac has a long-term view, sees what this can be in a couple of years. Gave me a shot to prove it." It was clear by his tone that he worshipped the old man.

"If they're too young," they looked full grown to him—like black-tinted German Shepherds. They were beautiful dogs. "What about him?"

Stan looked over to a small pen just inside the fence where a puppy lay napping with his chin resting on a small stuffed animal. "Vizsla. Hunting dogs. Picked him up in Choteau. Shouldn't have, but have a friend back east thinks they'd be good military war dogs. Promised Mary I'd try one and there he was, so I had to get him. She named him Gibson."

"Friend back east..." He was so gruff that it was hard to imagine Stan having a girl.

"Retired librarian. Funny lady."

Okay, so much for that idea. Nathan nodded back toward the resting dogs, "Is there a star of the group?"

"Bertram there," he pointed at the pack with his hooks, which told Nathan nothing. "Far and away the smartest of the lot. Watch."

Stan picked up a ball, then a second one. All of the dogs were instantly on their feet, ready to play—except the puppy still asleep in its pen. Stan heaved the first ball high. Five of the six dogs raced after it, striving to grab it out of the air. The sixth dog still sat on its haunches, looking from Stan's face to the ball in his hand.

Stan winged it low and fast. Before he even released it,

Bertram was on the move. Reading Stan's body language on the throw, he snagged it out of the air before it had traveled fifty feet, despite the wide angle and high speed that Stan had heaved it at. He dropped the ball at Stan's feet while the other dogs were still wrestling over who could keep the first one.

The two of them had settled into a game of catch of their own —a game that had shown so much of how Stan felt about his "best dog" that Nathan had felt he was intruding to watch more of it. Rather than retrieve his car, he had left the two of them to their game.

That had been yesterday. Today, of all odd places (one of the last he looked), Nathan found his car in the dim confines of the garage—no daylight yet through the windows. His Miata was parked among the ATVs that weren't all that much smaller. Doug had made good on his offer and the flat tire was repaired and back in place.

The gas was full.

It was all set to go.

JULIE WAS ALWAYS THROWN when she ate at Henderson's. The contrast was so sharp to her own home experience that it almost gave her a sense of vertigo—like she was barrel racing and hit the turn wrong.

At home, no one interrupted Dad during a meal. Matters unrelated to the farm or an upcoming rodeo were rarely discussed. The latter was the only time she had a real place as she was by far the best rider in the family and her display of ribbons and prizes were a point of family pride. There was a gap there that continued to irritate her father: the Miss Rodeo Montana award. Or even— never said aloud of course—the coveted Miss Rodeo America award.

She hadn't cared about manners and world affairs and "representing fine American traditions". Instead she'd gone for the only prize she really cared about, and come closer to winning than she'd ever expected. She'd taken home Third Prize for Barrel Racing at the Calgary Stampede. The foot-tall bronze statue of a cowgirl and her horse carving a hard turn around a barrel held the place of honor in her bedroom. She'd beat out any number of professional riders for that coveted win. When she died, she was taking that statue to the grave with her.

At a Henderson Ranch meal there were so many conversations that she didn't know which to follow. Topics ranged all over the frontier from lame horses to the tourist economy to international news. Devin and Drake were either a goldmine (or maybe they were a landmine) of Hollywood celebrity gossip—at least about who was sleeping with who. It was both funny and just a little creepy. No one could ever pay her enough to put up with that. Being three-time top rodeo rider of Teton County had gained her far more notoriety than she liked. She had sight-unseen proposals from as far away as Bozeman and Missoula—not to ride, but to wed.

Mac Henderson didn't even make any attempt to corral the conversations. It was just crazy. Though the guys, even Patrick, were better behaved around Emily, which Julie appreciated.

But the most disorienting thing of all was Nathan's absence. The straw wasn't deep enough for her to have missed him on the floor of Clarence's stall. If he wasn't here, where had he gotten off to? She wanted to ask Ama, but she was at the far end of the table taking care of one of her granddaughters. Emily too was at that end.

Patrick and the non-twins were busy dissecting Tom Cruise's latest *Mission Impossible* performance and debating that if he got to choose any one of the female costars, which one should it be.

Chelsea was teasing them about which man the female costar should choose, and how it shouldn't be Tom because "he was getting so old. Still cute, I mean I'd trip him if I hadn't met Doug, but seriously? If you guys want to pretend you're over fifty and would have a tenth of the chance that Tom would, go for it."

Mark and his dad were discussing possible fishing trip plans for guests. For a change, Mark's ever-present mirrored Ray Bans were dangling from his shirt's collar rather than hiding his steel-gray eyes.

"For the back-country fly fishers, there're several fine spots up towards the falls. Stan did a great job fixing up the fishing cabin last winter," Mac said in his easy manner.

Stan, as usual, made no comment though he was listening in. He wasn't a fisherman, that she knew of, but he appeared even more bored by the on-going Hollywood discussion than she was.

Mark's speech was more clipped, more…recently ex-military. "Need to look into back-country permits. Helicopter them in for a true wilderness experience. Scout some lakes, fish them a bit to see what's biting."

Mac had slapped Mark on the arm knowing exactly what his son was up to. "You never were made for just sittin'."

"Except along a trout stream."

Julie had never been one for "just sittin' " herself. And she realized that's what she was doing, even though breakfast was already done. Another very non-Larson style activity, still at the table after the meal was eaten.

She rose to her feet and cleared her place over to the sink. Still no sign of Nathan. It wasn't as if he was duty bound to show up. And it definitely wasn't that she wanted to see where that first hint of a soft kiss might have led if Clarence hadn't taken exception to him.

It definitely wasn't that.

Mac flagged her down halfway to the back door.

"We need to talk, girl. Come along to my office." He led her back through the ranch house and to the grand double staircase that swept up from the front entrance. The sunrise was shining in through some of the high windows, lighting the big foyer like a cathedral.

She'd never actually been upstairs in the house since the Hendersons had taken it over.

"We used to sneak in here when we were little kids," she told him to hide her nerves. "Big, spooky old place to a little girl, but I always liked it, too. Even then I could see the house's bones were good under the age."

Mac nodded. "Bart Sr. offered it to me when I retired. How could I refuse? I'd saved his son during Desert Storm when we were forward deployed past Saddam's lines. Nothing Bart Jr. wouldn't have done if our positions had been reversed. But his dad was—still is—one of the big ten owners in Montana. Legally made this place mine as long as me or mine are working it. Can't sell it except to him, and only for any added value. Fair a deal as I've ever been offered."

Almost a tenth of Montana private lands were owned by ten major holders. She'd always wondered how the Hendersons had afforded such a big spread. Neither theirs nor the Larson land was anywhere near the top ten category, but they were two of the bigger ranches around for a long ways. Her family had done it by moving onto the land back when Custer's Last Stand at Little Bighorn and the Great Sioux War were passing into history. Back when no one had cared about this stretch of the Montana Terri-tory except the "injuns"—who long since had been moved onto reservations or forcibly relocated.

"It had gone fallow," Mac continued telling his ranch's recent history she barely recalled. "Only thing that saved the place is how remote it was. 'Fix it up however you like,' he told us. Five years back, he brought his grandkids out to ride horses. They were our first clients, insisted on paying. 'Don't give anyone no charity they haven't earned,' was one of Bart's rules."

At the head of the stairs, the transition was dramatic. She

vaguely remembered cobwebbed corridors and a long attic of weathered gray wood.

The attic was now a big airy room with five big pedal looms and a couple of smaller ones. Dark cherry wood and bright maple, they stood on a floor of polished oak beneath large skylights. Tall windows, glowing with the morning sunlight, offered a sweeping view only a little less spectacular than the one from up at the cabins. The walls were hung with Cheyenne weavings: deep red, black, tan, and gray. Some were bright and new, probably Ama's work. Others looked to be museum-quality heirlooms.

"There's such a sense of belonging here." Julie wished she could somehow wrap this space around her and hold it inside so that she'd know it was always there. Mac gave her the time to walk through, brush her fingers over the rich colors and tight-woven geometric shapes, and pretend for a moment that she had such a depth of history.

The Larsons were Minnesota dirt farmers who followed the cattle west in the late 1800s. They'd only arrived in Minnesota after working their way across from some long-lost Scandinavian famine. Their history hadn't moved with them. Ama's had; Julie could feel it in the air.

"Thanks for that, Julie. We've worked hard to create that," Mac sounded as if he still didn't believe that they had. She remembered what he'd said about how a father worried, at least some fathers.

Taking his hand for a moment, she looked at his lined face. "Your son and his wife could have chosen anywhere in the world to live. They chose here. You done good, Mac."

He nodded, looked aside for a long moment, then nodded again. "Come on back," his voice was rough as he guided her along the corridor.

To the other side of the main stairs from the majesty of the weaving, a door led to a cozy hallway adorned with family pictures and a few smaller wall hangings. This was the family's private space, separate from all of the splendor downstairs. The dimensions were smaller, more human. The architecture simpler. This was their home.

How did that feel, having a home? She had the house she'd grown up in, the bedroom that had been hers since the day Grandma had passed when Julie was four. But this was different.

Home meant someone to live with, didn't it?

"You're going to be a 'hard woman' soon," her father had taken to saying. A hard woman: unmarried, alone, bitter. Too hard for any man to want her.

It wasn't true. She knew it wasn't. But sometimes she worried that it was.

And then Nathan had cooked for her and done it like she was special. Kissed her softly as if that's how she *deserved* to be kissed.

For the first time in years, perhaps ever, he made it possible to imagine "home."

NATHAN SAT on a hay bale in the equipment garage and looked at his car parked among the ATVs. In front of him was a helicopter. Behind him, an entire array of machinery that he couldn't begin to name. The metallic red Miata MX-5 fit in here just about as well as he did—not at all.

It had been a crazy purchase for someone who so rarely left the city limits. He'd put more miles on it the two days of coming here than he had in the year before, maybe the two years before.

And now?

He should get in the damned thing and just drive away. Just go. Don't even go up to the house to get his knives or his clothes, because she was up there.

Just slide open the big door and fire out of here.

What the hell was he playing at anyway?

Julie was a startling woman. A breath of fresh air that he liked more with each passing moment. But how fair was what he was doing?

To either of them?

She was right. He'd be gone. Sooner or later, probably sooner, and then where would he be? Where would they be? They'd both be even more miserable than if he left now. Just toss the dice and start over.

Somewhere.

Seattle or Portland? They were supposed to both be hotbeds of foodie innovation.

So was Brisbane, Australia. But he didn't *want* to go to Brisbane, Australia.

Back to the city?

He'd go insane.

And if he stayed here? Great Falls or Boise? Or was Boise in some other state?

Even crazier.

Maybe he should just drive until he ran out of gas, or money, and start over wherever chance landed him.

Not cooking. He'd liked cooking for Julie. He liked watching her eyes slide shut as the flavors overwhelmed her.

But a restaurant? Never again. He'd sooner herd cattle from hell.

He stood up.

That's what he'd do.

He took a step toward his car.

"I'll just start the engine and go. See where the road leads me."

It was good. It made sense.

He reached for the door handle.

It was the right thing to do, for him. For her. Cut it off before he did more than kiss her. Before he fell for her like he'd never fallen for a woman before.

He could see that, too. Really falling for her. And *then* having to go.

Best to just do it now.

Best to—

"There you are."

Nathan almost shouted in pain at the interruption.

If Mark Henderson noticed anything out of the ordinary, he didn't comment on it.

"I'm going up. Want to come along? Help me roll this out." Mark opened the equipment bay door in front of the helicopter, letting a slash of hard sunlight slice through the air. He signaled for Nathan to help push without waiting for an answer.

Not knowing what to do, or even how to speak at the moment, he pushed where Mark said to push. Together they rolled the helicopter out of its garage bay and into the brilliant morning sunshine radiating from low in the east.

The sky was shockingly blue, horizon to horizon it looked like spilled paint.

∾

HALFWAY ALONG THE UPSTAIRS CORRIDOR, Mac led Julie through a doorway into a small office. It was almost comical it was so plain. Two steel desks, a couple of big file cabinets, and a view back into the sloping hillside. One desk was neat as a pin, the other looked as if it had been through a train wreck—a wreck that was still in progress.

"Didn't want this to be nice. Get work done, then get out in the sun where I belong. That desk is for doing the books," he waved a hand at the neat one. "This one here is for thinking."

She suddenly felt uncomfortable. Why were they meeting in his office? Was there something wrong with her contract? Or with her work? She needed this to succeed.

"I figure that running a ranch should be done out on a ranch, not locked up in some pretty office," Mac had read her surprise at how plain and cramped the space was in the otherwise expansive house.

"Dad's the same way. I think his office might have once been a broom closet. We kids always clear out when he goes in to deal with the paperwork because he usually comes out in a foul mood."

"Happiest when he's out and about," Mac nodded and sat down at the "thinking" desk, which she'd take as a good sign, and indicated for her to sit across from him.

Julie tried to shunt the huge wall of worry aside and answer Mac truthfully, which wasn't a very comfortable feeling when it came to her family.

"I'm not sure happy is a word I'd ever apply to Dad, but *content* might work." During rare moments.

"That's something you learn in Special Operations. You work hard, you train hard. But there is a time when you have to celebrate being alive. Really let your hair down and kick it out a bit. You ever do that, girl?"

The only image she could conjure up was galloping on Clarence over the empty fields. She wasn't sure if that counted, so she shrugged uncertainly.

"You should do it, Julie. I'm serious. Take that young man you're so worried about and go play."

She wasn't worried about Nathan. Not really. Though she wished she knew where he was.

Mac fished around on the desk until he unearthed a pen and a pad of paper. He made a clear spot by shoving some of the journals, notes, catalogs, and a couple of books about snipers over on top of more of the same.

He plopped the pad down on the desk and raised his voice to carry over the helicopter that was passing close over the ranch house.

"So, here's the problem I'm thinking on."

≈

NATHAN TRIED to remember how to breathe, "I thought you were going to hit the house."

"Not a chance. I missed it by over twenty feet," Mark actually swooped back down toward the ground on the back side of the big ranch house until they were skimming mere feet over the grass. "God it feels so good to fly again."

"How long has it been?"

"Days, maybe weeks. How about you?" Mark swooped low over the cabins.

"I flew to Paris about a decade ago and spent five years there."

"Airliners don't count. Sardine cans of the sky."

"Then," Nathan swallowed hard and hung on to the edges of his seat, "never."

The Bell JetRanger had three seats in back and two in the front. Mark sat in the right-hand seat and Nathan had the left. The clear plastic window offered him a fantastic view—a clear vision of whatever Mark was about to ram them into. But each time, at the last moment, he swooped aside. Not in hard, panicked moves, but as if it was the most natural thing in the world.

The engine and rotor were so loud that he could still hear them despite the heavy headset Mark had given him.

"Do you always fly so close to the ground?"

Mark's laugh was bright over the intercom. "Depends on the mission. You fly a firefighter helo a hundred feet above the flames, give or take. I've spent most of the last five years up in a command plane. To you that would be two engines with propellers on fixed wings. About a dozen seats, but I needed it for speed and range, not for people-carrying. I flew that within a thousand feet or so of the fires. Far enough to stay out of the way of the helos and airtankers."

"There's no way that we're a hundred feet above the ground," their flight path slewed across a broad pond just over the rise behind the cabins that Nathan hadn't even known was there. It looked as if there was still ice around the edges. There was also a sagging dock that was going to need some work before it could be a decent swimming hole.

"Do you skate?"

"Like Rockefeller Center? Ice skating? A couple of times, if she was cute enough to talk me into it. Fell down a lot."

"Midwinter there's good skating on this pond. I'll get you some hockey skates and we'll have a game," he climbed up the far berm and headed out over the fields.

"Sounds good." And it did sound good. Too bad he wasn't going to be here by then. Nathan actually shivered when he thought about how close he'd come to not even being here by lunch. It had been a close call. Whether that was good or bad was a question he couldn't deal with, especially while occupied with hoping he'd live through the next thirty seconds.

"On a mission, trying to stay out of sight, we'd be more likely to fly here," and Mark carved a turn around a tree, then slid down until it looked as if the skids were brushing the grass.

Mark's smooth moves still appeared casual, but Nathan could feel the silence of intense concentration settle over him. Nathan looked over but Mark's mirrored shades reflected the racing prairie as if the landscape had become his actual eyes.

"It takes a lot of control. Have to think without thinking. Every movement is critical." He narrated between shifts and jogs as he cleared the ground by feet and hummocks by inches.

Nathan felt a little seasick when he looked down. The window by his feet was so close to the rushing ground that all he could see was a blur—except when he blinked. Then, like a freeze frame, he felt as if he was standing on no more than a stepstool above the ground—the moment before it *rushed* out of sight underneath them.

"Goddamn it, Lucy!" Mark cursed sharply and did something to the controls that jerked them harshly upward.

They cleared the cow's massive horns by inches.

Far out—on Henderson land—Lucy was grazing on winter grass.

Mark circled her once from a couple of stories higher in the air. The cow watched them balefully, but kept chewing on her latest mouthful.

"It's the curse of the demon cow," Nathan shuddered. "You shouldn't have brought me along. She seems to know where I'm going to be and just shows up."

"Nah, I needed you as a second set of eyes."

"To avoid stray cows?"

"Need to scout out some fishing trips. Promised Dad I'd lead one now and again. Do you fish?"

"I cook."

Mark gave him a long, assessing gaze. "Heard some about the meal you made for Teton County's most eligible."

"Did she like it?" Nathan knew she had, but couldn't help himself. He was so pitiful. Hadn't he been on the verge of leaving for her own good just a few minutes ago?

"Mom said a real lack of leftovers came back from the dinner. So I'm guessing the answer is yes. Don't you know?"

Nathan decided to keep to himself how truly pitiful he was about wanting to please Julie. Actually, it was something of a surprise *quite* how important that was.

Mark swooped low over the broad pastures that looked to go on for miles. The mountains that had loomed so close all week were getting even closer. Thankfully they now flew several hundred feet above the rolling prairie.

"A chef really only lives for two reasons. If he's insanely lucky or practices for a lifetime, he may create a new flavor or a new dish that will outlive the moment of creation. The other reason is to make people happy with his food. Regrettably, knowing that he'll probably never achieve the former, he is constantly convinced that he can never achieve the latter."

"You really need to get a life, Nathan."

"Tell me about it."

Mark laughed easily enough.

"Instead, tell me what we're doing out here."

"We're on a fishing expedition."

"Fishing for what?"

Mark's sigh was unexpectedly deep. "Fishing for a way that I can survive retirement."

FOR OVER AN HOUR, Julie worked with Mac on the future of Henderson Ranch. First, they'd verified that all the orders were in place for the yurts: bunks, fixtures, bathrooms, and the yurts themselves. They'd opted for all five the same, the medium-sized twenty-foot diameter ones which could comfortably handle up to six people with a cozy sitting area for rainy days—though the main activities on those days would be down at the ranch house.

There was already a shower at the back of the main house. It had been for the hands to clean up back when the place still ran cattle. Mac added fixing that up to her to-do list, which had saved the size of the bathroom building up on the slope, though Julie wasn't sure about that choice yet—when you had children with you, a shower close to hand seemed preferable. The spring work-load was shaping up well for J. L. Building.

Then they'd looked over some of the ranch's prime recreation spots. They both knew the good trails that were a mix of prairie to gallop on, woods to mosey through, and the occasional vista. But there was only the one remote fishing cabin out by the waterfalls.

"I'd like to add one a year. First, maybe a hunting cabin back against the primitive area."

"Next, out by Old Baldy," she tried to be careful about not overstepping her place. But each cabin would be a couple months of good work for her if she did well on these first jobs. "There are some great trails back there. The guests pay for the ride out to the cabin, then the horses get a day or two of paid rest while they hike themselves up the trails."

"Make them happy to spend more for something that costs us nothing extra but some feed and a guide. The businessman in me calls that a win-win."

"Nothing comes for free." Then Julie nearly choked on her own words, because they were her father's.

"Nothing but the best things. Those are always free." So not her father.

Julie didn't know what to say to that, so she kept her thoughts to herself. It sure wasn't part of her experience. There was a cost, a trade-off to every decision in the Larson household. Pursuing her own future also earned her the brunt of Dad's disapproval. While her brothers seemed to appreciate his focusing on her for now, she sure didn't.

After she and Mac mapped out a couple more ideas—she was pretty pleased at coming up with geocaching of historical sites and especially spectacular views. Once the course was set, it would be a whole day horseback quest that didn't even need guides except as protection in case they spooked a bear. Could even change it up each year with new sites and new routes.

Finally Mac tossed down his pen and pad, then pulled out a desk drawer, leaned back, and propped his feet on it.

"Like the way you think, girl. You know this land better than I do."

"No, I don't."

"Ama and I have been here for just over fifteen years now, you've been on it your whole life."

"I spent most of the time over there," she pointed in the direction of Larson land.

Mac rocked his chair back on its hind legs and looked straight at her with steely gray eyes the same as his son's. Other than that and his powerful build, they barely looked related. Mark had

Ama's dark straight hair rather than Mac's graying blond. Though Mac still looked dangerously military, there was a soft kindness to his face that balanced him out. Mark's steel-eyed gaze unnerved her even more than Emily's used to.

"That's not my point. You know the land, the Big Sky country. I came from Chicago. No way you'd ever guess how I became a SEAL, so I'll just go on and tell you."

Julie kept her smile to herself. By his casual manner and willingness to take the time to tell a story, he fit right in. Somewhere along the way he'd become Montanan, whether or not he knew it.

"I was headed to California to become a surfer bum. Fresh out of Oberlin, liberal arts education in French literature, and absolutely no skills."

"You're telling me you got Ama because you were a surfer bum turned SEAL?"

"No, I met Ama before I did either of those. My car broke down in Cheyenne, Wyoming, during the Frontier Days, so I wandered to the rodeo while they were replacing my starter motor. Ama was a native performer there and I'd never seen anything so amazing in my life as that tall Native American beauty. I was done and gone before her dance was half over. She'd never traveled but wanted an adventure, so she went to California with me on a whim. We both sucked at surfing, but I can't begin to tell you how good that woman looked in a bathing suit."

Julie tried to picture Ama Henderson as a bikini-clad surfer babe and simply couldn't conjure up the image. She was still beautiful, but she embodied the serene matron of the spiritual connection to the ranch as if she'd never been anywhere but on this land.

"While we were surfing off Coronado," Mac was tipped back and studying something far beyond the ceiling. "I'd watch the SEALs run on the beach during the day and sweep up all the great women in the bars at night."

"But you already had Ama, right? She doesn't strike me as the type to get swept up too easily."

"True. I had her, but I wanted to keep her, too. That's how I became a SEAL. Did it for her, and whenever I had to dig down and find that extra motivation, just thinking of her did that for me. We made a good life together. She and Mark joined me overseas whenever it was safe. Neither of us knew crap about ranching before Bart gave us the place to run. Learned a lot, but we weren't born to it the way you were."

"Well," Julie thought about the ranch house, the property, the cabins, the horses, and the plans they'd just been working on for the future. "I think you've done a fine job of it, Mr. Henderson."

"Thanks, Julie. Means a lot coming from you," he thunked his chair down into place. "Enough jawing, as they say. Let's go get 'er done."

"Sure thing," Julie rose to her feet.

As Mac led her back along the corridor and down the stairs, he muttered as if speaking to himself, "Whole life changed because of a shorted-out starter motor."

Julie missed a step and might have tumbled to the bottom if it hadn't been the last one.

All because his car broke down.

"Now this *is* a sweet spot." Nathan lay back in the grass and watched a lone cloud slipping through the blue sky like a giant cotton ball.

Mark had landed them by a high lake well to the south of the waterfall. With the excuse, "Just need to see what's biting here," he pulled out a fishing pole he'd stashed aboard the helo and was soon casting a line out over the pristine water.

It was a fair-sized lake, wandering back into the deep trees for almost half a mile. While Mark fished, Nathan had explored. A lively creek drained to the north. He pulled out his phone and snapped a couple of pictures of Mark casting, thinking he'd send them to his friends still in New York—they'd never believe where he was—except he'd have to wait to send them until he found a signal again.

"Welcome to the wilderness."

He'd finally returned to the helo, grabbed a horse blanket from the supplies in the back, and lay down on the grass to watch the day. He hadn't truly stopped since getting here. Cooking with Ama to feed the hands. Talking to Julie. Kissing her. This morning's pre-sunrise "horse" lesson, provided equally by both the woman and the horse in question. Except for his sore butt, he thought it had gone well. Clarence wasn't nearly as intimidating close up as he had been in the evening light out on the road.

Nathan was utterly exhausted by the uncertainty of his life. His struggle to leave this morning without even seeing her one last time had almost broken something inside him. He had nowhere to go. Nowhere to be. Whatever came next—

Mark's soft whistle from fifty feet along the bank had Nathan looking back down from the sky. A trio of the ungainliest animals he'd ever seen had wandered down to the lakeside not a hundred years away.

"Moose?" he whispered. He'd never seen a moose.

"Elk," Mark whispered back. "I think. Not a lot of either in Iraq or Afghanistan."

The trio ignored them as they waded into the frigid water. There was a baby that was nearly as big as Clarence, a monstrous bull with a rack of horns which might even be bigger than Lucy's, and the mama in-between. "What do they call the mother?"

"A cow. Bull, cow, and calf."

"You're closer. Does she look demonic? I have really bad luck with cows." They'd been slowly raising their voices toward normal speech, but the elk's, or moose's, reactions were only a twitching of the ears.

"Usually people worry about the bull," Mark checked for him. "Looks more like she's just happy to be in a bath and away from

Junior." The young one was playing in the shallows, barely in the water up to its knobby knees.

"An elk family," Nathan sat up and shot a photo with his camera so that he could ask Julie when he saw her. If he saw her. If he didn't just grow a pair of balls and climb in his car to go as soon as Mark flew them back. He took another, this time of the angler and the critters together. Actually, that one would make a great publicity shot; he'd even caught the nose of the helicopter in the frame. Even if he left, he'd send it to Ama for the Henderson Ranch website.

"Or moose. I'm really not sure."

"Maybe it's some kind of weird crossbreed that only happens in Montana. A melk?" He could picture it being a melk.

Then with a flick of water, Mark's line snapped tight. In moments it was racing off his fishing reel.

"Grab the net!"

"Don't you have to land it first?" But he tossed the horse blanket back in the cargo hatch and dug around until he found a net.

Mark was slowing the spool, but the line was still growing longer. Nathan didn't like the angle.

"It's going straight for the moose, or elk. Don't let it—"

But it was too late, the racing fish had dragged the fishing line across one of the moose's legs. The big bull levitated straight out of the water with a loud sound that was half bray and half honk.

When it landed back in the water, it glared in their direction.

"Uh-oh!" Nathan began edging back toward the helicopter. "I've had some experience with this. If Lucy had looked like that, not even Julie could have rescued me. Let's go."

"But I've got a fish," Mark's voice was nearly a whine. But he too began backing away. As he did, it must have moved the line, this time the big bull didn't levitate, he roared.

"Mark. Forget the damned fish." Nathan had reached the passenger side of the helo and tossed the net into the foot well.

"Aren't you supposed to face down wild animals?" But Mark didn't sound so sure even as he said it.

"Haven't you ever seen the videos of moose crashing into each other with their antlers?"

"Forgot about that." Mark made some decision, then hurried up to him. "Take the pole. Don't let go." Then he raced around the other side and climbed in. Within moments, the helicopter's engine whined to life and the rotors began turning slowly. Too slowly.

Nathan climbed in on the passenger side, feeling like a complete idiot for still holding the pole out the open door.

The moose twisted in their direction, bellowed again, and began clambering up toward the shore.

"He's coming this way, Mark. Get a move on."

When the calf tried to engage his dad in play, the bull nipped him sharply on the butt and the calf squeaked in pain and surprise.

"I know how you feel, buddy."

By the time the bull reached the shore, Mark had the rotors going.

There was some momentary slack in the line. Nathan prayed that the line had simply broken. He fooled around with the handle until he figured out how to wind in the line.

As the rotors wound faster, so did he.

The melk (eoose? whatever) also took that as his cue and moved more quickly along the shore in their direction. The closer it came, the bigger it looked. Its huge rack of antlers were massive curved plates big enough to serve a suckling pig on, with sharp points sticking out from them. Its bulbous nose pulled back over bared teeth as it bellowed out a warning that seemed to shake the hills.

The line snapped taut and the pole bent, the sudden tension almost yanking it out of Nathan's hands.

"Let out line. Let it out! That button on the right. Press it!"

Mark shouted over the blast of engine and rotor noise that was now beating on him.

Or was it the noise of the moose's pounding hooves as it shifted from a walk to a trot after it reached the grass?

"Damn! That thing is huge! It's coming our way. Get us out of here!"

"Almost…" Mark was doing things to the controls, but none of them were getting them aloft. "Don't touch the spinning reel with your bare hands, you'll get a bad slice. Ease on the brake. Not hard or you'll snap the line."

That last sounded like a good idea to Nathan, but he did as he was told.

The moose went from trot to run. Then it lowered its head to ram them just as Mark got them aloft. The moose's blow caught the skid squarely on Mark's side and knocked them through the air toward the lake. The impact had Nathan whiplashing against Mark and then being almost ejected, along with the fishing pole, out the door on the other side. No time for a seat belt.

Mark managed to get a little more height and turned the nose to face the angry bull. The second blow shattered the small window by Nathan's feet when the moolk rose on its hind legs to pound home a final blow.

Again they were pushed toward the lake.

Mark finally was able to lift them out of the moose's reach and get them out over the water.

The bull stood at the lake shore looking big, dangerous, and triumphant—which it should, because it completely ruled the lakeshore. The cow had herded the calf off under the trees somewhere farther along the shore.

"Do you still have it?" Mark shouted.

"What? My heart? My life?"

"No! My fish."

Nathan could only stare at him.

"Reel in. See if you've still got it."

Nathan cranked on the reel until the line went tight again. "It's still there."

"Good," Mark looked at the tip of the pole and flew sideways in the direction it was pointing, easing along just ten feet above the icy water. "Keeping reeling it in."

"I can't believe we're doing this."

They crisscrossed back and forth above the lake, chasing the fish as Nathan kept shortening the line until finally the line was straight down into the water and he could see the fish struggling and splashing just below the surface. Then Mark descended as Nathan reeled until the helicopter's skids were in the water.

"Hey!" Lake water was splashing in through the shattered window and soaking Nathan's sneakers.

"Sorry, forgot about the window." Mark eased up a few inches, which didn't help much. "I need two hands to fly."

Nathan could barely hear him over the rotor's roar. Neither of them had a free hand to pull on the headsets.

"So pole in one hand, but don't lose it. Grab the net with the other."

It took Nathan a couple of tries, but he finally snagged the fish in the net. It was big for a rainbow trout—longer than his elbow to his fingers. He'd never seen a live one. It was beautiful— nothing in common with the ones in the New York fish market. He finally understood why it had been named rainbow: color glistened down its side, especially an iridescent pink.

For lack of anything better to do—at Marks' instruction—he grabbed it by the tail and brained it against the edge of the door.

"Dinner!" Mark sounded utterly delighted. Though Nathan suspected that he'd be the one who had to cook it. Maybe he'd do a simple white wine and thyme poach, let the gentle fish speak for itself. Though browned in clarified butter with a sage-mushroom-cream sauce, using wild mushrooms and farm fresh cream, also sounded good.

Nathan tucked the pole, the net, and the dead fish back

between the seats, then closed the door and pulled on both of their headsets and his own seatbelt. As the adrenaline drained away he realized that he was actually happy.

Mark circled back up over the still-glowering moose, standing with its feet just into the lake as if ready to come after them at the least sign of weakness.

"At least I know what a truly angry animal looks like now," not that a soul back in New York would believe it. Then he started laughing.

"What?" Mark was smiling.

"I never knew why they call it fly fishing."

Mark guffawed as they turned back toward the ranch, the chill wind whistling through the shattered window and over Nathan's soaking wet feet.

～

"WHAT THE HELL did they do to my bird?" Doug was scowling at the sky.

Julie looked up just as the helicopter passed by low overhead. There was a big crease across the nose and one of the windows was broken out. Nathan waved cheerily from the passenger seat, but they were gone before she had a chance to respond.

At least that explained where he'd been all morning.

She didn't know why she cared.

No. She *did* know why she cared. Some terrified corner of her heart had feared that he'd gone. Over dinner last night she'd heard his love for New York City. He didn't miss it, or he didn't seem to, but he knew its terrain as intimately as she knew the Montana Front Range. It was a part of him.

There hadn't been time to hunt him down or his car—the hay loft had been her idea, but she didn't know what the boys had done with it last night. So all morning she'd worried over it. There'd been no sign of him in the kitchen or crossing the yard.

Not once had he appeared to scan around for what she was doing —something he'd done constantly, even when she wasn't speaking to him.

Preparing the holes for the yurt platforms' concrete footings, ones that would be stout enough to support full cabins in the future, was a three-person job. And she had to take advantage of the help while she could get it rather than hunting for him.

Mac was on his backhoe operating the big auger. It crunched through the last of the frozen ground like it was shaving ice at a county fair for snow cones, then quickly cut down into the rich soil.

She and Doug concentrated on bending and wiring up the rebar internal framework, then placing them in the finished holes and slipping sixteen-inch cardboard Sonotubes over that to define the post for the concrete pour. She'd gotten everything pre-staked and run one of Mac's flatbeds all the way into Great Falls to get the rebar and Sonotube she'd needed. Splicing in a temporary power pole, they had the juice they needed to run saws for slicing the tubes and cutting the rebar.

At this rate they'd be ready for concrete in just a few more days. Then she could start on the yurt platforms.

And what had Nathan been doing? It wasn't that she expected him to be working. He was...she didn't know what he was. He wasn't on vacation. He was helping Ama with the cooking and had now gone somewhere with Mark. But he also wasn't leaving.

Doug held a freshly bent length of rebar in place and she wrapped a thin wire around to secure it.

What *was* Nathan up to? With his fine food and his soft kisses. He wasn't trying to bed her, or if he was, he was going slower than molasses in January.

More to the point, what was *she* up to? She never let a man close unless she knew what she wanted from him. But she had no idea what she wanted from Nathan Gallagher. She—

"Don't need to strangle the poor thing," Doug interrupted her thoughts. She'd wound the wire so tightly around the next rebar joint that it was never getting away.

"Maybe it deserves it. Besides, I don't want it going anywhere." Though it definitely hadn't needed the three extra wraps before she twisted it off.

Doug bent and placed the next piece before speaking again, barely louder than the steady grind of the big auger chewing up the next snow cone layer before getting down to the dirt.

"I'm maybe not the best person to speak to about these things, Julie. But I'm willing to try if it'll help."

"What things?" Another piece of rebar cinched down within an inch of its life.

Doug sighed, "And Chelsea wonders why I leave her to do the talking."

Julie was irritated with herself for any number of reasons, prime among those being caught thinking about a man when she should be thinking about work. After they dropped the rebar cage into one of the holes and slipped over the piece of Sonotube, she made a show of pausing, going to the cooler, and getting them each a bottle of water.

Mac eased the auger to a stop and clambered down off the backhoe to stretch for a moment and drink some water with them.

Suddenly she had an audience when she really didn't want one.

Down by the garage, she could see Mark and Nathan closing the equipment bay door after tucking away the helicopter. He waved with one hand and held up a dinner-sized trout with the other. She didn't want to draw everyone's attention down there, so she just gave a nod that she hoped he'd be able to see, then returned her attention to the project.

"Making good progress," Mac started the conversation.

"Seem to be," Doug agreed and emptied half of his bottle of water.

"Slow but good."

"Uh-huh."

It wasn't slow at all. They were well ahead of her planned schedule. To make sure, Julie began mentally counting number of footings to go in her head when she happened to look up and see that neither man was looking at the worksite progress. Doug was avoiding her gaze and Mac seemed fascinated by the two men and a fish that were headed into the house.

"I'm talking about the foundations," Julie kept her tone business-like.

"Sure," Mac agreed but she knew better than to trust that.

"Seriously, that's all *I'm* talking about."

Doug harrumphed.

Mac looked down at the latest hole fully prepared for the concrete truck. "Well, then I'll change 'slow but good' to 'incredibly faster than expected' but work isn't what any of us are talking about."

"I am," Julie tried, but knew it was lame. "Okay, I'm so not." Some part of her was near to panicked over Nathan's sudden disappearance and she didn't like that one bit.

"Now you're talking," Mac agreed.

"No, she isn't," Doug idly kicked some dirt back in around the outside of the Sonotube. "Now she's just feeling helpless. That one I know. Chelsea bowled me over in the first ten minutes."

"First two minutes," Mac corrected him.

"Maybe not even that long," Doug agreed. "Damned if I knew what to do about it though."

When had she *known?*

Julie swallowed hard and bent down to strangle a fresh piece of rebar with a tie-wire.

She didn't *know* anything. Because there wasn't anything to *know.*

CHAPTER 8

*I*t took them three hard days of labor to get the rest of the footings in place and Julie could feel the ache in every muscle.

No morning horse trainings because that precious hour before sunrise was one of the few chances to calculate what other supplies were needed. No pleasant evenings over a fine meal, because that's when she was able to work on Emily's office. No time for Nathan—which sounded like a good thing, but didn't feel that way at all.

The midday temperature was up into the fifties, which reduced them all to shirt sleeves. Her hands throbbed from working the rebar despite the heavy gloves.

For three days she'd worked like a mad woman and successfully avoided three things: the question of her attraction to Nathan, Nathan himself, and sleep. Her mind had become an endless churn of why Nathan hadn't tried to seduce her after that dinner and what was she going to do about it.

That night, she wouldn't have gone with him even if he had tried. She was still fairly certain about that. But for three days now he hadn't done a single thing except be friendly and make Ama's ranch food—which had always been a treat—even better.

If he were to ask right now, she just might go willingly. Perhaps even very willingly.

There was a round of silent nods with her, Doug, and Mac after they finished the last footing prep. A careful scan of the hillside revealed six clusters of footings springing up through the grass and mud—five for the yurt platforms and one for the common bathroom. Not a single marker stake left, every single one had been augered, rebarred, and Sonotubed.

The three of them began cleaning up the site. Restacking extra supplies. Moving the heavier tools like the rebar bender and cutter, both of which they were done with for now, into the bucket of Mac's backhoe so that he could drive them down to the barn.

She paused to slam back half a bottle of water that did nothing to soothe her parched throat.

And then it struck her: had Nathan been playing some kind of waiting game? Knowing that she was churning away inside and it was going to twist her up? But even as she thought it, she remembered his promise: *No games.* Besides, it didn't sound like something Nathan would do.

Let your hair down and kick it out a bit, Mac had told her. Maybe he was right.

She looked down at the main ranch house and recalled how Nathan had looked that morning—three days and forever ago—sleepy and holding the covers tight about his neck. How could so much be packed into a single morning? A horse-interrupted kiss, the fear of him leaving, and her impossibly huge relief to see him flying by overhead.

Only now did she admit to herself that she'd had an image of another way to wake him besides kicking the foot of his bed. For just a moment, less than a second, she'd had an image of sliding under those covers with him.

Take that young man you're so worried about and go play.

What if she did? She had an errand down Great Falls way. She'd been planning to make a morning run—down and back in one shot. What if...

"Go, Julie."

"What?" she looked at Doug but he wasn't explaining himself.

"Get yourself moving, girl. Doug and I've got this," Mac gave her a small shove to get her moving. She barely managed to hand off the last spool of tying wire and the cutters before she headed down toward the house, still unsure of what she'd do when she got there.

NATHAN WAS SLICING a loaf of fresh-baked sourdough, while the stew he'd made for lunch bubbled away, when Julie came striding through the back door of the kitchen. She wore her Ford baseball hat and was covered in dirt as usual. Heavy leather gloves clasped a half-finished water bottle like she could do war with it as her sole weapon.

She looked absolutely fantastic.

Meeting her halfway between counter and door, he did the only thing he could think of: he wrapped his arms around her and kissed her. He hadn't even recalled sleeping last night, not with Julie and his own future both all stirred up in his thoughts.

Having decided not to leave had opened something in him. For three days he'd wondered what fit there. It was an open spot that Julie slid right into.

She made a pleased "Mmmm" sound and wrapped her own arms around his waist. Had a woman ever felt so right in his arms? She fit there like...like...the trout had fit in an amandine sauce.

When she broke it off, his head was spinning from the impact.

His nervous system had just been hit by a stampeding herd and showed no sign of recovering.

"Come with me?"

"Anywhere." He needed her. Now. Blindly. He didn't care what or where or how. He wanted to be beside her. To touch her hair. To watch her blue eyes slowly shift when a reluctant smile finally reached them. To take her body with his until they both cried out like—

"I have to run into Great Falls."

"That's..." he tried to remember his route here, but couldn't. Great Falls was somewhere beyond Choteau. It was, "...a ways."

"Yep. Couple hours either way."

"Love to." As long as it was Julie Larson leading the way, he'd follow.

She nodded, then started for the door. Halfway there, she looked down at herself. "I need to go home and change."

"Should I bring anything?"

"Your car keys if you're willing to drive." Then Julie hesitated for a long moment before continuing softly. "Might bring along a toothbrush too."

Nathan grabbed that as well as a jacket, a fresh shirt, and a small box of protection he'd left in his suitcase. He stuffed them into a knapsack and hurried out to hunt down his car. This time, it was oddly parked in its own bay of the garage, just sitting there ready to go. He followed Julie's truck over to her ranch.

It wasn't a big place, and definitely not a showpiece like Hendersons. But it looked homey. A comfortable two-story. Maybe a little small with four grown kids, but it was pretty with the sky blue siding and white trim that seemed so popular along the Front Range.

Julie tried to have him wait in the front drive, but he figured that wasn't fair. He didn't want her to face her family alone while a "young man" sat waiting out in his car. It simply didn't feel right.

However, he hadn't counted on meeting them all at once. It

was only when he and Julie walked into the kitchen at the end of the Larson's lunch (which locals called dinner) that he remembered the stew bubbling away on the kitchen counter. Well, it would be found and consumed shortly, so no need to panic there.

Introductions were made. "Nathan has agreed to drive me down to Great Falls for a morning meeting. I have to go change." It didn't fool anybody.

"I'll be quick," she whispered and disappeared from the room like a shot.

Five sets of eyes turned on him and their reactions were all different.

Mom looked pleasantly surprised.

The twins looked ready to rough him up, maybe just for the sport of it.

Nathan had expected Julie's father to be the worst of it, but he was all polite manners: shaking Nathan's hand in greeting, offering him dinner even though it was clear they were already done, and giving him a glass of lemonade when he turned down the food.

It was the oldest brother, Matthew, who looked the most displeased. He rose silently from the table and stood just as silently with his arms crossed until he looked bigger than Lucy or the moolk that he and Mark had barely survived out at the lake.

"I don't think we've met," her father started off the conversation. Which was better than the "Who the hell are you?" that Nathan had been expecting.

"I'm staying up at Henderson's. You may know my brother, Patrick, sir," Nils Larson was definitely a *sir*. "I'm out visiting," though he decided to leave out that he was from New York. From Julie's comments he'd guess that while an outsider might be unwelcome, someone from New York City or Los Angeles would be considered certifiable. Or perhaps eligible for target practice— Matthew certainly looked at him that way.

"How are you liking the ranch lifestyle?"

"I see much to recommend it. Except for an," he made a guess, "elk that Mark Henderson and I ticked off the other day."

"Good man. Served his time and then some. Have you served?" But Nils glowered at his sons. Apparently none of them had either and that looked to be a bone of contention.

Matthew opened his mouth and Nathan hurried his answer to keep the peace.

"No, sir, I haven't," Nathan changed back to his earlier topic quickly. "The elk took exception to Mark's fishing methods and head-butted our helicopter before we could escape aloft."

"Head-butted a helicopter?" One of the twins remarked in surprise.

"Great big antlers," Nathan held his arms out wide. "Like great curved platters with spikes."

"Moose, not elk," Matthew growled out.

"Oh. Thanks. I've lived most of my life in cities, so I wasn't sure. Mark's fish dragged the line across the bull's legs while it was browsing in deep water. It was very unhappy about it."

"Do you fish?"

"No sir. I cook."

"Like at a restaurant?"

"I did. Not anymore." Could he sound more useless if he tried? "I'm helping Ama Henderson while I'm here."

There was a shift in the room and Nathan could feel it. It was like when a star reviewer was spotted in the restaurant. Everything shifted. Tension went from typical service-scaled worry to full-blown flambé. The only step beyond that would be fire-in-the-kitchen panic.

"And what are your inte—" Matthew had been leaning back against the kitchen counter, but now stood straight to tower over Nathan. Maybe there was a step beyond fire-in-the-kitchen panic —something like *Oh god! Oh god! We're all going to die.*

"We've got to run," Julie breezed into the room, now carrying a small backpack. She'd changed and washed her face, but he could still see the dirt line along her neck. Thankfully riding to his rescue rather than wasting precious moments to shower.

"Did you eat yet?" Nils Larson's manners stepped back in.

"We—" Nathan started, but Julie jumped right in.

"Ama fed us. We're all set. Come on, Nathan. I've got a whole list of errands in the city."

"The city?" That only had one meaning to him—New York.

"Choteau is the town, Great Falls is the city. Helena is the capital and Bozeman is too far away for anyone to think about," she was speaking fast, obviously trying to hide her nerves. She turned to her family, "Nathan wanted to see some of Montana while he was here so I agreed to play tour guide if he'd help me with my errands. Gotta go. C'mon, Nathan."

She was halfway to the door before Nathan had time to turn and shake Nils hand again. "Pleasure to meet you, sir. I look forward to a chance to talk."

"You may count on it, young man."

Matthew made the moose look timid.

JULIE COULDN'T BREATHE. Couldn't move fast enough.

Nathan pulled his keys out as they crossed the front porch and she grabbed them out of his hand.

"Get the gate. Make sure it latches behind you." The top was down so she vaulted over the door and slammed into the driver's seat.

Then couldn't find the key hole.

Nathan leaned over the passenger door and pressed a big button marked "Engine Start" and it purred to life.

She didn't need purr. She needed *roar*.

He strolled to the front gate as if he had all day and her family wasn't at the windows, breathing down her neck. She never should have brought him here. She never should have brought

133

him with her. Was it too late to pull out? Leave him back at Henderson's?

But as she rolled through and he (finally) closed the gate behind him, her truck was now home and she wasn't. There was no way she could take Nathan's car without him and she actually did have to go to Great Falls.

"Take a breath. First gear. Clutch out with a little gas." Nathan had climbed into the passenger seat without her noticing. "It's fine, Julie. Let's just get some distance so that you can breathe."

She managed to get them moving, working her way up through the gears until they were flying down the road—washboard and pothole nothing more than low spots to fly over. She finally caught her breath when they reached the pavement and she could really open up the little car's engine. She still needed *roar* but it was too well mannered an engine for that. However, the speedometer said they were doing eighty (a speed far beyond the one at which her truck would try to shake itself to death) and she felt much better.

"They seemed nice enough," Nathan was the first to break the silence.

"Ha!"

"I mean for people who didn't know what to do with me. Your big brother—at least I assume that's who he was by his sheer size, almost as big as Mark Henderson—couldn't decide what kind of machine to feed my soiled remains into: a combine, a scythe, or a shredder. Your father would make a fair job of auditioning for the role of a space alien bearing nasty body probes and a memory eraser—except without the memory eraser. Thankfully his manners were too good to start right away. I think the twins would help hold me down for either of them."

"Matthew?" Julie puzzled at that one. "He's always been the only one I could ever talk to. Not even Mom, who is like a straight line to Dad. You actually talked to Dad?"

"Let's just say that if I ever have to meet him alone, I want Stan to show up in my place."

"I can't believe you met them at all. That definitely wasn't part of the plan."

"We were just supposed to sneak off to Great Falls and have amazing sex?"

Julie could feel the heat rising to her face and couldn't do a thing to stop it.

"Wow! Brighter red than the rising sun."

"When did you ever see the rising sun?"

"When someone kicked me out of my bunk in the middle of the night to go be bitten by a horse."

Julie stomped on the brakes, skidding the car to skewed halt.

"What?" Nathan had one hand braced against the dash and the other at the center of her chest as if to protect her. His touch calmed her like a bucket of cold water.

"Clarence," she felt foolish for startling Nathan. "I forgot about Clarence."

"Julie," again he used that calm-down-a-riled-bronc tone of his. "I'm sure Chelsea will pamper him plenty."

Chelsea would. Julie had taken to keeping Clarence there because it was the only way she got to see her horse. She was rarely home while the sun was up—there was just too much going on at Henderson's. She glanced at Nathan then turned away. Way too much...yet also not enough or why was she here.

She looked back the way they'd come, four long black skid marks that would have everyone down this way talking and wondering for months to come. "How could I forget about my horse?" It was no longer a worry, but still, it just wasn't like her. She turned to Nathan, "How did I do that?"

Nathan's soft laugh made her feel more at ease. "I never knew quite how good a compliment could feel. I'm so distracting that Julie Larson thinks of me even before her horse."

It was true. He leaned over for a kiss. This time his hand traveled up her ribs, caressing, testing, until it reached her breast. Her soft moan matched his.

The car jerked when her foot slipped off the clutch and then the engine died. He held her for a long moment before collapsing back in his seat.

"Gods but I need to get you in a hotel room soon."

She couldn't agree more. Her hands were still clenched on the steering wheel and the gear shift, though her body was humming and she could still feel the imprint of his hand on her breast. "Not in Choteau. Everyone there knows me and reports would flow back to my family so fast it would make our heads spin."

Nathan groaned dramatically, "I'm supposed to keep my hands off you until Great Falls? How far away is it?"

"How fast is your car?"

"What about the speed limits?"

"This is Montana. Those are really just suggestions."

"Even with New York plates?"

Julie laughed, finally feeling like herself for the first time since Clarence had nipped Nathan's butt. "Oh, city boy. There are so many things to fix. Are you really worth the trouble?"

"Let's get to Great Falls and find out."

CHAPTER 9

"The Hotel Arvon?"

"It sounded nice." Nathan had never heard of it, but once they were in close enough range to get a phone signal, he'd done a quick search. All, absolutely all of the other top-rated hotels in town were the big chains. It didn't bode well for the city. But the Arvon was a recent restoration of the original 1890 hotel and sounded promising. Even more promising, they'd had a room available on a half hour's notice.

Julie had done an impressive job of finally proving exactly why he'd bought a sports car even though he rarely left the city and never broke the speed limit. With the top down and the wind in her hair, it was hard to believe he was cruising through Montana and not a car ad. Truckers had popped their horns in loud blats of appreciation for the vision as Julie whipped past at speeds he hadn't known his car could go. With the heater on and the growing warmth of the afternoon, it was a very comfortable ride.

"Nice?" Julie protested. "It's the best hotel in town. Can you afford it?"

"I never spend money except on cooking. That plus a rent-controlled apartment for five years. So, a lot of it ended up in the bank for some reason. Besides, I'll be damned if I'm going to take you somewhere less than the best."

"Oh, Nathan," she said it on a happy sigh.

It wasn't New York, but it also wasn't New York prices.

The block it was on wasn't very impressive and that worried him. The hotel itself was a three-story, chunky brick building; only copper decorations along the roofline that were long gone green gave it any relief. Or maybe it was green paint. It was sandwiched between a used furniture store and an electrical supply, but the hotel frontage itself looked cheery and welcoming. There was nothing else particularly attractive in the area except an old railroad station a few blocks away. The main street they'd come in along was a mix of old brick and modern that lacked the frontier-town feel that's he'd been expecting.

Once inside, the hotel was a welcome mix of modern with red leather furniture and Western art on the walls. Julie was practically vibrating with impatience while they checked in. The clerk didn't even blink at the small knapsacks they were carrying instead of luggage.

When they hit the room, Julie hit him.

Full body slam!

Arms, legs, lips—she was everywhere at once. It was like being attacked by a whirlwind of spring and sunshine.

Nathan tried to slow her down a bit.

It wasn't working.

There was a frantic edge to her that had him trying to ease back even more. She had his jacket off and his turtleneck as well. Her flannel shirt was wide open, revealing a flat stomach, a fit body, and a very nice pair of breasts in simple white cotton.

"Julie."

She didn't respond, just continued her attack.

"Julie!"

Still nothing.

He hooked his hands under her arms, lifted her up, and set her back down with a little space between them. She was nearly as tall as he was, so he didn't get her moved far, but it helped.

"Julie."

"What? I thought you wanted to have sex," her eyes were narrowed in confusion.

"With you? Absolutely."

She tried to surge at him again, but he kept her at bay. "Then what's the problem?"

"With *you!*" Nathan couldn't believe that he was holding off a gorgeous woman who was throwing herself at him.

Julie merely looked bewildered.

He took her hands in his and led her to a couch. She tried to protest as he pulled her down beside him rather than toward the king-sized bed. He resisted the urge to close her flannel shirt. Her body was a hell of a distraction, but he guessed that pushing her away a second time would be a bad idea.

"Julie. Talk to me."

"About what?"

He laughed. "That's a good question. Talk to me about...why you're here?" She'd been manic since she'd walked into the kitchen in the middle of his lunch preparations.

"I'm here to..." But she stalled out. "Because...I'm so sick of being a good girl!"

That came out with a blast of anger he wasn't ready for.

"I'm starting my own company, which my father hates. I won't sleep with every man who thinks I should, which they hate. I won't marry someone I don't care about, which my father (again) hates because he wants the help on the ranch. Cattle are more work than you can imagine. Mac and Emily and Chelsea all want me to be madly in love with you. And they—"

"Wait, what?" He almost missed it going by in the tidal wave of angry words she was suddenly flooding out.

"*You'll find* him, *Julie. Remind her that she likes you, Nathan. Isn't he just the cutest thing?*" She did a fair running imitation of each of the three in turn. Then she huffed out a hard sigh. "Then—" she shrugged.

"Then you decided that if you just screwed me and got it over with, they'd all leave you alone and you could go back to work."

"Yes. Maybe...I don't know." Then she thumped her forehead against his bare chest and left it there. Then she groaned as if in pain. "Real nice for you, huh? I'm sorry, Nathan. You deserve someone better than me."

"That's hard to imagine, anyone being better than you."

"Ha!" But she didn't raise her head and it was a bitter sound.

He slipped his arms around her and brushed his hand down her smooth glory of hair and onto her back. "I'm serious."

"So am I," she mumbled against his chest.

He tipped her back until he could see the blue of her eyes. There were tears lurking there. Of frustration, of rage, of sadness? He didn't know, but he didn't like them.

Brushing gently at them only made them start to flow. Crying woman. What to do with a crying woman?

Nathan kissed her on the forehead and then on each salty eye. "Julie?"

"Yep. Julie the mess here." She didn't even appear to be aware of the tears.

"What the hell have the men of your past done to you?"

"Screwed me and done," the harsh edge in her voice cut at him. He knew men like that. Too many. Braggarts in the kitchen about what babe they'd scooped up at some bar. He figured that both sides got what they deserved out of those kinds of places—he'd done it more than a few times and could never seem to scrub off the feeling afterward. Not who he was anymore and *definitely* not who Julie was.

"I want to make love with you."

"But you just said—" she blinked at him in confusion.

"Do you want to make love, *with me?* Not some male, but with me?"

"Oh!" She patted a hand on his chest a few times, the warmth of her fingers trickling over his skin just like the tears still sliding down her cheeks. "With *you?*"

"Uh-huh."

She looked him in the eye, really looked at him for the first time since the horse stall three mornings ago. Apparently not trusting herself to speak, she finally nodded.

He'd prefer the words, but didn't want to push his luck. Besides, she was more of an actions-speak-louder-than-words gal.

So, he scooped her in his arms—and almost dropped her on the floor when he stood. Sweeping a grown woman into bed always looked easier in the movies. Julie was giggling by the time he deposited her on the mattress.

Not exactly the reaction he'd been hoping for.

~

No one had ever carried Julie anywhere. No one except Nathan the White Knight. It was simply too funny that all of her childhood princess dreams were coming to life with a New York chef. That he wasn't carrying her across the room to save her, but rather to ravage her willing body only made it all the funnier. White knight with a tinge of the rutting cowboy—which actually got him into the quarterfinals for prince charming, maybe the finals.

He stood, looking down at her for a moment. Not cowboy-working man buff, just a good solid man. One whose dark eyes were watching her, asking permission one last time.

In making it wholly her choice, even with both of them already half undressed, she knew what she had forgotten. She didn't want a man—she wanted *this* man. The one who somehow already knew her well enough to understand that she'd lost that distinction. Well, with his help, she'd found it again and she knew the real answer.

Taking his hand in hers, she tugged lightly. "Yes, Nathan. With you."

He huffed out a big breath like he'd just finished a cross-country cattle drive. "Well, that's good news." Then rather than lying down upon her or undressing her the rest of the way, he sat down on the edge of the bed. Men, Montana men, always seemed to know what they wanted and simply took it. Happily along for the ride, she'd almost always enjoyed herself. At least the act itself, though the aftermath was typically far less charming.

Nathan instead brushed lightly at her hair, then trailed his curled fingers behind her ear and down her neck, watching his own hand. When he finally leaned down to kiss her, it was with that same impossible gentleness that he'd demonstrated before.

"Nathan."

"Uh-huh?" he shifted his attention to her neck.

"I already said yes."

"Uh-huh." But he didn't speed up any.

She half feared he never would. Sex wasn't supposed to put a girl to sleep. It was—

Then he kissed more deeply. And then more. He built slowly from an arroyo trickle into a melt-out torrent. One strong arm about her waist, the other lifting her from the bed until she was as much in his lap as lying beside him.

"It's been a long time, Julie. I don't want to scare you or mess this up."

"You couldn't," and in that moment she knew it was true. Both parts were.

And he didn't.

Being made love to by Nathan wasn't about *to*—it was all about *with*.

It was impossible to ignore the joy he took from every caress he gave. His joy at every one he received was equal. It unleashed something inside her.

She wasn't some horse being ridden, no matter how expertly, by a cowhand.

When it came to making love, Nathan made it as perfect as the best horse and the best rider flying along in unison. One moment he was the one in control, the next it was her, and there was no break of stride as it shifted back and forth between them.

The lines and roles blurred so thoroughly that it was mere chance that she was one who landed astride him for the final race to a glorious finish. Together they rose and clung, gasped and moaned. Most importantly—absolutely the first time ever for her —they both gave.

~

WHEN JULIE slowly fluttered down upon him as gently as a leaf caught in the lightest of breezes, Nathan wondered if now *he* was going to be the one to cry.

How had he missed this? How had he gotten so far in his life and never had an experience like this one? Her body was a work of art: strong, lithe, and masterfully formed. Julie was painted in the fairest of shades except for the alarming intensity of those blue eyes that she didn't close until the very final throes shook her. The woman within was both sweet and fierce, with a big dollop of impossibly dynamic—all at once. He'd never had so much fun having sex or been wracked by such a powerful release.

Thinking that he knew who Julie Larson was, ranked as perhaps the most presumptuous thought of his life. She tasted of salt tears, warm skin, and—he buried his nose in the crook of her neck...and sneezed—dirt.

She looked down at him curiously as he sniffled.

"What? Are you allergic to me?"

"No," he couldn't help sniffling again. "Just to the places you didn't wash off in your hurry to scoot me out of your kitchen."

"You mean my hurry to rescue you from my family?"

143

"Oh, absolutely. Life and limb at risk. Dead without you. Which actually may have been closer to the truth than I'd like to think about."

She held up an arm, which sported a ring of dirt where glove would have met sleeve. "Not exactly charming."

"Utterly charming." It made him like her even more. Julie wasn't the sort of woman who felt a need to primp. Again, she was just so absolutely herself.

"I need a shower."

"I'll help," then that charming blush of hers lit her face. "Never showered with a man."

She shook her head, unleashing a cascade of hair over his face. "Skinny-dipped, but that's different."

"Skinny-dipped. Like outdoors with no clothes on?" He pictured Julie instead of a long-legged moose stepping into a mountain lake. "I definitely have to give that a try."

"You've never done it?"

"Well, the problem was we could never agree on where to go. The Jacqueline Kennedy Onassis Reservoir in the middle of Central Park seemed disrespectful, even discounting the thou-sand-odd member audience you'd have on any typical day. The Conservatory Water was always a possibility, but the model-boat sailors have rules about these things. There's a very nice fountain at Lincoln Center, but would upset the opera patrons something awful. And in the East River or the Hudson you'll just get run over by a Circle Line tour boat if you aren't poisoned by whatever is floating down the river."

She propped her chin on her palm to look down at him.

"You have sharp elbows."

Julie didn't apologize or move. "I don't get you, city boy. How have you lived your whole life like that?"

He shrugged, which only let her elbow dig in a little deeper. "Born and raised to it."

She shrugged as if it didn't make any sense to her. Then she pushed off and rolled out of bed. The scenery in this hotel was really excellent.

When he finally mustered the energy to follow her, he realized it was even better than he imagined. The shower was separated from the bath by floor-to-ceiling glass. He checked the slowly fogging mirror. Yes, it was definitely him in it. He looked back through the glass. There was definitely a drop-dead gorgeous, all-American blonde in there. He just couldn't reconcile the two being in the same place.

Once the mirror fogged out and he'd joined her, it was less hard to imagine.

～

"That. Was. Spectacular!" Julie eased down into a back booth at the restaurant. Her body was still splendidly liquid. "I knew that chefs were good with their hands, but what you did in that shower, that was almost better than that meal you cooked me."

She could still feel the heat. The man-in-control that she hadn't met in bed had definitely entered the shower. If she didn't know him so well, he'd have looked dangerous as he stalked into the glass enclosure. Never once speaking, he'd manhandled her in the most incredible ways, making her body arch and shudder with just a washcloth, soap, and hot water. Her release hadn't been as big as the wonder of having him inside her, but it was a good thing he had strong shoulders to hang on to or she'd have been down on the tile floor while she begged for mercy. Or begged for more. She couldn't remember which she'd asked for.

"I didn't even know there were things like that to feel."

"Better than riding a horse?" Mr. Dark and Sexy hadn't completely gone away yet.

She threw up her hands. "Okay, you got me. That was *at least* as good as riding a horse. Even at a full gallop during a summer sunrise."

"I guess that's as high as a mere man can aspire."

Julie laughed. She couldn't seem to stop smiling around Nathan, even when he was being a little grumpy. No man had ever affected her that way. She hadn't even paid any attention to where he led her.

"Hey, this is nice."

"Welcome to the Celtic Cowboy. It's what sold me on staying here. Nathan Gallagher and Julie Larson—umpteenth generation Irish and cowgirl. Seemed like a natural."

Julie was on the verge of commenting about how *natural* had nothing to do with the heat they'd generated between them, but the waitress arrived and she'd save those thoughts for later. Like when she had enough blood sugar to go another round with Nathan upstairs.

She checked the unlikely name on the menu that the waitress— wearing cowboy boots and an Irish green polo shirt—delivered. The downstairs restaurant at the Hotel Arvon really was called the Celtic Cowboy; Nathan hadn't been fibbing. A dark walnut twenty-stool bar commanded one side of the room. It had at least that many beer taps down its length, the wall of bottles behind were mostly whisky, and the four big screens were running basketball and rugby. Tables clustered beneath Western-style lights and a band was setting up in the far corner with a harp, fiddle, and a keyboard.

It was early evening; they'd spent almost an entire afternoon in bed or the shower. A dozen or so patrons were scattered about the room and more trickled in from the fading day.

"Can I start you with something to drink?"

"A pint of Ivan the Terrible."

Nathan looked at her strangely, "Excuse me?"

"Beer. Stout, a good one."

"You drink a beer called Ivan the Terrible? What the hell planet am I on?"

"Montana," the waitress glared at him in mock disgust.

Julie tried to explain, "Big Sky Brewing Company. Great beer. Used to ride rodeo with the daughter of. They have beers like Pygmy Owl, Slow Elk..."

The waitress added in, "They also have specialty beers like Olde Bluehair and Buckin' Monk."

Nathan looked as if he was being cornered. "How about a whisky? Something Irish?"

"Chicken," the waitress laughed at him. "Sure you don't want a glass of Moose Drool? It's a very smooth brown ale."

"No, I've had enough to do with mooses to last me a good while."

"The plural of moose is meece or meeces," Julie corrected him incorrectly. He'd told her the story of the Great Moose Encounter, and if the moose could mess with him, she didn't see any reason not to do so herself.

"I've got just the thing. And I've always used meeces for the plural," the waitress said perfectly deadpan and was off without giving Nathan a chance to choose his liquor.

"You do things differently here in Montana," Nathan was watching the fine things that heeled cowboy boots and tight jeans did to the waitress' retreating figure.

"Hey!"

"Like the way you make love, Julie Larson," his dark eyes turned back to her and she wondered if he'd even been conscious of where his eyes had tracked. He now looked at her with an intensity that almost made her look away and definitely drove some heat to her cheeks. "Never experienced anything like it in my life."

Neither had she, but she couldn't think of what to say to that. Talking about sex was another thing she had no experience with beyond, "That was good." The nicer guys would eventually think to ask, "Was it good for you?" Though she doubted if they ever heard her reply.

"Women usually..." he ground to a halt. "Shit! I'm sorry. I seem to say the clumsiest things around you."

The waitress was back with a beer and a whisky. She thumped them down on the table, then put her fists on her hips and looked down at Nathan. "Try that."

"Told you," Nathan winked at Julie. "Montana is very strange."

"Ignore him," Julie told the waitress. "He's a city boy."

Nathan sipped his whisky, closed his eyes for a moment, then sighed happily. "Now *that* is a fine bit of Irish—even if I'm not familiar with it."

"That," the waitress was beaming, "is Logan Bar twelve-year-old. Distilled by Bridget MacDeaver...right here in Montana." She turned back to Julie. "Just flag me when his jaw stops flapping in the breeze and you're ready to order," then she sashayed off.

Nathan sniffed at the glass again, shrugged, and then raised it toward her in a toast. "Seems there are several things to like about Montana." He made it sound as if he was talking much more about her than the liquor.

She tapped her glass of stout to his tumbler and looked down at the menu. Any other man saying that line would have been talking more about the whisky than the woman. Had her bar really been set so low that someone less than the wonderful Nathan Gallagher, from New York City (the good lord save her), could step over it? Sadly, past experience already answered that. Wasn't going to ever happen again though.

NATHAN SIPPED THE WHISKY. He rarely drank it anymore—it had been his poison as a young chef. But he'd learned a lot about them in his younger days and this was a fine one indeed.

Montana. He didn't know what he'd expected, but this certainly wasn't it. A Celtic Cowboy bar, a truly fine single-malt, and Julie Larson.

He had only begun to learn the curves that made up her body. They were enough to make a man go mad. It practically had. *Women usually—Idiot!* But it was true. All the women he'd ever been with, from high school to the Cordon Bleu to the hostess in the back booth at Vite had a *studied* beauty: plucked eyebrows, makeup, carefully stylish clothes. Even the sous chef he used to screw in the walk-in fridge wore a tailored blouse and lacy underwear while they worked together over the cook line.

Through the glass of the hotel's shower enclosure had stood Julie Larson—a woman who was nothing more (or less) than she appeared to be. She worked hard, got dirty, and had the incredible body to prove it.

He'd bet his last bottle of Château Margaux Bordeaux 2005 that she'd actually meant it when she said she didn't know what passive-aggressive games were. They were part of every interaction in the restaurant business. Piss someone off, and the fish arrived to the line overdone, forcing the whole table to be refired so that everyone could be served together. Break up with someone and you could find that your lockbox of truffles was "accidentally" put away in the freezer.

Julie was as straightforward as she appeared. It had overtaken him as he moved to join her in the shower. Maybe he'd gone in hoping to prove that she hadn't just negated the value of every single relationship in his past by shining such a bright light on the present. Instead, she'd responded with such an absolute honesty that he'd sought to do for her what she'd done for him—purge her past until it washed down the drain.

How could the prior men in her life not see her for how incredible she was? How many men were like his fellow, bar-hopping chefs, or worse yet his little brother?

Damn it! She deserved better than that and he'd done his very best to give it to her.

Now, across the rim of a whisky glass, he studied her while she read the menu. Her pale blonde hair fell in a smooth cascade down either side of her face. She wore a flannel shirt that was just open enough to provide a splendid view of her collarbone. The curves below were lost in shadow and closed buttons. No coy games. No teasing cleavage.

"What are you looking at, city boy?" she didn't raise her head. "Because you sure aren't looking at your menu."

"Prettiest woman who ever let me take her to bed."

"Skin deep, Nathan."

"On most women I can tell you that's far more true than you think." Even the nice ones. There was always a deeper layer with a hidden agenda. "You, I'm thinking your beauty goes all the way to the core."

"Pretty speech. If you're trying to get me back into bed with you though, it's not going to work."

"That's not what I was say—"

Then she looked up and grinned at him. "Not until I've had something to eat anyway. But keep trying, Nathan. I'm discovering that I like the way it sounds."

She flagged down the waitress.

"I'll have the Ploughman's Lunch. And I don't think my friend is quite awake from his afternoon endeavors, better give him the Irishman's breakfast."

"Need him to wake up some, honey?"

"Don't know as I'd survive if he woke up more, but I'm willing to risk it. Maybe I wore him out."

"Not a chance. Around you I've got plenty of..." Nathan then glanced up at the waitress' knowing smile and shut up.

CHAPTER 10

"We've got one more stop before we leave town," Julie settled into the passenger seat of Nathan's car. It might have looked like a clown's car to her, lurched sadly sideways on the road that first night, but it had a solid, comfortable feel that she could get used to in a hurry. It also didn't rattle as it labored along. Instead, as Nathan eased it through Great Falls, it slid along smooth and quiet.

He looked good. Their first stop had been at Hoglund's. First they bought him a good denim shirt and jacket, and a decent pair of work boots. Not even cowboy boots, just some good leather Red Wings that he could tromp through the spring mud or ride a horse with.

Her attempts to get him a decent hat had been thwarted when he reached into a small cubby behind his car seat and produced an Indiana Jones-style hat. He'd tugged it on and given her a smile that was at least as charming as any Harrison Ford look. She'd tried on a Falcon hand-tooled leather hat—perfect for going about fancy—but her budget couldn't justify it.

"Someday we'll get you a real hat and boots."

"Sure thing, lady," with a brim-tug right out of the movie. He made it funny, but she found it harder to laugh this morning than she had last night.

Last night.

When did a girl ever have a night like that? Yes, they'd made love again and it had been as tender as the earlier time had been wild. Then he'd held her and they'd just talked. That was something that was wholly outside her experience. A couple times she and her big brother had run into each other during a late night raid on the ice cream and talked about nothing much through a bowl or two, but never a lover.

She was a ranch girl—up before the sun and gone to bed not long after it set. If she and Nathan had slept more than a few hours last night, she'd be surprised. Instead, she'd spent the night curled up against the man who could make her feel...she didn't know what. Cared for? Important? Lucky?

The problem with Nathan wasn't that he didn't talk. Most men —now *she* was guilty of the same kind of generalities that Nathan was always making, which made it easy to forgive him—didn't talk about how they were feeling. Growing up with three older brothers and a passel of field hands, she'd learned to read men. Men not like Nathan anyway.

Nathan did talk—and about what he was feeling. Sometimes he did it too well.

Over dinner, and afterwards as he nursed his lone whisky, he'd finally told her about New York. The amazing restaurant scene and all the wonders that the city had to offer. But also the disappointment, the loss, and the confusion he felt were all laid out on the table for her to see. He'd never been anything but a chef.

"Cooking for you was the first meal I've cared about, really cared about in months."

If she hadn't already been soft in the head for Nathan Gallagher, that would have done it.

Once through Great Falls, where the two-story brick of Old Town gave way to suburbia and strip mall, he followed the signs for Malmstrom Air Force Base. It was only a mile or so before the houses became closer together as they neared the base.

It was that hint of sadness in him that she'd spotted before, that loss of joy in cooking. It was also her own revelations about her upbringing, about her marginal value in the Larson household and finally realizing, as she told the story, that she'd started J. L. Building as an escape plan that had made them especially gentle with each other last night.

Afterward, curled up, Nathan had told her about being a young chef. A multi-generation Irishman who cooked fine French food in Paris and New York.

That had been the problem that she didn't know how to wrangle. It was so easy to hear his passion for cooking and for the energy of the city. Somewhere in the night she'd finally understood. Someday, perhaps someday soon, Nathan would be gone— back to his beloved city.

Then Julie Larson would be down the shitter. One choice was to push away now, hit the ground hard and let the bronc finish out its dance alone. The other was to hang on and enjoy the ride as long as it lasted.

She never knew when to let go, or even how to. Not in rodeo, not in work, not in relationships—even the marginal ones. Without asking, she knew that she'd be holding on to Nathan Gallagher until the last possible moment.

The trick was figuring out how to make sure the fall didn't break her at the end.

Nathan had followed Julie's directions to Malmstrom AFB. Apparently there was some delivery to pick up for her loft office project with Emily. They had taken turns on the drive down making up bizarre possibilities from a science fiction plasma rifle to a personal-sized ICBM—Minuteman missiles in their silos was the whole purpose of Malmstrom. Getting to know Emily, none of the ideas had sounded quite as implausible as they should have.

The gate guard looked very serious and very armed when they rolled up in his red Miata.

"We're here to pick up a delivery."

"Post office is back that way half a mile," the guard indicated with his rifle, not quite raising it all the way to point but making it clear he didn't have time for this shit.

Julie leaned over, "I was told to ask for Quartermaster Belkin precisely at eleven o'clock." The clock on the dash read 10:59.

"Stay here." The guard retreated to his shack and the phone.

"I think we're in a movie," Nathan teased Julie. He'd hardly gotten a laugh from her all morning, probably because she was tired. He was used to short hours, but that didn't explain how he was feeling. There was a euphoria that was hard to deny.

To hold her close all through the short night had been more than a gift. It had been a chance to pretend that there was something in his life that could be normal. That maybe there was a future even if he couldn't see it. He'd been at the ranch for a week (about five days more than he'd expected to be welcome), barely seen his brother, slept with the most incredible woman, and cooked. By god, he cooked. He'd enjoyed himself more making breakfasts with Ama than he had in his last six months at Vite.

And her laugh. Julie Larson had been so serious when he met her, like it had been driven into her soul. Every laugh he'd been able to elicit had been a glimpse of simple, purest joy.

The guard came back, looking pissed. "Through the gate. Stop there," he jabbed a finger at the spot next to his Humvee. "Do not get out of the car. Do *not* piss me off. Someone will be here in five minutes."

The thrum of a helicopter sounded low overhead.

"What the hell?" the guard was looking up at the big aircraft with two sets of rotor blades.

"What's wrong?" Nathan wished he hadn't asked when it drew

the guard's attention back to him. The man's rifle looked far more real and dangerous than on some movie screen.

The helo slewed around and began to settle inside the perimeter fence, just beyond the parked Humvee.

"We don't have any Chinooks here. Just Hueys. And Air Force birds are gray, not black."

"Whose are black?"

The guard just scowled again, raised the gate, and waved them through.

Nathan looked at Julie, but she had no more of a clue than he did. He didn't know about helicopters and apparently neither did she. He eased his Miata forward.

After it landed, a rear ramp opened and lowered to the ground. A woman in uniform walked down the ramp and waved them forward.

Nathan checked the rearview. The guard had at least transferred his scowl from them to the big helicopter. There wasn't a marking on it. No white star. No numbers. Just pure black.

The woman didn't just wave him to the ramp, but up onto it.

Julie shrugged and they rolled forward. The inside of the helicopter was two Miatas long and there was at least a foot to either side of his car. Every surface was covered with a pipe, a cable, a piece of shining equipment, or a warning sign. Just past the nose of his car was a pair of mounted machine guns that looked as long as a person, thankfully not pointed toward them.

"Howdy y'all," a tall blond man in a cowboy hat strolled into the cargo bay while the ramp closed behind them. "My name's Justin and you must be Emily's contractor. Not quite what I was expectin'. Good choice in hats though."

Flummoxed, Nathan just hooked a thumb toward Julie. "She's your man...so to speak."

"Howdy, ma'am. Not *a' tall* what I was expectin'. Though not any big surprise with the stories I've heard about Emily Beale."

"Pop your trunk," the woman in uniform told him.

He did, but when he went to get out of the car, she just shook her head.

Justin and Julie were talking horses at some sort of esoteric level that sounded like a foreign language.

The woman and another crew member piled several boxes into the back. He could feel the car settle—they might be small, but some of them must be heavy. Another crew member started chatting with him about how he liked his car and how it handled on the open road, making it so that he couldn't follow what else was going on.

Less than two minutes later, the ramp was lowering and he was being guided backward down the ramp and into the real world of bright sun and scowling gate guards.

"Next time y'all are in Austin, you just call the ranch and we'll show you some *real* horses," the big guy doffed his cowboy hat to Julie, then strolled back to the cockpit.

The rear ramp closed and the big rotors, which had never stopped spinning, hammered the air down on them hard until he backed far enough away. Then they were gone back into the sky.

"You've got to be asking yourself, 'So, who are we'?" he asked the glowering guard as they rolled out through the gate. He answered his own question before he slipped out of earshot. "We're just folks."

Julie's laugh cheered him immensely as he headed toward the highway.

"So," he asked once they were on their way, "who were those folks?"

"No idea. But if we're ever in Texas and want to go to one of the top horse-breeding ranches in the country, Justin just gave us an invitation."

Nathan turned to look over his shoulder as if he could see what's in the trunk, "Any guesses?"

"Emily told me she had some friends who could help with

electronic security for her office. I guess she meant the US military."

"This happen to you much? Is Montana really like this?"

"Oh, sure. All the time. You should stick around, city boy."

The warm fun of cuddling together, going into a cowboy outfitter like he'd never seen before, and cruising with Julie beneath the sunshine, ripped away in the chill air that seemed to descend on the car as they reached the highway.

Stick around. It was the one thing he couldn't do and they both knew it.

CHAPTER 11

*T*heir escape ended the moment they crossed back onto Henderson land. They'd been gone less than twenty-four hours and Julie felt as if her entire world had shifted.

A huge load of supplies had arrived, including all of the material for the yurts' platforms. For the last eleven miles back to the ranch, they'd eaten a cement truck's dust on its way to pour the pilings for the yurts and the common bathroom.

When they arrived, Chelsea, Doug, and Patrick were putting the saddle horses through their paces, shaking off the excess energy of a lazy winter so that they'd settle down for the tourist season. She envied them that. The non-twins and Mac were rebuilding one of the truck's engines. Stan was doing what he did every day, working with his dogs. Ama had updated the website and was taking reservations.

And she and Nathan had somehow forgotten how to speak to each other. They'd each tried to start conversation on the drive back, but nothing had caught.

Emily met them at the barn. "Sometimes, the best way to move very valuable equipment is in plain sight." The two of them helped her carry everything up to her unfinished office—it had walls, windows, and a secure door, it just didn't have an interior yet.

When she went to check on Clarence, Nathan followed her into the stall. As he held and kissed her, Clarence didn't make any comment. Which was good, because she was too busy melting against Nathan's wonderful body to protect him from her horse. Then, still with no idea what to say to each other, Nathan rubbed Clarence's nose and left the stall.

"What's happening to me?" she asked Clarence as he nuzzled up against her. She hid her face in his mane for a long moment before going to snag a treat from the bin in Chelsea's office.

She was thankful for the quiet moment she had with Clarence while he crunched on a couple of sugar cubes and a carrot. It would be her last for a while.

Julie threw herself into the work. When the first of the summer's guides and a maid had arrived, Julie sicced them on the cabins. First they painted the doors and trim while she finished out the Ponderosa's bathroom. Then they cleaned and prepped them for the first guests. One of the guides was a contractor during the winters and along with the twins, once the truck was running again, they tackled the decks.

Over the next few weeks there were only rare occasions that she saw Nathan. He would smile and wave. On the rarer occasions when they got close, there was a hug and a kiss. In those moments, she could rarely do more than cling to him.

"It's just a busy time," he whispered.

All she could do was nod before rushing off to whatever crisis called next.

When the yurts were delivered, they performed exactly as promised. The first one went up in half a day. The others took even less time now that she'd figured out the tricks.

The first time she saw Nathan up on a horse, it almost killed her. He and Mark were soon trotting around the corral, even a brief canter. She could only watch out the Larch cabin window; watch as her heart ached.

"He rides well," she told no one before going back to tackling the busted pipe under the sink. And he did. She could see from up here that he sat the horse solidly. And they'd put him up on Red, rather than an old-timer like Daisy. Red was an intermediate horse, but still Nathan looked comfortable. Then she noticed that he was wearing his Indiana Jones hat and for reasons she couldn't explain to herself, she started crying.

"Morning, Julie," Mac blustered into the cabin.

She turned away and wiped her face but not fast enough. She couldn't stop the tears.

"Easy, girl. Easy."

"I'm not some damned horse, Mac," but her voice choked and stumbled.

He fumbled about for a moment, then held out a paper towel at arm's length as if she was a pissed-off grizzly. She used it to blow her nose into and wipe her face.

When she'd cried at the hotel, Nathan had held her. And the memory of that hurt all the more.

She ran a splash of cold water, then regretted it when she heard it splattering inside the cabinet where she'd removed the busted U-joint.

"Something you want to be talking about?"

"Not really."

Mac watched her in silence as she sponged up the freshly spilled water under the sink and squeezed it into the bucket she'd prematurely moved aside.

She slipped on the new joint and tightened up the fittings. Then she wiped everything down with her tear-stained paper towel and turned the water back on full. She let it run for a full minute, checking for drips or water squeezes around the plastic washers. Nothing, all good. She stuffed her tools in her tool belt, dumped the bucket's contents down the drain, and turned off the water. One last check, the U-joint and her face were both dry now.

Mac was still there, leaning back against the counter. "Think we need to talk some, girl."

"I don't have time."

"Fine. You're fired."

"What? But I—" she waved a hand helplessly at all of the unfinished tasks.

"Until you talk to me some, girl, you're off the clock. Period." This wasn't his friendly rancher tone. It was his retired Navy SEAL tone.

She covered her eyes for a long moment. "I really don't want to talk about this."

"Tough."

Julie turned to stare out the window.

Nathan was following Mark out of the corral and into the first pasture. At an easy jog, they soon disappeared over the first rise.

"That was supposed to be me."

Mac was nodding when she turned, "Wondered what was up with you two. Looked like that trip to Great Falls didn't go so well so I decided to keep my trap shut."

"No, Mac. No. It went..." how was she supposed to put words to it? It was the best memory, maybe ever, in her life. "It was perfect."

"Then, pardon my language, what the hell, Julie?" He folded his arms over his big chest.

"You know his background?"

"Some fancy-pants chef in New York. Damn good one according to his brother."

"I went online and looked up the restaurant he used to work at. Top twenty on almost every website, top ten in some. That's in New York, Mac. He's one of the best chefs anywhere. There's not a chance of him staying in Montana."

"And if you went with him—"

She tried a scoffing laugh to hold back the tears. It worked, barely. "I'd wither and die."

He nodded slowly, "Yes. I kind of imagine you would. Even your father isn't rooted to the land the way you are. That's the thing about you that so confuses the young men who come sniffing around. None of them understand that about you."

"Nathan does. He's going back to New York and he didn't even ask me. At least he could have asked." And she had to turn away because the tears were back and she couldn't stop them.

"He is? He never said."

"No. Not yet. But it's obvious. I can't imagine it will be long now."

"Fight for him, girl."

"How?"

Mac was silent long enough for her to wipe her face again and look over at him.

"Am I supposed to go out and become a Navy SEAL?"

"Now you're trying to steal my tricks. They're the sort that will only work for me. We're just going to have to find you your own."

"I won't trick him," her protest was sharp. That had been part of what he liked about her. No games. Not even if it broke her heart.

"Wouldn't be you to use tricks," Mac confirmed. "We'll just have to think on it a bit."

"Better hurry," she waved a hand out the window. Two tiny figures on horses topped the next rise, then disappeared out of sight.

~

NATHAN ALTERNATED between having the feel of the trot and then completely losing it.

In one moment he understood why Julie talked about Clarence the way she did. Red would be striding along, following the line of a small stream that wandered down out of the far hills, and it would feel as if he could sink right down into the smooth leather of the saddle. The horse's muscles working in perfect sync with his own.

Then it would all go to hell and he'd be bouncing so hard that he could barely stay in the saddle. It was a miracle that his tail-bone didn't break as the powerful horse slammed up against him every billionth of a second. It was only after the fifteenth or sixteenth transition that he caught on to what was happening.

Red was toying with him. Red was shifting his stride on the sly, hoping to abuse the beginner. A couple more changes that Nathan managed to catch onto more and more quickly, then Red settled down. The glance that the horse cast back at him looked very amused.

"Ha. Ha. Ha." He told the horse. Just as he'd told Julie when she'd started her lesson with *This is a horse.* She felt so far away. He knew she was busy, but that wasn't all of it. He should turn back, track her down, and ask what was going on.

Ask her to go with him? Go where? New York? She'd shrivel and be bitter the rest of her life. She was the one with a business, with family and a place. Not something he was going to find out here. He'd barely talked to his brother in all of his weeks here. They were friendly, easy enough with each other to joke around, but they weren't friends. That had been a hard discovery. He and his little brother had so little in common anymore. The decade apart—him in his restaurants and Patrick on Montana ranches—had put so much distance between them.

But there was something, even if he wasn't sure what, that he and Julie had to talk about.

He looked around and he wasn't so sure that he could find her even if he wanted to. He and Mark were out on the open prairie. The mountains were ahead of them, but behind him there was no track through the winter-dead grass. Because he'd been preoccupied with Red's games, he hadn't been paying attention. This wasn't New York where, if he got totally turned around, he just had to walk to the next street corner and read the signs.

He'd never been so far from everything. Out here there were no fences, no ranch house or cabins. There was just brownish-green grass with the first hint of purple flowers, soaring mountains, and the biggest sky in the world. Except it wasn't far away, it was somehow strangely all...closer. As if he could reach out and touch every piece of the most expansive place he'd ever been.

He wanted to stop and appreciate it, but Mark had kept them moving at a trot for a while now.

"What's the rush?"

"Just passing on the favor, buddy."

"What favor?"

"My parents took over this spread when I was a 'cow'—means it was my third year at West Point. Their first ranch hand was a real old-timer. Crotchety son of a bitch, must have been eighty if he was a day, but that man could really ride. I came out for my first visit to see the place, so impressed with my hot school and that I'd be a 'firstie' soon—a senior at the best military academy there is. I *knew* I was hot shit and could do anything."

"Is that where you met Emily?"

"No. I missed her somehow. She was a freshman plebe my senior year. Damned woman did what I couldn't—was made First Captain her senior year, top of the school. Only woman so far to pull that off."

Nathan sighed with relief when Mark eased them back to a walk and his butt could start recovering. Though now there was a side-to-side roll that started sandpapering his inner thighs.

"That old bastard put me up on the orneriest horse on the place and made me ride him. Looking back, he was probably no worse than Red there, but I'd never so much as seen a horse. I can tell you that I fell off a bunch more than the one time you did."

"How many times did Emily fall off?"

"Never," Mark sounded totally disgusted as they continued

along the stream up toward the mountains. From that one helicopter flight, Nathan had enough of a feel for the size of the ranch that he doubted they'd reach the hills today. "What's your secret?"

"Julie said it was about confidence. She told how horses aren't *thinking* critters, they're *feeling* critters. So I'm trying to be confident. I also don't want her laughing at me if she sees me riding."

"Impressing a woman is a good tactic. Did that by rescuing Emily from a bunch of Thai hill-tribe opium runners."

"I'll make that my Plan B."

Mark turned them back toward the ranch, then rode up close beside him. "Ease up on the reins a bit. Make sure you stay solidly in your stirrups. Even looser on those reins."

It felt wrong. Red would be breaking back into a trot if Nathan didn't rein him in soon. He wasn't ready for more of that yet.

"Lean forward a bit. Perfect," Mark drifted back a couple feet.

Out of the corner of his eye, he saw Mark whip over the end of his reins, smacking them hard against Red's rump.

"Go on!" Mark shouted as Red leapt straight into a gallop.

Nathan took one glance at the greening grass racing by without the relative safety of a helicopter wrapped around him and knew he didn't stand a chance if he fell off.

Confidence. Like seasoning a dish with panache. It wasn't about the carefully measured spoon, it was about having confidence.

Red stretched out his stride and the world moved even faster. The horse's ears—what Julie had called the windows to a horse's emotions—slowly swung from back hard the moment Mark smacked him, to forward as he lowered his head and they sped over the prairie. Up one rise and down the back side. Sweeping by a family of small deer too startled to run and a wild rabbit that shot away fast enough to avoid being trampled.

He eased up in the saddle a little more, gave his hat brim a tug to make sure it stayed in place, and it felt like he was flying.

It wasn't as good as making love to Julie Larson, but it was right up there.

~

JULIE WAS up on a ladder with her head sticking out of the central hole of the yurt when she heard the thunder. She checked the sky, stark blue except for a couple of cumulus bumpers too small to hold any water.

Steady thunder. Not big enough to be a stampede, but plenty to be—

Two cowboys shot up over the back of the rise. With a swerve and a *Whoop!* they swung to either side of the yurt. One had been wearing a black cowboy hat, the other...an Indiana Jones one.

"Nathan!"

At her shout, he turned to look up at her and that was his undoing.

Red carved a hard turn to the right to match Nathan's weight shift. Except Nathan didn't lean into the turn. Instead, he continued in a straight line as the horse ran out from under him. He was pitched down the slope, which was all that saved him. Instead of going splat onto flat ground, he rolled and tumbled and spun until he came to a stop well down the slope.

She slid down the ladder, raced outside, vaulted over Doug working on the porch, and was at Nathan's side while he was still just blinking in surprise.

"What happened?"

"You fell off."

"I know that. I thought I was doing so well. How did I screw up?" He sat up slowly, testing himself as he did so. She sat close by him, ready in case something was really wrong. But other than a few winces and groans, he appeared unscathed.

"You okay, buddy?" Henderson trotted up close beside them; he had Red's reins in one hand.

167

"Idiot!" Julie tried not to yell, but watching Nathan fly through the air and tumble like a broken rag doll really threw her. She'd seen more than one rodeo rider broken or crippled by less.

"Which one of us?" they asked in unison.

"Both! You," she aimed a finger at Mark, "for teaching a beginner to gallop."

"He didn't teach me. He just whacked Red with his reins. Why me? All I did was fall off."

"You," she couldn't help herself and hugged him because she was so glad he was okay. "For being stupid enough to go riding with Mark on your first time out."

"It's a mistake I won't be making again," Nathan glared up at Mark, who just grinned.

"Next time, it's with me or no one."

Nathan looked at her. That smile of his slid to life, then he leaned in and kissed her on the nose. "That's a deal."

Julie had no idea what in the world to do with him. She wanted to smack him, hug him, and take him right here and now. Most of all she wanted to keep him as close as she could for as long as she could.

CHAPTER 12

*T*he next day the yurt topping-off party was a big occasion. He and Emily chased Ama out of the kitchen and spent all of that same afternoon creating a feast.

"You really cooked at the White House?" Nathan had never actually met one of the White House chefs and it took him over an hour to stop feeling clumsy beside her.

"For just a few weeks. Private chef to the First Lady," Emily didn't make it sound like a very nice experience, but he had to ask.

"What's she like? The First Lady?"

"I've known three of them. The last one and the new one are both wonderful. I cooked for the one before that." Her tone put a clear, end-of-discussion period at the end of it. She'd cooked for the one who'd died at the White House—that must be a bad memory indeed. He remembered it only vaguely; he'd been surviving his Parisian servitude at the time.

What he discovered as they cooked together was that she was an unconventional chef, clearly with no formal training—with an exceptional palate. That was the one thing that was hardest to teach, but Emily didn't need any instruction there. Her looser style forced him to adapt. It was fun, especially working on the flavor profiles together.

As executive chef at Vite, he rarely cooked *with* anyone. They cooked *for* him. Tasting and seasoning with Emily was a reminder of what a joy it was to work with a truly talented chef who was more of a partner than an underling. He hadn't had that since he and Estevan had worked together at the ill-fated *Le Carte Blanche* just off Wall Street.

Because the day was plenty warm for eating outside, Chelsea improvised a horse cart for them and they hooked up Red—one of the few horses also trained to a full harness. Reconciled to his bumps and bruises, he let Red know that there were no hard feelings with a carrot *and* an apple.

"Gonna spoil that horse," Chelsea chided him.

"That's the plan," Nathan agreed.

By keeping a weather eye out the window, he could gauge when the last yurt would be done. They made a pretty little cluster atop the hill. The mountains, their ice-capped peaks glowing in the afternoon sun, shone in a brilliant backdrop. The tourists were going to love it from their very first sighting. They might end up even more popular than the cabins.

Timing it right, they delivered the feast up to the yurts just as Julie slid the last acrylic skylight into place and secured it in position.

All the ranch hands came up, even Stan with his favorite dog Bertram.

Nathan helped Chelsea drop the sideboard on the wagon and turned it into a serving station. They uncovered platters of pasta with meatballs, pesto chicken skewers, and shish-kebab veggies still hot off the kitchen grill. Sometimes comfort food was called for, but he and Emily had elevated it a couple notches while they were about it.

Nathan had even tracked down a case of Moose Drool in the pantry and loaded it into a cooler of ice.

He'd also seen to one other detail for later. Thankfully, Patrick had been out on another supply run this morning and had been able to bring back the one special ingredient he'd been lacking—which Patrick had delivered with only a brotherly ration of grief. Nathan couldn't resist peeking in his pocket to make sure it was still there.

The party quickly settled down to a lot of weary people sitting on the edge of porches that still lacked railings or chairs but had a view to die for.

He sat next to Julie, trying to hide the winces from yesterday's fall that aspirin had been unable to relieve.

"You load up a fine chuck wagon, Nathan," Julie spoke as she devoured her meal like the hungry worker she was.

"Glad you like it. Emily might have helped some."

"Best meatballs I've ever had."

Nathan tried not to cheer, those were completely his—except for a bit of the spicing in the red sauce, but he wasn't going to mention that.

Mac thumped a hammer on the porch a few times to call everyone's attention. Even though there were only ten or fifteen of them, it took them a while to settle down. The sun was bright and warm, the new spring grass was brushed with the purple he'd only noticed this morning. Ama had said that within a week the prairie would be purple, gold, and red with wildflowers. That's a sight he wouldn't mind seeing.

Mac thumped his hammer one last time, then tossed it down on the decking.

"First, thanks go to Nathan and Emily for this fine feed."

"And Red," Chelsea called out, slipping the horse a palmful of carrot sticks.

"And Red," Mac agreed happily.

"I hooked up the wagon."

"Shutting up now, Chelsea."

"Yes, boss."

Nathan liked how easy they were with each other.

"Next, I want to thank you all for busting your asses to get this ranch ready for the spring."

"You mean *you* busting *our* asses," Tweedledee shouted out.

"Mine's still broken," Tweedledum agreed.

"Hush or I'll bust 'em again."

"Too late," Dee. "Still busted," Dum.

"But the one person I want to thank more than any of you lot is the lady who really made it happen, Julie Larson," and Mac started the applause that swept through the crowd.

"Long way to go yet," she muttered under the applause. Her face was brightly flushed.

"But where would they be without you?" Nathan couldn't believe that she didn't see how little would have happened without her skills and drive. "Remember that, Julie."

She nodded uncertainly.

"Don't you see the value you're bringing here?"

A shrug.

"Crap, woman! I bet Mac wishes he could find five more just like you, or even one more. Except there isn't anybody like you."

The applause ran long but finally tapered off some time after she'd gone from flushed to beet red. She didn't speak again until other conversations resumed and some of the hands went back to the cart for thirds.

"Stop selling it, Nathan. I can get that out of the back of a horse anytime I want." Then she grimaced, "Sorry. I just have a mental to-do list in my head that could kill a Triple Crown Winner."

"A Triple Crown..."

"Kentucky Derby, Preakness, and Belmont Stakes," Julie explained with her *oh-city-boy* sigh. "If you get a horse in a decade who can win all three, you've got something really special."

"Come by Aspen around sunset and I'll show you who I think is so special."

"You looking to get laid?"

He reached into his shirt pocket and handed her a single, perfect, red rose petal.

∿

JULIE ARRIVED at the Aspen cabin just as the sun was shifting behind the Front Range crags. Getting past the steps was hard. She wanted to protect her heart, but—she had to admit as she ascended the steps to the front porch—she wanted Nathan more.

Inside, there was a cheery fire. Though the evening was warm enough that it wasn't really needed, it looked mighty cozy. No Nathan in the kitchen. No food on the table, which was just as well. She'd barely worked off the fullness from the amazing spread Nathan and Emily had delivered.

Then she spotted a yellow flower petal in the middle of the floor—a daffodil—and another. Not red roses, but sunny, spring daffodils. She never told anyone that they were her favorite, but somehow Nathan knew...or just got lucky. The trail led to the bathroom where a towel and a fresh bar of soap had been laid out on the counter. The shower ran hot when she tried it. She managed a laugh past the tightness in her chest, wondering who had helped Nathan turn on the water heater.

It felt so good to be clean that she stayed under the spray far longer than she normally would have. She let the water run hot until she knew she was avoiding whatever came next. With a slap, she stopped the water and dried off. A terrycloth robe hung on the back of the bathroom door. It felt sinful to pull it on over bare skin; she'd never worn a bathrobe at home.

She ventured out of the bathroom, still holding her one red rose petal, and spotted a second trail of yellow daffodil petals leading up the stairs and into the main bedroom. Whatever thin temptation lay along the first petal trail, leading to escape, wasn't enough to pull her aside.

Upstairs, unable to believe what she was seeing, Julie stopped at the threshold. Nathan sat in a comfortably worn armchair beside the bed, reading a book. Looking as if that was simply where he belonged, at home, waiting for her. The room was lit with candles and a single oil lantern dialed barely bright enough to read by. The light curtains had been drawn over the last hints of the sunset. The pictures of the ranch and Montana history blended into the shadows. The big bed had been made up with spring green flannel sheets and one of Ama's showpiece Cheyenne blankets.

The daffodils led to a vaseful of red roses on a small table at his side. No one had ever given her flowers, never mind roses.

Nathan's smile was brighter than the lantern. He closed his book, reached out, and missed dropping it on the table by more than a foot. When it hit the floor, they both jumped, then shared a laugh in surprise.

"I've imagined you here so many times since that dinner," his voice was rough as he clambered to his feet.

"So have I," but she couldn't get herself moving again. Across this threshold would be an incredible night. And then what? The lost chef—spooked by a cow and never ridden a horse—him she knew. The man who galloped across the prairie, laughed with the hands over a beer, and now waited for her with a vaseful of flowers and a smile full of promises—him she didn't know at all. Who would he be in the morning? Worse, *where* would he be?

He rose and moved until he stood just over the bedroom's threshold from her.

"What is it, cowgirl?" Nathan tucked her hair behind her ear.

Not trusting herself to speak, she let the warmth of his touch pull her into the room, into his arms.

She could feel Nathan's strength and his confidence as he pulled her against his chest. It was as if their awkwardness with each other since the trip to Great Falls had all been in her imagination. He held her more tightly than ever before, practically crushing her against him.

His kiss made it impossible to remember the world outside the bedroom door. In here there was only him. And he made it clear that, as far as he was concerned, there was only her.

Julie took a brief side trip to bury her face in the roses. They really did smell utterly incredible, just like in the novels and movies. She set her one petal close beside the vase.

Nathan led her to the bed and it was a hundred times more momentous than leaving with him for an out-of-town tryst. She didn't help him undress, but she couldn't look aside as he did. He'd become stronger, more solid in the weeks that he'd been here. More real. The last of his clothes hit the chair, except for one sock that landed on his forgotten book on the floor.

Never had she been so aware of a naked man. His unthinking power, his confident stance, his *incredible* maleness. How had she ever pictured him as belonging in a clown car? His presence filled the room and chased away shadows.

When he brushed her robe off her shoulders, it wasn't with greed, it was with reverence. He didn't untie it or tug it down to expose her breasts. Instead he nuzzled one bare shoulder, then the other. He eased it off her in such small stages that she couldn't place the moment when she transitioned from dressed to naked, from hesitant to gasping. Not until the robe lay in a pool about her ankles did he stop uncovering her inch by inch. Then he looked up at her with those dark, hungry eyes from where he knelt before her.

"You are the most beautiful thing I've ever seen."

"Thing?" Julie was amazed that she could still speak.

"Better than any sunset or the finest meal at Le Bernardin."

She had to laugh, though it was hard to find the breath to do so. "I'm guessing that last one means something."

Nathan smiled. "Best restaurant in New York. It's one of only six Michelin three-star restaurants in all of New York. One of the very best in the world. If I could be anyone else, I'd be Eric Ripert —the head chef. But if I was, I wouldn't be here with you."

She wanted to look aside from the intensity of his gaze. Needed to look aside. But couldn't. Nathan Gallagher of New York City might well be the best *thing* she'd ever seen as well.

Without breaking eye contact, she eased backward onto the bed and under the covers. He followed her slowly.

Each place he touched her, she placed a wall around—to both preserve it and keep it safe against the unknown future. His hand, endlessly tracing the curve of her hip until it was sealed as surely as the prairie by a winter's hard frost. Where his head lay between her breasts as he listened to her heart until the sound was swallowed by the vast emptiness of the Montana prairie.

And when he finally took her, when he filled her heart like no one ever had or could again, that too she locked away behind the hard mountains of her soul. She locked it away though it was bigger than the Montana Sky.

❧

WHEN HIS RINGING phone woke her, the world was still dark beyond the curtains.

"Murmph," Nathan said into his phone once he recovered the screaming thing from his discarded clothes.

Julie checked the time. Too close to sunrise to sneak back home and pretend she hadn't just spent the night on Henderson Ranch. Not too late to snuggle back under the covers with Nathan for a few minutes.

"Who?... Estevan, you asshole... What's wrong with me? It's the middle the night is what's wrong with me... What do you mean what time zone am I in? Montana. Whatever zone that is... I know. Crazy, right?"

The more Nathan woke up, the farther away Julie felt. Estevan was clearly a friend. A friend Nathan had never mentioned. From a past that was suddenly in bed with them.

She slipped from between the covers and out into the chill morning air. The cold bathrobe brought goosebumps, though none as much as Nathan's loud exclamations.

"You did? You actually broke off and started your own restaurant? Who's your backer? Oh, she's good. What's your take on it? Sounds fair... No, French puts you right up against Vite. You need your own voice in there..."

She closed the downstairs bathroom door, which reduced Nathan's voice to a distant rumble. A quick shower to wash off the night muffled him briefly. His questions had turned to excitement in just the two minutes she'd been under the water. On her way through the kitchen, she spotted a small bag of bagels. Where in Montana had Nathan found bagels? Oh, it was Nathan. He'd probably made them himself. There was no jam or butter in the fridge. The only thing there was cream cheese, which her mother had only ever used for making cake frostings.

Nathan's laugh boomed through the bedroom door and down the stairs, "No, shit? How is this my fault?"

She was almost out the door—chewing on her first bite of the dry, oddly dense bagel—when she heard the one thing she'd been hurrying to escape.

"You need me in New York by when?"

NATHAN WAS STILL SCRATCHING his head when he hung up the phone.

"Can you believe that bastard went and—" He turned, but Julie wasn't there beside him to hear what he had to say. Not her, not her bathrobe. But he could smell her, could feel her. It was the best night of his life: making love to her, holding her while she slept upon his shoulder. He'd spent hours imagining them like this, night after night. Waking together morning after morning.

Even asleep, he could feel her strength where his arms hooked lightly around her. How could someone so strong be so womanly at the same time?

And now all trace of her was gone as if she'd never been here.

No—she'd left her roses.

Maybe she was downstairs eating breakfast. He hadn't set up the coffee machine, but he should have.

Dressing quickly, he tossed the Zane Grey western back on the bookshelf, swept up her vase of flowers, and trotted down the stairs.

No clothes in the bathroom. No sign of her at all, except that on the kitchen counter there were only three of the bagels he'd made for her. Not four.

He stuck his head out the door; the sun was just putting the first hints of pale blue into sky—only a few stars struggled on. Down below, he could see Doug and Chelsea turning the horses out of the barn and into the pasture. Stan was feeding his dogs.

And the bright *whirr* of a screw gun told him that Julie was already hard at work up at the yurts.

He had cursed Estevan for calling so early and now he cursed himself for not waking up sooner. He'd missed his chance to see Julie Larson wake. To make love to her as the sun rose over the distant horizon.

Turning back, he cleaned up the cabin quickly. The only thing he couldn't quite figure out was the untouched cream cheese. Why would she eat her bagel dry?

Out the front door, he turned to head up to the yurts. To at least say good morning or...but he saw the backs of the non-twins and a couple of the other hands already past Aspen on the trail up to the construction site.

Instead, he tossed Ama's Cheyenne blanket over one shoulder, picked up his bags of supplies and laundry, and turned for the main house and the kitchen.

The kitchen.

Two weeks from take-over to open. No wonder Estevan was panicked. He had plenty of connections to staff up. The money woman was a responsible one and had taste. The front-of-house renovation would be a real pinch, but that was a given on a fast open.

It was an idea he and Estevan had figured out over a bottle of wine and three a.m. pasta a couple years back.

"How can we open a place and not bleed capital for three months while we build it out and get everything in place?"

They'd chased Estevan's question for half a bottle and straight into leftover chocolate-and-Courvoisier mousse before Nathan had finally seen it.

"Do a pop up!"

"Feh!" Estevan had been disgusted. "I don't want a pop-up restaurant—there one day and gone the next. I'm talking about a permanent, fine-dining, linens-and-wine steward sort of place."

Nathan recalled he'd been tired and drunk enough to barely hold onto the idea, but he'd managed. "I am too. You pop-up in your future space one night, and then you don't tear it down. Make improvements every day, but cook and serve every night. It gets the cash moving."

Estevan's askance look had motivated him.

"Get the customer involved. Give them little feedback cards with every meal. And not just on the food, but on the décor, the attitude, what wines and liquors to stock. Even if you ignore them, they'll feel like they helped make it what it is. We'd get customer loyalty out the wazoo. And they'd forgive a lot of the mistakes that usually happen with a new place."

Now, after all this time, Estevan was really doing it. Doing it, and told Nathan that he was expected to show up and help. It would be his kitchen as well. The old dream of running their own restaurant was finally coming true.

Nathan got everything put away at the ranch house and was toasting a bagel by the time Ama came in.

"I was thinking cheese-and-mushroom open-faced omelets and Potatoes O'Brien," he told her while he watched the coffee pot fill. The ranch hands had emptied it and not bothered starting a fresh pot. They'd be back from their start-of-day chores for breakfast soon.

"No bagels?"

He split another of the ones he'd meant for Julie and slipped it into the toaster for Ama before pulling a whole bag of them out of the bread drawer. She smiled and began washing and cracking eggs. What he wouldn't give for some lox, capers, and slivered red onions right about now, but the nearest supply of those was two thousand miles away.

Two thousand miles.

He began washing and dicing potatoes.

Estevan was choking on the menu ideas. Nathan could feel it. He was going to serve the same things they'd cooked at Vite. He was a creative chef, but didn't trust that. Any pressure and his friend scampered for familiar ground.

This is all your fault. Nathan's fault because of his dropping off the face of the planet—as Estevan had called Montana—had put a different kind of fear into Estevan. A fear that he would never have the guts to open his own place and would then end up feeling as lost as Nathan had.

Estevan had begged him to come back and help. "At least through the open. I've got a couch. Come on, man. Together we can build the menu the way it should be. You owe me, bro."

And he did. Estevan had gotten him through the door at two different restaurants before Vite. Had listened and commiserated each time another relationship had collapsed. Nathan was far closer to Estevan than his brother. Who seemed just fine out here in Montana. He'd never fit anywhere in New York, not the way Nathan had. Ranch life really did fit his little brother.

The next thought should be that it didn't fit himself.

He diced up some onions, tossed them on the griddle...and nothing happened. He'd forgotten to turn it on. Chef's rule Number One: first thing you do on entering the kitchen is fire up all of the ovens and burners you're going to need. He lit the griddle and shifted over to rounding up the spices while it heated.

Ranch life didn't fit him. He wasn't a rider...he'd proven that yesterday. It had been exhilarating; with practice it might even be fun. But he could see the natural riders and the trained ones. Julie, Doug, and Chelsea all rode as if born to the saddle. No one else on the ranch, not even the two summer trail guides rode the way they did.

Everything here was foreign. He'd asked for different, but frankly, he was having trouble keeping up with it. For the first week, well... He'd been such a wreck that it shouldn't be a surprise that he'd been going through detox—not from drink, just from the standard chef's high-adrenaline, sleep-deprived lifestyle.

The only times he slowed down, felt as if he really belonged anywhere, were with Julie. But the morning-afters were proving to be rough.

You gotta come back and help me, man. I signed everything this morning. You're my first call. I open in fourteen days.

Fourteen days. He could do that, then come back to...somewhere he didn't belong in the first place. He'd only been here...

"What day is this, Ama?"

"Wednesday."

"No, what date?"

She didn't look up from the grill that he'd completely forgotten he'd fired off. The onions had added a bright sizzle and tangy bite to the air. In chagrin, Nathan got the peppers and potatoes on the grill before turning to the omelet pans.

"April 30th."

"It's..." *what?* This time he almost lost the whole bowl of eggs to the floor. Hadn't he left New York in the first week of April? A month. Somehow he'd come for three to four days and been here a month. The way the time had slipped by, he couldn't account for it. A week until that first dinner up in Aspen. Another several days had led them to Great Falls. Had he really let two weeks of busy go by before last night? Apparently he had.

He couldn't keep floating through life on someone else's charity. He had to find a city and a restaurant where he could earn his way. Where he belonged rather than out on some Montana Front Range spread beneath a sky so big that it still shocked him every time he looked up.

"Here she is, Ama, just like we promised." The non-twins came in through the back door making a show of escorting Julie between them. "She resisted."

"I already had a bagel," Julie's protest didn't make the non-twins release her.

"Without any cream cheese," Nathan teased her.

Tweedledee looked at him through narrowed eyes, "Why would you put frosting on a New York doughnut?"

"Heathens," Patrick said coming in behind them. "I warned you, Nathan. These guys are nothing but heathens."

"I have work to do," Julie cut for the door, but the others grabbed her.

"If you work on this ranch," Ama said quietly, "you eat in my kitchen."

Nathan figured it would take a braver man than he was to argue with Ama when she used that tone. Maybe she'd gotten it from her SEAL husband.

"But—" Julie was apparently impervious to even that.

"Girl! Sit!" Maybe Ama had *given* that tone to her husband so that he could become a SEAL.

◇

JULIE SAT, then wished she could switch sides, but it was too late.

It was hard watching Nathan as he moved about the kitchen. Something was wrong. He usually looked so smooth, as if he was dancing. This morning something was distracting him badly...and it wasn't her.

He'd teased her—which she'd let slide off—but he hadn't really looked at her. Not even his usual easy smile. He was thinking hard about something that wasn't her.

She sat and watched her worst fear come to life across the width of the Henderson's kitchen. His friend's phone call this morning.

A chef calling from New York.

It was like the call of milking time. All of the beef cattle could spend the entire summer wandering aimlessly over the prairie and rarely be seen until roundup time. But the hundred head of dairy cattle trooped to the barn twice a day like clockwork to be fed and milked. You had to go.

The call had come. Nathan would be gone. Very soon.

All through the meal she did whatever was needed to appear normal. Growing up with three big brothers and her father, she'd learned young how to keep everything inside.

After the meal, Nathan caught up with her just outside the door. She didn't even give him time to speak—didn't know if she could bear to hear his voice saying those fatal words.

"If you're going, Nathan, then go. I heard the call. I know what it means. Have a good time." She searched for one more thing she could say without revealing the pain, the flaming geyser of agony. *Have a good life? Go to hell for breaking my heart? Ask me to go with you?* She couldn't do that last one. She knew that.

But he could at least ask!

He didn't.

"Thanks," was all she could manage past the layer of rock she had wrapped around herself last night to keep her heart safe.

"Hey, Julie," Emily passed them on her way toward the barn.

"Can you give me a hand with something when you have a chance?"

"Now's fine," she needed to run, far away. "Bye, Nathan."

Then she turned and walked toward the barn. No one would be able to see what was going on inside her. Not even Emily.

CHAPTER 13

*N*athan made the mistake of turning the car right when he hit the main road and going to Helena. He'd figured the state capital would have the best flight connections. Besides, it wouldn't feel right going to Great Falls without Julie.

At least he got to prove that the last big, white cow barn on the road from Choteau to Augusta was indeed the one at the turn toward Henderson Ranch. But that wasn't the mistake.

His real mistake was not checking the flight booking more carefully. Great Falls had a one-stop flight to La Guardia, six or seven hours depending on the layover. Helena's only real choice was to fly the wrong way first—through Seattle. It was twelve hours, two stops, and no better connections. He'd driven an extra forty miles to end up with a flight that was going to take double the time. For reasons that completely eluded him, he had to travel a thousand miles further west to Seattle to get back to JFK.

And he spent the whole time puzzling over what Julie had meant with that deadpan, "Bye, Nathan."

Not, *See ya, city boy.*

No, *Come back fast.*

Not a hug. Not a smile. Nothing except, "Bye, Nathan."

As if he'd been a nice screw, she was done with him, and she'd really meant goodbye. But it didn't make any sense.

Unable to sleep on the redeye—how was he supposed to sleep as he was flying over Montana again—he began working on a menu. Something had to distract him.

Nathan started with a classically French menu. He made a dozen different attempts to veer that one way or another, but couldn't seem to find it. Estevan, like most of New York's finest French chefs, was Hispanic—one of the weird truths of haute cuisine. The flavors of Estevan's youth had no place in a French restaurant...but what if they did?

Nathan began listing ideas, crossing out more than he kept. Snails in salsa was ridiculous, but a slow-simmered pozole beef stew reworked with a Burgundy wine had possibilities. Coq au Vin, made with a yellow Oaxacan mole. Instead of Courvoisier-chocolate mousse, a chili-chocolate one.

Mexican-French Fusion. He paid for some airborne internet time and did some searching. There were a couple people trying it, but none in New York and none doing it high-end. Of the few he found countrywide, most were panned. But there were a couple good ones. Someone had proved that it worked, but it wasn't even enough to be a trend yet. Estevan was a good enough chef that maybe he could turn it into one.

By the time Nathan reclaimed his knives from checked luggage and the cab got him to the city, it was eight a.m. Six a.m. back in Montana—time to get up and cook. He headed straight for the restaurant.

He found Estevan crashed out on a sagging settee at his new place halfway between Ripert's Le Bernardin and Keller's Per Se, and not too close to Hell's Kitchen. It was an amazing location... and a total wreck. It looked like a cattle stampede had come through.

"Hey!" He kicked the settee just as Julie had kicked his bed a lifetime ago to introduce him to her horse.

"Buddy, you came," Estevan's groan was dramatic. "What time is it?" He looked at his watch then collapsed back onto the broken settee. "Wake me some time past noon."

Nathan kicked the settee again, which may have been a mistake as he was still wearing the heavy boots that Julie had made him purchase in Great Falls. Standing in the heart of Manhattan, it was hard to believe that he'd ever shopped at a place called Hoglund's.

The heavy blow was too much for the settee. Something inside cracked, then the whole thing gave way, ejecting Estevan into a line of chairs that weren't much better than the settee.

"What?" Estevan yelled without opening his eyes as he rubbed at his banged elbow.

"It's time to cook."

"It's eight in the morning."

"Exactly," Nathan could get to enjoy this. "Let's see the kitchen."

Estevan staggered to his feet, lurched into the kitchen, and punched the coffee maker—literally. It seemed to be a random act until Estevan did it again and the power light flickered on.

"Cold or hot?" Estevan held up half a pot of blackened sludge.

"I'll wait."

Estevan poured one chipped cupful, looked around the wreckage vainly for cream or sugar, shrugged, and took half of it in one swallow like bad medicine. Behind him, the machine cycled to life and began dribbling hot coffee onto the empty burner. The reek of burned coffee filled the air before Estevan could dump out the half pot of cold and slam it back into place.

"Time to cook?" he looked at Nathan through the one eye that might have been starting to wake up.

Nathan knew how to cure that. He handed over the stack of recipes he'd spent the last half of the flight writing down.

187

Estevan grunted at the first, went quiet by the third, and by the fifth was starting to smile.

"Amigo! *Muchas gracias!* But why not espazote leaves here in the Tarte Flambée? It would go well with the bacon and onion."

"Because I didn't think of it."

Estevan grinned at him. "You and me. Two weeks. This will be spectacular. Mexican-French fusion, but all the way high." He wrapped Nathan in a bear hug and pounded on his back as if he wanted to break some vertebrae.

"Simple ingredients," Nathan managed once Estevan released him. "But perfect preparations."

"Yes. Yes. Haute cuisine, but with a big punch of Mexican flavor."

Nathan looked around the kitchen. "Where are we going to cook? We need to test this."

Estevan kicked an oven—the door fell off with a crash. "The crew hits in an hour. By tonight, we'll have enough of a kitchen to start testing. By three days, the kitchen will be done and they will start out front. I *knew* you would come back. Help me start breaking down this old equipment. The Irish owner was so cheap that he never fixed anything. I have to replace it all."

"Hey, I'm Irish," Nathan couldn't help laughing.

"Get some whisky in you, then you will be." They went back a long way, long enough that they'd helped each other dry out before they became true chef-alcoholics.

"It's a good space. Show me your layout."

Estevan found a magic marker and began drawing directly on a countertop. They soon scrounged up a tape measure and were making adjustments to the layout of the cook line.

Open in two weeks.

You and me.

I knew you would come back.

Nathan didn't know quite what was going on. Except that he

knew Estevan would never get this place open in time without him.

"Montana? Really?" Estevan began throwing rusted and broken utensils into a huge garbage can.

Nathan didn't want to talk about it. "It's where I ran out of road."

CHAPTER 14

*J*ulie stood in front of the last yurt and looked around her, unsure of what to do next. Every bunk was in place, every heater tested, every screw tightened. Ama had done one of her Cheyenne patterns in tile for the communal bath and showers. That alone was so beautiful that the yurts could well become the preferred rentals.

There were already tourists in three of the cabins—she'd finished the Ponderosa bathroom with only a day to spare. Next week, the first of the yurts would be occupied.

Down in the big corral, one of the summer guides was doing a basics class for the new guests. The kids were making better of it than their parents, but she could hear their laughter.

The ranch was waking up, but the springtime was slow. The local farmers were starting to worry and the part-time Montanan preoccupation with the weather had taken on a full-time choke-hold. The spring rains had yet to come. The doomsayers were already calling for a dry year, her father was on the fence, and Mac was still hopeful.

She had another day or two of work on Emily's office. A few

touchups where Patrick had backed the baler into the corner of the barn.

But nothing major.

Nothing to hold her here.

She'd been too busy to line up other jobs. For the last two weeks since he'd left, she'd purposely kept herself too busy to think. Except at night, after driving past the darkened Aspen cabin, to go home and lie in the silence of her bed.

"Damn you, Nathan."

He had given her so much in so little time. The way he saw her: more beautiful, more capable, stronger than she could even imagine. The way he'd held her. The way he'd loved her.

But not enough to stay. Not enough to ask her to go with him. Could she survive out from under her Big Sky?

She'd never be able to leave Clarence. So what would he do? Become a stabled New York horse, only allowed to see the sun when trotting slowly through Central Park? She could see him even now, pastured in with the other Henderson horses. She'd barely ridden him in the last hectic weeks and it had seemed too cruel to leave him alone on the Larson ranch. And that would be far less cruel than some big city stable.

Mac came up the hill with another group. Only Aspen and Larch were still empty. Not able to bear it if they were headed for Aspen, and definitely not able to bear any more of Mac's gentle probing, she tossed her tool belt in the back of the truck and drove down the track to the barn.

The sooner she finished Emily's office, the sooner she could get off Henderson land and away from all of the reminders of what she'd had here—however briefly.

But today, she couldn't even face that.

Instead, for the first time in weeks, she went up to the corral. She didn't even need to click her tongue to call Clarence over; he spotted her and cut through the herd at a brisk trot.

"Just you and me again, my big man," Julie scrubbed at his nose, then apologized for not bringing a carrot. "Stay there."

She doubled back to the truck and grabbed an old horse blanket she'd been using when she didn't want to scuff up the new flooring with her tools.

Clarence followed her on the other side of the fence until they reached the gate. Once he was through, she tossed the blanket over him, then climbed the first couple rails until she could hop on bareback.

She gave him a nudge with her knees.

His ears twitched forward and in moments they were off.

CHAPTER 15

"*D*os artichoke empanadas and *tres* crispy duck quesadilla," Estevan called out the firing order.

Nathan slapped three duck legs on the big griddle. Miguel began on the empanadas.

"I swear to god, *mi amigo.* You ever get tired of this, you should become fancy pants consultant for opening of restaurants. You can charge a ton. *Si?*"

"*Si,*" Nathan agreed because it was easier than arguing with Estevan.

"And 'meals half price while under construction.' Brilliant, Nathan. F'ing brilliant. At the real open, there won't be any sticker shock at the real prices."

They had a packed the house on the first day and with the open kitchen plan—it had taken an extra two days to knock out the wall but it was worth it—they could hear the excited buzz. It wasn't just French-Mexican fusion cuisine, it was French-Mexican fine dining. Tall walnut tables and minimalist chairs, set in a space with twinkle lights and still untouched bare brick walls. Next week they'd clean up the brick. After that, add fine linen and better service ware. Then...

The upbeat energy of being able to see the kitchen played off the attentiveness that even a French *maître d'* wouldn't be able to fault.

Rather than a breadbasket, every table was started with quail-and-black bean grilled jalapeño poppers with just a little of Estevan's killer-good secret salsa recipe. It was served in classic dimpled French escargot plates of the finest porcelain.

There were some fine wines coming out of Mexico and one of Estevan's more comely cousins was also a top-notch *sommelier*. The beautiful steward—as well-versed in beer as in wine—was proving to be very popular. Like so many Mexican restaurants, Estevan had made it a family operation as much as possible. But he ran them through hard-core training on proper deportment and fine service, right down to the daily lecture on dish ingredients and the best ways to describe each one. The typical Mexican casual was replaced with elegance.

"C'mon, *amigo.* Give," Estevan called out between orders.

"What?" Nathan tapped one of the lobster tails but decided it needed another thirty seconds in the pan.

"I know what you are thinking of when you go quiet."

"Shut up, Estevan."

"*La mujer bonita. La jolie femme.* The pretty lady cowgirl."

"I should never have told you anything. Leave it." One late night, so late that he knew Julie would be waking up soon, he'd told Estevan just a little.

Some of it had sounded stupid, sitting here half drunk in a Manhattan restaurant. The way she looked when she rode. Her easy confidence around the cows and horses. The way she had seemed so a part of the land.

Nathan stayed focused on the six sauté pans lined up in front of him, each with a different order. He was having a hard time keeping them straight. It was as if the edges were blurring.

Was he so out of practice? It had been years since he'd even had to think to keep a dozen separate orders all firing at once, just at this one station.

And now all he could think of was the way that a blonde cowgirl had smiled at him while eating a meatball.

∼

AFTER CURRY-COMBING CLARENCE and getting him settled back in the Henderson's barn, Julie headed home. It was after dinner, after dark, even after Dad had finished the books and gone in to watch a game on the TV along with his sons.

Julie dug around in the refrigerator and unearthed a piece of meatloaf and some leftover mashed potatoes. She didn't even bother with the gravy, just nuked them in their plastic containers and sat down alone at the dinner table.

She was halfway through the meal before she became aware that she wasn't alone. Her father was leaning against the doorway, just like the weary cowboy that he was. He was tall, taller than Nathan, almost as tall as Mark. She knew he was impossibly strong, but he wasn't built big. She'd gotten her leanness from him.

"Can see you're unhappy, Julie." It was so rare for him to actually call her by anything other than "girl" that she didn't look away. In a house full of men, "girl" had always been sufficient. "Anything I can do about it?"

She shook her head. "I wish there was, Dad." She looked back down at her plate and really wished there was.

"Got to do with your little company?"

She shrugged. "Not really."

"'Cause I was chattin' with Vern about the kinda work you're doing for Mac. He sounded mighty interested. You should give him a call."

Julie looked up at him. She'd hoped for recommendations from Mac, but never expected one from her father.

"Their property is off a ways. Not sure if that's a good thing or a bad."

Vern's spread was as far the other side of Choteau as they were. Sixty miles by the crow from here. Well clear of the Front Range. Well clear of the memories. She liked...and didn't like that part of it.

"Got to do with that young man."

He didn't make it a question so it was hard to shrug it off.

"He worth it?"

She could only nod.

"He's gone back to New York?"

Even the nod was beyond her.

"Not coming back."

Again not a question.

"Shit!" Then after a long pause, he spoke softly. "I'm real sorry, Julie."

By the time she could trust herself to look up, her father was gone.

~

THE NEXT MORNING Mark nearly steamrollered her into the ground as she came into the barn and he was headed out.

"Hey, Julie! Help me roll out the helo." It wasn't a request, it was an order.

In five minutes, with hardly another word, Mark was in the air and headed East—fast.

Emily was waiting for her when Julie reached the new office. It had changed a lot over the last six weeks. The battered loft filled with the unwanted refuse of a horse barn was now unrecognizable.

Up the stairs above the two tack rooms and to the right was a set of cubbyhole shelves and hanging pegs for coils of rope. Leather strapping had a different shelf for every gauge. There was even a big bin of old horseshoes to be given to eager kids to hang on their walls at home.

To the left was one of the strangest rooms Julie had ever been in—never mind built. From the outside, it looked wholly innocuous. She'd sided it with old barn lumber and normal-looking windows. But she'd found (and Emily had been thrilled with) special glass that looked mostly black from the outside—as if the lights were always out inside the room—but offered full visibility from within.

The parts she'd picked up at Malmstrom AFB with Nathan offered an entire layer of electrical silencing. Nothing done inside the room traveled out except as an encrypted signal up to satellites via a few small antennas she'd mounted beside the solar panels. No emissions to detect. Even the fresh air system was a crazy collection of electronic filters and wave disruptors that she didn't begin to understand, but the installation instructions had been clear enough for her to install them.

Inside, Emily' seat commanded a jet black cocoon of enough electronics to make an alien spaceship look average. What made it even stranger were the views out the windows overlooking the horse stalls, and the skylight on the sloping ceiling that allowed a view of the fields and sky.

When she'd asked, Emily had laughed. "Nothing mysterious. I do tactical consulting on complex missions for my old unit. Since I refuse to leave my children in order to do that—the whole idea behind leaving the Army in the first place—they built me this. Well, you built it, but they paid for it. It's a tactical command center."

Which had prompted Julie to add a small wooden plaque outside the door which read "Tac Room" to go with the two larger "Tack Room" signs below.

The door was open when she reached the top of the steps.

"I like my sign," Emily greeted her and waved her to a chair.

"I hoped you might."

"What's left?"

Julie ran down her punch list, which was actually depressingly short. She'd be done with all of her Henderson Ranch contract work by midday.

Emily nodded, "Good. There are some people who want to talk to you."

Some traitorous part of Julie lit a brief candle of hope—that she squashed as fast as she could.

"No, not Nathan. I'm sorry."

"That's okay," Julie got her stone walls back in place around her heart. "Who? Certainly not Mark. He lit out of here like his hair was on fire."

"I sent him on a mission."

Julie eyed the darkened computer screens behind Emily.

"Not that kind of mission. He'll be happier once the tourists are here. He's better with the kids than I am. Little children, fishing trips on horseback, the helicopter tours that Nathan thought up—"

"That Nathan thought up?"

Emily nodded, "We're also going to start offering, for a fee of course, heli-transport from Great Falls International Airport to the ranch. It's not a Black Hawk, but Mark will welcome the air time. I think I've probably flown enough for this lifetime. If it goes well, I might get him a bigger helo that can take more than four passengers. But then again, more trips will help keep him busier."

Julie was still pondering Nathan thinking up helicopter tours.

"Are you ready?"

Julie shrugged. "Since I don't know what for, bring it on. Is it something else to fix?"

Emily smiled, which Julie was learning to be a rare enough occurrence to be noteworthy. "In a way. Chelsea, you're up." Emily called out one of the inside windows after opening it.

There was a very Chelsean cheer, and then the pounding of

booted feet up the stairs. "You're finally done?" She burst into the room with more energy than Julie would ever have again.

Julie nodded. Most of her words had flown away with Nathan.

"Yes!" Chelsea did a fist pump followed by a little clog dance around the room before plummeting into a chair. "Please say yes. Please. Please. Please! Please...PLEASE!"

Julie almost laughed, another thing that— She chopped off the thought. "To what?"

"I need an advanced rider."

"For what? A pony express run? Closest point of the old route is probably Big Sandy, Wyoming. That's a ways off."

"Oh, wouldn't that be so cool if the Pony Express had run through here. We could offer Pony Express rides and—"

"Chelsea. Focus," Emily not only smiled but might have been fighting a laugh.

"Right. Sorry. We're trying to draw an expert-level crowd. That's a new market segment for us. The only person we really have to lead those kind of rides is Doug and he needs to be here to run the ranch. Mac said that I had to wait until you were done with the spring work because your brain might explode if we gave you another thing to think about, but now that you're done can you think about it. Right?"

Julie tried to absorb the strangeness of the request. "How often?"

"One a week, probably three-four days each trip—right through the high season. You know this country better than anyone. Ama wants to do more riding, too. The two of you could scout together, maybe lead them together sometimes. When you're here, well, Doug said he's never seen anyone better at talking down the feistier horses and he wants you to work with them when you have time. Then there's the breeding program we want to start up and— Oh crud! Doug wanted to talk to you about that later. But that's in there too."

"I have a business..." though Julie couldn't imagine anything she'd like to do more. Working with the horses was beyond a dream come true.

"That's my part of it," Mac was leaning on the door frame.

She hadn't heard him come up the stairs behind her. Maybe she should have left a squeak or two in the staircase. Though Mac had been a Navy SEAL, so it might not have made any difference.

"The management of Henderson Ranch," Mac pointed at himself and then up toward the house, indicating Ama. "We're thrilled with the work you did, but we can't afford you full time."

"That was my point," Julie hoped she could make one now that Mac's presence seemed to have silenced Chelsea. "I need to go find some work. I've gotten a good taste of building and find that I like it. Though a less crazy schedule wouldn't hurt me none."

Mac smiled. "Yep! This spring was a real stretcher that I don't want to repeat either. What I meant to say is that we can't afford you full-time as a building contractor alone. But if you wanted to mix that up with the trail rides and horse work," he gave one of his eloquent shrugs. "I think we can make that work."

"Full-time? Here? At Henderson's?"

Mac nodded, "Got a place picked out for you, already know you like it." He nodded up toward the cabins on the other side of the barn.

Julie looked out the skylight window. She was glad it faced away from the cabins—away from Aspen where...

He couldn't mean that.

If he did...

No! Impossible! She never could.

The skylight faced toward Larson land. And somewhere far to the east, a construction job on Vern's ranch. He was a good man. His older son was married and Julie liked his wife well enough when they met at church socials or the county fair. The younger son wasn't a complete troll either.

"I—"

"We're going to clear out of your way," Emily stood up and made shooing motions at the others.

"You get the trim and such finished in here. And just think on it."

She really didn't need to. What she needed was to be far away, but she nodded. Emily Beale wasn't the sort of woman to argue with.

Mac gave her a nod and a smile, then departed, probably assuming that of course she'd take the offer.

Chelsea made praying motions and whispered, "Please, please, please," another half dozen times as she backed out the door. Chelsea, at least, knew it wasn't as sure a thing. Though Julie had rebuffed her attempts to talk about "things" several times since Nathan left, she would miss Chelsea.

"Two nights, Julie," Emily said when it was just the two of them. "I want you to sleep on it for two nights. Because I know that's all it takes to change a person's life."

When she was gone, Julie couldn't find the energy to move.

Two nights.

Exactly the number of nights she and Nathan had had together.

She'd wait because Emily had asked, but then she was gone.

~

"WHAT THE HELL, BUDDY?"

Nathan startled up as the big voice boomed forth in the restaurant.

All other conversation immediately died and the patrons were all staring at the big guy in a jeans jacket.

"Mark?" Everyone in the restaurant wore upscale chic, even the tattering of some patron's clothes had been done by a designer. Mark Henderson looked big, burly, and completely out of place in his ranch attire. "What are you doing in New York?"

"Damned if I know," Mark brushed by the hostess and the waiters. Somewhere along the way he acquired a beer. He plucked an empty stool from one of the high-top tables just as its occupant headed off toward the restroom. Mark carried it to the center of the servers' station and dropped onto it.

It was the exact busiest point of the entire restaurant. It was where the three different legs of the cook line came together in front of the expeditor—which was Estevan because they hadn't found a good one that they could afford to steal yet. The expeditor finished the plating and made sure everything was perfect before sliding it across to the waiters. Sliding it to exactly where Mark had unknowingly parked himself.

"Hey. Get out of the way," Estevan flapped a hand at him. He couldn't do more because every patron was staring into the open kitchen to see what happened next.

Then Nathan recognized Mark's look, the look of a man who had just been head-butted by a moose and still kept his wits about him regarding his precious fish.

Mark knew *exactly* where he was sitting.

Nathan tipped his head to come back into the kitchen.

Mark sat through another long sip of his beer just to make Estevan crazy, then came around the side, still carrying his stool. He plunked it down just barely out of Nathan's way.

"What do you mean that you're damned if you know why you're in New York?" Nathan dropped three salmon fillets in butter with just a sprinkle of fresh-ground guajillo red pepper.

"Emily told me to come. Not a chance I'm going to argue with that woman. One thing I've learned about her over the years, she has a habit of always being right. I don't mess with that."

Nathan nodded as he spooned the butter up over the fish in fast little strokes to keep it moist. Too much liquid escaped from the first layer of the flesh if he didn't. The goal was a perfectly seared finish on one side, and a consistently moist bite from top to bottom. The butter gave a more luscious mouthfeel than white wine. It also played better off the artichoke salsa served alongside it.

Then he remembered Julie crowing with delight over proving Emily fallible.

I do like you!

He accidentally splashed a scoop of butter onto the burner rather than fish. Someone, probably him, was going to have to clean that up after the stove was cold. The butter smoked and tickled his nose as it burned off. Almost made him sneeze like that time with Julie when—

"So what did Emily have to say?" Because he certainly wasn't going to ask after Julie.

" 'Get on a plane, go find Nathan, and fix this.' I think those were her exact, and only, words. So what the hell am I fixing? And why did I have to fly two thousand miles—on a commercial jetliner, for cripe's sake—and track you down to do that?"

"How *did* you track me down?"

"Emily did one of her things with your phone's location from up in that room Julie built for her. Said you've barely been out of this building for two weeks."

Nathan cracked his neck. His shoulders hurt like hell, which they hadn't since he'd quit and driven to Montana. Hunching over a hot cook line did that to a guy.

"Where's my fish?" Estevan managed to keep it below a shout.

Nathan looked down. Scorched and dry. "In the crapper." He began knocking pans into the waste bin so that he could refire the whole order. In the process, he accidentally grabbed a duck confit and knocked it into the trash as well, which was going to screw up a whole other table's sequencing.

"Basket case," he called out. There were nights when a chef turned all thumbs. There were only two approaches that Nathan had ever found would work. One: plow mindlessly ahead while the disaster rippled through the service for an hour or more, all the way out to the tables, before it finally tapered off and resettled.

Or two: cry "Basket case" and get the hell off the line.

Estevan was muttering foul imprecations as he juggled the line in order to take over the position himself. "Get out of here, Nathan. And take this asshole with you."

"Sorry, man."

Estevan shrugged. It happened, just never to Nathan. He'd set up the system at Vite, but he'd never had to call it on himself.

He returned the stool to the perplexed patron who had only just returned from the restroom.

Nathan swiped a beer from the bar and led Mark out the front door. It wasn't a warm enough evening for New Yorkers to use the outside sidewalk tables, but after Montana it seemed almost balmy.

"Find me and fix this?"

"That's what she said," Mark toasted him and drank. "Any idea what it means?"

"Yeah," Nathan sighed, then returned the gesture and drank himself. "Yeah, I think I do."

CHAPTER 16

*J*ulie hadn't been able to stand it. There wasn't a way she could stand waiting a whole second day.

Dad had silently lent her a hand loading her truck. There wasn't that much to load. She couldn't take Clarence, not until she knew the lay of the land at Vern's ranch, so it was just her work clothes and her tools. The old Ford cringed under the load, but stood staunchly by. She had the money in her pocket to rebuild the engine—Mac had paid her off yesterday afternoon—but she didn't have the time.

When everything was loaded, they stood awkwardly in the front yard close beside her truck.

"Mac called me about the offer couple days back," her father finally grumbled out. "Told him I hated to lose a hand as good as you, but it sounded like a better fit than this place will ever be. Or Vern's. You sure you're making the right decision in turning him down? He's a good man. Good spread. I know your mama would like having you close to home."

Julie studied her father's grim face. It was perhaps the longest speech she'd ever heard from him. And it was definitely the closest Nils Larson had ever come to saying he'd miss her.

It touched her that he tried.

"I'll still see you and her at church, Dad, and the Choteau socials. First rodeo coming to Great Falls is but a handful of weeks off. Besides, I'm just sixty miles off." Not New York or some other impossibly faraway place. "Have to come back and get Clarence at some point."

"You thinking of taking up racing again?"

Julie shrugged. She'd liked barrel racing. It tested a horse and rider's cooperation like no other rodeo event. The men's event of bronc riding and tie-down roping was as much about raw nerve and real guts as anything else. Women's barrel racing was about pure horsemanship.

"You were good, Julie. I was sorry to see you quit after that third you took up in Calgary."

"The pro riders, Dad. The ones who don't have to work for a living. Can't go up against them."

"S'pose so," he shrugged, but it was more like he was sorry she'd quit. "Well, you take care, Julie. You need anything, give a call."

"You too, Dad."

He wrapped his arms around her for a moment and patted her on the back.

She breathed him in deep so that she could keep that memory close. As close as those memories she'd kept of Nathan. The problem was that after two long weeks and starting a third, those memories were already starting to fade.

Julie was losing him and couldn't bear it.

Her Dad let her go.

They exchanged nods, then she climbed in her truck and headed out. He opened the gate, where Lucy stood waiting to get back in.

He shooed the cow into the yard, then closed the gate behind her after she pulled out.

He didn't wave.

∼

JULIE WAS LESS than a dozen miles of dirt from Vern's ranch when a helicopter came in low and fast from behind her.

It swooped by so close above her truck that she ducked even though she was inside the cab.

Then it soared upward until its nose was almost straight at the sky. The tail kicked around, and it dove to land not a hundred yards directly ahead of her.

Julie slammed on the brakes to avoid ramming it before she recognized the crease in the nose. The passenger's foot window had been replaced, but the moose's dent in the nose definitely marked it as the Henderson's helicopter. Which now completely blocked the dirt one-lane.

She knew that Mac couldn't fly anything like that.

There was only one person aboard—though she didn't know why she'd expected anything else. Emily or...

Mark Henderson climbed out before the rotors had fully stopped. He stalked up to her truck window and rapped his knuckles on the glass.

The window crank had fallen off while crossing all of the rough roads and gone somewhere under the seat, so she opened the door wide enough to be heard.

"Go away, Mark."

"Not a chance. Turn this truck around."

"Not a chance."

He looked up at the sky and growled. Then he yanked the door open so abruptly that her hold on the inside handle almost tumbled her to the ground. Once she had her balance back, she reached back into her tools and grabbed the first thing that came to hand.

A crowbar. God was definitely laughing her butt off over this scenario.

"Out of my way, Mark. I mean it," she brandished it high, just the way Nathan had waved it at Lucy that first evening she'd met him.

He sighed, then made a sudden move to grab it. But she'd out-maneuvered enough cows and fought off enough rutting cowhands to not be such easy bait.

She dodged clear, but not before she whapped his butt a good one with the side of the bar.

"I have had enough of this shit!" Mark shouted down the long stretch of empty road. Then he spun too quickly for her to follow.

He swept her legs out from under her so fast that she had no way to recover. She landed hard, flat on her back. When she managed to open her eyes, she lay in a cloud of dust and Mark was tossing her crowbar back into the toolbox in the truck bed.

Just for fair play, she spun around, hooked his ankles with hers, and sent him toppling as well.

"What the—" Mark snarled from the dirt.

"Three older brothers," she sat up and rested her elbows on her knees. "You?"

"A whole line of Army hand-to-hand combat instructors that I'm going to have a hard word or two with next time I see them." He sat up opposite her and began dusting at his arms and legs. Even his sunglasses had a patina of dust on them.

"I can't go back, Mark. I just can't face it. Your dad, with the best of intent, was going to offer me Aspen. I can't go there. I can't stay there, can't even look at it. There were too many good things in that cabin."

"Yeah, a certain hospital bed comes to mind," Mark smiled to himself.

"A hospital bed. What was the other one?"

"The other what?"

"Emily said there were two nights that changed her life. Mine were a Great Falls hotel room and the Aspen cabin."

"She said that?" his smile looked awfully pleased. "Back of a Black Hawk helicopter would be the other."

"Should have guessed that one." Julie shook her head. "But you two got the end of your story. How do I go back when the rest of my story isn't there? I want that job. I want it so much. I love your ranch. And the people. The horses. It's all so perfect and it's all so ruined," her throat cracked hard but she couldn't stop it.

"You never give the hell up," Mark practically shouted. "I should have lost my commission for the hospital episode and we both should have for the second one. I lied my way into the White House to get her and almost got us both killed. You never give the hell up."

Julie cringed under the tirade Mark unleashed on her. But he was right. She had given up. Maybe too easily. She'd quit the barrel racing because of the truly exceptional women who were full-time riders. It wasn't that they were just the pro riders who didn't need to work. They didn't need to work at anything else because they *were* the top women's pro riders. And she'd finished third against them. If she'd been willing to give up everything else, she could have been as well.

But she was giving up the sweetest job offer there ever was because she couldn't face all the *good* things that a man had given her. That was so wrong.

And if she wasn't going to give up the job at Henderson's...

Then she certainly wasn't going to give up so easily on the best thing to ever happen to her. She stood and dusted herself off.

Mark eyed the hand she offered him carefully, then grabbed ahold and rose as well.

"If he's not in your helo, then where the *hell* is Nathan Gallagher?"

Mark's smile was radiant. "I dropped him at his car in the airport parking lot, so he's about an hour behind me. Or was before I had to come chasing after you."

She climbed up into her truck. "Get out of my way, Mark."

He held up both hands in mock surrender and backed away

while she maneuvered a five-point turnaround on the narrow dirt lane. And headed back.

She worked the truck up into third gear and wished for a fourth, fifth, and sixth while she kept the pedal down hard. Let it rattle and moan.

He didn't drive to New York. He flew.

Mark had had to go and get him, so he'd probably dug himself in pretty deep.

But he left his precious car here.

Maybe he'd thought that he'd fetch it later like she'd thought of fetching Clarence in a few weeks.

But he hadn't taken it with him. Some part of him had known he'd be back.

Just like some part of her had known not to move her horse.

She leaned low over the driver's wheel, hoping that would get her a little more speed back to Henderson Ranch.

CHAPTER 17

*N*athan sat on the porch of Aspen and watched the weather rolling in, darkening the afternoon. He didn't know where else to go. The last twenty-four hours had been so strange. In a way, the least strange thing had been Mark hunting him down all the way to New York City.

For the entire trip back he'd been obsessed with that one little phrase of Julie's, her confession of: *I do like you!* Somehow, that seemed bigger than their trip to Great Falls or even making love here in the Aspen cabin. Emily had told him to remind her that she liked him—and to not let her forget. Somehow he had been the one to forget and now it was time to remind them both. If she gave him the chance.

Nathan was now betting every single choice on that memory —thank god Mark had come to New York to knock some sense into him.

But the mad race back to the ranch had run into a major issue: Julie was nowhere to be found. Not even all of Emily's military equipment could find her, probably because Julie was somewhere that didn't have cell reception.

While Nathan drove, Mark had flown his helicopter from the

airport. Once it was determined Julie was gone, Mark had tracked Nils to the Larson's calving barn and found out where she was headed. Emily called Nathan to report that Mark had taken off in the helicopter to chase Julie down at about the same moment Nathan turned off the highway at the big white cow barn. He'd almost run into the gun-shot stop sign.

He didn't know the roads well enough to chase after her on his own. If she came back, there was only one place he could be sure she'd eventually go, and that's what drew him back to Aspen cabin.

Nathan had raced the Miata along the highway, but the wash-board roads from Choteau forced him to what felt like a painful crawl—no matter what the speedometer said otherwise. It was the longest thirty miles of his life.

Now, at the cabin, holding his breath, all Nathan could do was wait.

Emily had locked herself in her office and was probably doing marginally legal things to track Julie for Mark to intercept. Mark hadn't called to report his success or failure. Chelsea had swung by with Doug to offer him a few words of hope that he'd barely been able to acknowledge. Nathan managed to wave back when Mac and Ama looked up toward him from the main house's back door. He'd have to go far to find stauncher friends.

Nathan spotted the returning helo first, a small white dot against the heavy gray clouds. He stood and watched, holding onto a porch post because he didn't trust his knees.

He felt as out of balance as that moment last night sitting with Mark outside Estevan's restaurant when he realized his mistake.

Being a New York restaurant burn-out had sent him scrambling to Montana in the first place. And in just two weeks of helping Estevan, he'd gotten sucked right back in like some sick drug addict. Didn't even see what he'd done until Mark pulled the plug on him. Estevan's restaurant was on its legs, the friendship debt was paid, and his job was over.

At the next revelation he almost laughed—would have if he wasn't so scared: if he never cooked in Paris or New York again, that would be fine with him.

From Aspen's porch, Nathan saw the helo land, shut down—but Mark was the only one to climb out. He was too far away to see clearly, but Emily came rushing out of the barn. She threw herself at him and he swept her tight into his arms.

Nathan would take that as a good sign. Surprising, but good.

An even better sign, he spotted the dust of a vehicle far out along the road that ran between Henderson and Larson land.

In minutes the dust cloud resolved to reveal an ancient beater of a pickup racing toward the ranch. Unable to stand any longer, he sat down on the top step and waited. His hands ached with how tightly they were clasped, but he couldn't seem to let go.

Closer. Definitely Julie's truck. It disappeared behind the bluff for an agonizing couple of minutes, then came racing up the main drive.

It didn't slow through the main yard, which sent Patrick skittering aside when he foolishly tried to cross the open expanse.

Without a single hesitation she roared up the frontage road by the cabins, sliding to a barely controlled halt in front of him.

He couldn't stand.

For a long minute she sat there, looking at him through the closed window, her hands clenched on the steering wheel.

Unable to tolerate it any longer, he managed to rise and walk down the steps.

She watched him as he stepped up to the truck's door. Still held the steering wheel tightly.

He opened the door as the first drops of rain pattered softly on the roof of her truck.

She was covered head to toe in dirt.

"Hey, cowgirl." She looked incredible.

"Hey." No "city boy". Bad sign? Definitely not good.

"You're all dirty again. What happened?"

She shook her head. Not relevant. Right. Time to talk about what was important.

"A friend called. He needed help opening a new restaurant."

"So you just…went?" Her fury sounded deep, but he could read the hurt behind it. Nathan had no idea how he'd ever done this to her. He could only shrug. However, pointing out that she'd told him to go wasn't likely to help anything.

Instead he tried to explain. "It was a dream he and I used to have long ago. I owed him. Even more, I owed the dream."

She watched him with those impossibly blue eyes.

"I almost got lost in it again. So dangerously close. But one thing stopped me."

"Mark."

Nathan laughed and shook his head. "Not even close," he reached out and tucked her hair behind her ear.

She leaned into it a little, but didn't let go of the steering wheel.

"All Mark did was remind me that Emily can be wrong."

"What does Emily have to do with this?"

"You said, 'I *do* like you.' You said that Emily got it wrong and that you do like me. Is that still true?"

After a long moment she nodded.

"The piece I didn't connect was that I like you, too."

"Well, that's convenient."

He laughed at her tone. He now knew a Julie Larson-tone when he heard one. He thought he'd figured out a way around that, but he wasn't quite ready yet. It was the chef in him. A meal had an order: a build, a fullness, until the final validation at the end. In a meal it was called dessert. Here in Montana, beneath the roiling clouds of the Big Sky, it was called the rest of his life.

"Will you come sit on the porch with me, Julie?"

She eyed the porch over his shoulder, then nodded cautiously.

∼

IT WAS HARD, but she managed it. Nathan offered his hand, but that was asking too much. She flipped a tarp over her tools in the truck bed to protect them from the increasing rain and then climbed the porch steps beside him.

Aspen cabin. It was so thick with memories, with feelings, with hope and despair. He was here, but she didn't dare let the hope out. If she was wrong, she would never rebuild the walls holding her together.

"How are you here?" *How* was as far as Julie dared go. She didn't dare guess *why*. It was too risky.

"Mark and I got drunk last night, very drunk."

"That explains the bloodshot eyes."

"Actually, we got drunk last night in New York. So I think that the bloodshot eyes is more from having a hangover during the flight back. Don't ever do that. It sucks."

"Does this have a point?" Nathan was here. In Montana. Why was she complaining?

"It does actually. Usually drunk equals stupid—sometimes really stupid. I lost a couple years' worth of brain cells to being a stupid chef. Then I quit, cold turkey on my own, and became a slightly smarter chef. For some reason, last night, for once in my life when it really counted, drunk equaled smart."

"What were you smart about?"

"Mark and I came up with an idea. It sounded beyond stupid at first, but we were just drunk enough to chase it around a bit. Once we had, it sounded smarter. Then a lot smarter. Mark called Emily to roust Mac and Ama out of bed because we were so excited about this crazy idea. It was past midnight here, but they said yes before we had it half explained. *That's* when we got stupid and *really* drunk. Celebrating."

"Celebrating what? You draw this out much more, Nathan, and I'm going to have to commit more bodily harm on you than I already did on Mark." The rain began pattering on the porch roof.

"I'm sick to death of New York, Julie. It's not just because of

217

you. Actually that part isn't you at all. I'm tired of the grind and the way it chews up good people until there's nothing left of them but a palate and knife skills. I spent the last year having no life outside the kitchen—a whole year of my life. It's not how I *want* to live. Yet cooking for you, I was reminded how much I love to cook. Just as you reminded me every day what it looked like to be intensely alive."

"And…" she meant it as a growl, but she was too keyed up for it to come out that way. It explained so much, right down to the whisky he'd never quite finished at the Celtic Cowboy, proving to himself exactly who was in control.

"Cooking classes."

"Cooking classes?" What did they have to do with anything?

"Uh-huh. Cooking classes at Henderson Ranch. They have that magnificent kitchen. And there are bound to be guests who aren't so hot on horses married to ones who are. Also Ama wants to cook less. So, Emily and I will step in there together. And I was thinking to rebuild that wagon we used for the yurt-raising party. You and I could fix that up as a classic chuck wagon. Then Red and I could deliver dinners to remote campsites. Set up someplace a couple hours' ride away as a kids' camp and serve them meals from a chuck wagon. Give their parents a little alone time in the cozy cabins. We can offer fully catered ranch weddings. We'll get some great photos when a couple of Mark's old firefighter friends get married out here this summer."

He kept spinning ideas as fast as Chelsea had, just…yesterday morning.

"During the winter season, I'd get guest chefs out here and we'd do two-week pro-level master classes. During harvest we could—"

"And you'd be happy doing this?" She cut him off before he completely overwhelmed her with his words.

He nodded.

"Here?" she felt the cabin behind her but couldn't turn to look at it. She couldn't manage more than a whisper, barely louder than the steady rain.

"What's with all the rain? I've never seen a drop since we got here except that first night's bit of snow."

Julie hadn't really focused on it. What about her question? Was he avoiding it? Her heart was feeling too jumbled to hold focus on that, so instead she answered his question. "It's the first heavy spring rain. Everyone has been waiting for it. If it holds for a couple of days, it will be a good year along the Montana Front Range. Another major dump in August and it will be a great year."

Nathan rose and walked away from her to hold his hand out past the edge of the covered porch. "It's warm."

"We call it the 'Million-Dollar Rain'. It sets the crops, fills the reservoirs, and changes the prairie from struggling to lush. In a couple days, you're going to see wildflowers like you never imagined in your life. The entire prairie blooms purple, red, and gold."

"I'd like to see that." Then he turned back to face her, nodding toward Aspen's cabin door showing that he hadn't forgotten her question. "Yes, right here. One condition."

"What's that?"

"You said that you like me, cowgirl."

"I think we already covered that."

"But do you love me, Julie? I couldn't go through that door ever again without you beside me."

She turned from Nathan and those dark eyes that looked at her with such sudden hope. She finally looked at the front door of the Aspen cabin.

Could she live here? With Nathan? With their children?

Looking out over this beautiful land?

She finally faced Nathan once more but could only nod. The answer to every single one of those questions was yes.

He knelt before her.

"Then will you marry me, Julie? Because I can't imagine life without you."

A nod was too little. Not nearly big enough to explain the protective walls around her heart that were crumbling to dust. Washed away by a million-dollar rain and the love of a chef. Then her freed heart found what to say.

"Oh, city boy. Yes."

They were the happiest words she'd ever spoken in her life.

ABOUT THE AUTHOR

M. L. Buchman started the first of over 50 novels and now as many short stories while flying from South Korea to ride his bicycle across the Australian Outback. Part of a solo around the world trip that ultimately launched his writing career.

Military romantic suspense titles from his Night Stalker, Firehawks, and Delta Force series have been named American Library Association's *Booklist* "Top 10 Romance of the Year" in 2012, 2015 & 2016. His Delta Force series opener, *Target Engaged,* was a 2016 RWA RITA finalist. In addition to romance, he also writes thrillers, fantasy, and science fiction.

In among his career as a corporate project manager he has: rebuilt and single-handed a fifty-foot sailboat, both flown and jumped out of airplanes, designed and built two houses, and bicycled solo around the world.

He is now making his living as a full-time writer on the Oregon Coast with his beloved wife and is constantly amazed at what you can do with a degree in Geophysics. You may keep up with his writing and receive a free Starter Library by subscribing to his newsletter at www.mlbuchman.com.

Continue the conversation at:

www.mlbuchman.com

IF YOU ENJOYED THIS, YOU MIGHT
ALSO ENJOY:

"*A*lmost home, sweetie."

"Oh joy," Jessica Baxter tried to clamp down on her sarcasm. It was a bad habit that worked fine in her social set back in Chicago, but sounded more petty with each mile they drove toward the Oregon Coast. She slumped down in the passenger seat of her mom's baby-blue Toyota hybrid. It still had that new car smell. As much as she'd dreamed of owning a hot sports car some day, she knew that she was enough her mother's daughter that this was probably the exact sort of eminently sensible car she would buy when her VW Beetle finally gave up the ghost.

Just like her mom.

Maybe she'd get it in red to be at least a *little* different.

Jessica sighed again, keeping it to herself so that she wasn't being overly offensive. Her mother was one of the many reasons that she'd gone as far away as possible for college and did her best to rarely return—she didn't want to turn into her mother and it was too easy to imagine doing so if she'd stayed in the small town of Eagle Cove, Oregon.

They were like twins separated by twenty-two years. The two of them had been able to trade clothes since Jessica hit puberty and had shot up to match her mother's slender five-foot-ten. Other than a very brief mistake of dying her hair black as part of a tenth-grade dare, which had turned her fair complexion past goth and into bloodless vampire, they were both light blond.

The one part of twin-dom that she couldn't seem to pull off even though she wanted to was Mom's casual-chic. Monica Baxter was always dressed one step above the world around her; not fancy, just really well put together. The closest Jessica ever managed was Bohemian-chic which wasn't really the same thing, but she'd learned to make it her own. Of course, Bohemian was easier on the budget and often available in consignment stores which had only reinforced her chosen style.

Jessica did her best to not regress as they drove up into the Coast Range that separated the beach towns from the rest of Oregon...and failed miserably at that as well. She felt as if she was rapidly descending back toward being a pouty, pre-pubescent twelve from her present urban and worldly thirty-two.

Why did crossing the Oregon state line always take twenty years off her intelligence?

Maybe it was only Coast County. Because of the landscape the Oregon Coast felt incredibly far from anywhere. The Coast Range topped out at a mere four thousand feet high, but only a half dozen passes made it through the three hundred mile range of rugged hills that separated the beaches from the broad farming and industrial realm of the Willamette Valley. The interior of the state might as well be in a whole other country for how little it had in common with where she'd grown up.

"It's so strange being back here," Jessica rolled down the window and sniffed at the air. The scents were so rich and varied that they tickled. Bright with pine. Musty with undergrowth. Damp. A first hint of the sea.

"Well, it has been four years, honey. That's bound to make it seem a bit odd. But I'm so glad that you came."

"Me too, Mom." Better. She managed to say it as if she meant it, however unlikely that might be. Chicago fit her like a…but it didn't. The city was…something she was not going to give a single thought to for the next eight days. If she didn't fit there and she didn't want to fit in Eagle Cove, Oregon, then where did she belong?

Jessica breathed in deeply this time, trying to clear her thoughts with the fresh air of the Coast Range and nearly choked herself on how green everything smelled. The harsh slap of the mountains was almost an affront. The two-lane road dove and twisted along narrow corridors sliced through towering spruce and Douglas fir trees. The babies were sixty feet high along the shoulder as the car twisted up toward the pass; the mother trees behind them were much, much bigger.

And it wasn't just the trees that were lush. As they wound deeper into the Coast Range, each branch became covered with mosses and lichens. It soothed her eyes, so used to towering concrete and glass, with a living tapestry of greens, golds, and silvers. Beneath the trees grew an impenetrable tangle of salal and scrub alder. Old barns on the roadside didn't have shingle roofs, they had moss ones; some of them were covered inches thick. Many RVs, left unattended in front yards for too long, had a sheen of green growth on their north side.

"I really want to hate this," the Coast Range had three times the rainfall of Chicago, often surpassing a hundred inches a year. She expected to feel the weight of all that biomass crashing down on her shoulders, but instead she noticed the start of a disconcerting lightness as if coming home was a good thing. Jessica did *not* like that encroachment of pending appreciation, perhaps even enjoyment, upon her *true* feelings. "But it smells so good. Like sunshine and new growth."

Her mother's laugh was amused as they twisted along the two-lane road slowly climbing up a narrow valley.

"I didn't mean to say that out loud."

"But you said it anyway."

"Not helping, Mom."

Thankfully her mother's laugh said that she had understood Jessica's response as a tease. Which it mostly was, partly.

Jessica didn't *want* to like coming back to the coast. She didn't have small-town dreams. That was the main reason she'd left Eagle Cove. She had big city dreams...which weren't exactly coming together for her despite her efforts over the last fourteen years. But scurrying home wasn't going to fix those. And the selection of men in such a tiny town was, to put it kindly, pitiful. Puffin High—

Why they hadn't called it Eagle High in Eagle Cove was a subject of heated debate by every single class.

Puffin High's problem was that she knew every male her age all too well. The only reason the town had its own high school was that it was too far away from everywhere else for busing to make sense. Her senior class had just thirty-four students. Grades seven through twelve numbered under two hundred. And she knew far too much about every single one of them.

Even more obnoxiously invasive on her sense of right and wrong, instead of dumping rain, it was a perfect day. The sun sparkled down revealing a thousand shades of green in the living walls that lined the road. The air coming through the open window was thick with pine sap and the gentle tang of rotting undergrowth. There was so much oxygen in the air that it made her feel a little giddy.

Yes, a perfect day, if she'd been alone...and still in Chicago.

"I could have rented a car and saved you the drive, Mom." Actually, her budget had been thrilled when her mother had offered to come and fetch her. Also, once in Eagle Cove there wasn't a lot of use for a car, except when the rain poured down. The whole town was only a few miles long and she could walk most places she'd want to go. As if there were any old haunts that she'd care to revisit. She'd made good her escape to Northwestern University's School of Journalism at eighteen but every now and then the town still sucked her back.

"Nonsense, honey. I'm always glad to drive up and get you. Besides, I needed a few things for the wedding."

"How many is this?" As if she didn't know. It took much of her journalistic skill to keep "that judgmental tone" out of her voice. Something her early teachers had dinged her on until she'd learned to eradicate it. But since she was regressing as they neared the coast, it was trying to make a comeback.

"Number four."

"Why, Mom?"

"Because I love the man." Her mother actually glanced away from the road to offer her a scowl. "I'd have thought that was obvious."

"It is. But you've divorced him three times."

"Because *your* father can drive a woman bat-shit crazy without even trying." They giggled together because that was an absolute truth about Ralph Baxter.

"I meant, why marry him again? You're both legal age, your daughter lives in Chicago," and wouldn't complain if she lived on another planet entirely. "Just shack up together. Then you

227

can lock the door whenever Daddy becomes too much like himself."

Ralph Baxter was always getting caught up in monster projects. Without a word of warning he would suddenly rip out the entire kitchen, once on the morning before a dinner party, because he'd thought of a better way to design it. Or he'd start building a new boat from scratch in the middle of the driveway, rather than in the generous side yard, which blocked parking near the house for months.

"Oh, honey. I'm too old fashioned a girl to 'just shack up'."

Which was almost believable, even in the twenty-first century. To hear Aunt Gina—who despite her name was as not-Italian as a pastrami sandwich—tell it, Monica Lamont had chosen Ralph Baxter as her sweet sixteen love. She'd never even shopped around. How 1950s was that for a woman who hadn't even been born then?

Jessica had shopped plenty, or at least window-shopped. She'd found only a few men worth the cost of trying on for size. Definitely not a one worth taking home to keep. She might look like her mom, all blond, tall, and waiflike—which she kind of hated though the men seemed to like it—but inside she wanted to be like Aunt Gina.

Luigina Lamont looked nothing like her twin sister...or Grandpop...or much like Grandma for that matter. She was a statuesque redhead, in every voluptuous sense of the word and completely lived up to her name: Luigina meant "Famous Warrior." Her merry laugh slapped up against you at the most unexpected moments and constantly poked at your ticklish spot until you were curled up on the couch begging her to stop. Unlike Mom and her serial marriages to the same man, Gina brought home plenty yet had only tried to keep one.

That "unholy disaster" (as the family tales described it) had produced Natalya Daphne Lamont—Jessica's three-hour-older (and Natalya never let her forget it) first cousin and best friend.

Just like Gina, Natalya didn't look like either her mom or Gina's brief husband. Maybe that was hereditary on that side of the family to balance out how much Jessica resembled her own mom and their shared grandma. Jessica had a sudden flash of her own future daughter looking just like her...and felt the world spin just a little at thinking about children at all.

"If I hadn't seen her come out between my legs myself," Aunt Gina would announce loudly, "I'd have thought I adopted the kid. Maybe I signed up to be a surrogate then forgot all about it."

Mom blushed every time Aunt Gina let that one loose in public, without understanding that if she didn't, Aunt Gina would have stopped long ago.

"Such an exotic offspring deserves an exotic name. Natalya for the Russian Bond girl in *GoldenEye* and Daphne for du Maurier the romance writer, *not* the nymph who had to turn into a tree to escape that lusty jerk Apollo." The fact that *GoldenEye* hadn't come out until Natalya had already been in grade school hadn't changed Aunt Gina's story one bit.

Maybe Jessica's own child would be lucky and take after Cousin Natalya who was slender like Jessica, but had all of the curves Jessica had prayed for throughout her teenage years but never been granted. Natya was also dusky skinned like a permanent tan and leggy like some French model. Jessica's and her mom's fairy light hair and Aunt Gina's mass of red curls had been transformed to a smooth cascade of dark chestnut on her cousin. Yet she and Jessica felt like twins from different mothers: one light, one dark, but much the same on the inside.

Jessica smiled at the sign as they cleared Maxine Pass: eight-hundred and three feet according to the sign. The "three" always made her laugh. It was like Becky, her other best friend from Eagle Cove, firmly insisting that she as five-four "and a quarter" as if it made a difference.

Maxine Pass was technically Maxwell Pass. Or it had been until the day that Aunt Gina had declared it just wasn't right for all of the passes to have male names merely because men were the ones who drew the maps back in the 1800s.

For her sixteenth birthday Jessica hadn't received her first kiss —already happened a year before—or gotten laid—two more years until that event. Instead, she'd been recruited for a "Mission!" At two in the morning on their shared birthday, Aunt Gina drove her and Natalya up to repaint the Maxwell Pass highway sign to Maxine. It had become a tradition that every time the highway department changed it back to Maxwell, the three of them would have a two a.m. gals' outing and change the sign once again. The highway department had given up years ago. A few of the more recent road maps had even changed the name.

"Girl Power!" they'd shout after each time they finished repainting the sign, usually about three a.m. Then they'd break out the thermos of hot chocolate and drink it from a shared cup while they admired their handiwork by moonlight.

One time Martin, the town cop, had shown up while they were doing it. Jessica and Natalya had ducked, but Gina hadn't slowed down a single brush stroke.

"Thought it would be you," Martin had observed through his open car window, obviously talking to Gina.

"Out of your jurisdiction, Marty," had been Aunt Gina's awesomely calm reply. She had always been Jessica's hero, but that totally clinched it. The town limits had been left far behind.

He'd joined them for the hot chocolate and had a good laugh at the "Girl Power!" chant.

Today Jessica just waved hello to the sign as they crested the pass and began their descent.

"Didn't you ever bust out, Mom?" Jessica tried to imagine her doing so, but couldn't quite conjure it up in her mind.

"Bust out? You mean cheat on your father? Never!"

"But what about between times, when you were divorced? That wouldn't be cheating."

Monica Lamont's lips thinned as she tightened her jaw and

finally shook her head in a sharp little snap. "I was only living in the other end of the house."

"What about with Dad? You and Dad could just...you know?" The thought of her parents having sex was uncomfortable enough that she couldn't quite say it aloud.

"Ralph says that if I feel so strongly about things that I have to divorce him, then I shouldn't be expecting any special concessions while we are divorced."

Jessica felt she had to side with Dad on that one. He'd become used to his wife's antics, but that meant he didn't get any either in the interims. No wandering for him—it had always been clear that Ralph Baxter was absolutely crazy about Monica Lamont. Jessica felt kind of sorry for him.

"Wait. You mean you haven't had sex in two years?" This latest was their longest divorce yet.

Again that little snap that made Jessica's neck ache in sympathy. Mom moved to the right as the road added a climbing lane to reach the six-hundred and thirty-four foot (not quite so much bragging) Rogue Pass. That name at least made perfect sense by Oregon standards...because it wasn't anywhere near either of the two separate Rogue Rivers in Oregon. A half dozen cars roared past. Mom always drove exactly at the speed limit instead of the nearly mandatory ten over that prevailed throughout the state.

"So you're waiting for the wedding night?"

This time her mom's nod was a little sad.

"I'm sure tomorrow will be a great night, Mom."

At that she smiled brilliantly. "If the past three are anything to judge by, yes, it will be. It's just too bad we had to delay it."

"Delay it? Wait! What?" Jessica bolted upright in the car seat and almost throttled herself with her seatbelt. The wedding was supposed to be *tomorrow*. She'd secretly planned on staying just one day past the wedding, and then catching the Airporter Express that wandered through the small coastal towns once a day. She'd already warned Natalya to expect her in Portland for the rest of the week until her flight back to the Windy City.

"Well, we were meeting with Judge Slater about the ceremony. As he performed the first three weddings…"

Jessica resisted pointing out that he'd done all three divorces as well. Maybe her Oregon civility was coming back. Yeah, like a toothache.

"…and he had all of the old records in a file; even had the new marriage license pre-filled out, the dear man. However, it turns out that the first time we were married was on July fourteenth, not July seventh as I had remembered. You know how your father loves the cycle of things. So we moved the wedding to next weekend to coincide properly with the original. I knew you already had your plane tickets, so I didn't see any point in telling you."

Didn't see any point? She'd have moved heaven and earth to— Actually, her mother was right because she'd purchased the cheapest non-refundable, non-changeable tickets she could find.

A week! She was going to be trapped in Eagle Cove from Friday morning until Sunday morning nine days later? Oh, that was so bad.

"I can't believe that we celebrated it wrong for all of those years," her mother continued, completely oblivious to the panic she'd just created. "The seventh was the date that had always stuck in my head for our anniversaries."

Mom's dropping voice spoke volumes. She'd always been terrible at keeping a secret.

"So why *did* the seventh stick in your head?" Jessica kept it as casual as she could, rather than rubbing it in that her mom always gave up whatever she was trying to hide. It must be the journalist in her coming out: ask the question and then wait patiently for a reply. Not pushing was another change between them. Jessica didn't feel as if she was mellowing with age, but perhaps she was. Being disillusioned at thirty-two was no more newsworthy than it had been at twelve or twenty-two; but a woman shouldn't mellow until...well, maybe a hundred-and-two.

On the back side of Rogue Pass, Mom concentrated on the winding descent. Jessica waved at a massive Roosevelt elk who grazed in a small clearing beside the road. Coming back to Eagle Cove might be only one step better than a nightmare, but it was a very scenic one. The road was soon joined by a stream rushing in a deep ravine on Jessica's side of the road; the problem was that they were both racing in the wrong direction—toward, not away from, her childhood home. The stream tumbled along almost as fast as they did down toward Eagle River which would eventually define the end of town where it opened into a broad bay before it reached the sea.

No one quite knew why the bay had been named a cove, but it showed that way on even the oldest maps. It gave the town an off-kilter personality to Jessica's mind, as if it was always seeking to find its true identity. No bridge crossed the Eagle to the wilderness area on the other bank. To reach that required either a boat or an hour drive back up to Highway 101, across the river, and then a long crawl back to the Coast over marginal logging roads.

"C'mon, Mom, give." Since not pushing at her mother had failed, Jessica went with regressing and shifted to the wheedling tone she'd perfected as a child. She might hate herself in the morning for slipping back into it, but it always worked. Sure enough, her mom gave in right on cue.

"July seventh was the one time we cheated. We didn't actually wait for our first wedding night," the blush on her mother's fair skin was almost bright enough to lighten the dark corridor between the towering trees. "Your father made it amazing. But that's also the day I became pregnant, though I didn't know it until after the wedding. All those years I was celebrating the wrong date. That's why we never fool around unless we're married."

"Sounds like you were celebrating *exactly* the right date, Mom."

She tried to pin down the exact date of her own first time, but it hadn't been all that memorable. Good, but "earth-shattering" was just another one of those 1950s' myths that didn't happen in the twenty-first century. Except, apparently, for her own mother. How unfair was that.

"Maybe," her mom admitted, "but we're going to get married on the fourteenth anyway."

"So, I'm a bastard?" Not that it bothered her, but she couldn't resist needling her mother about it. Maybe she hadn't matured all that much.

"Yes dear, but only by one week. I swear I didn't know." This time Jessica heard that her mom's confession was a sigh at Jessica's question rather than sounding contrite. Maybe it was time Jessica grew up a bit—even when in Eagle Cove.

"Does Aunt Gina know about all this?"

"No one does, except your father and now you. You only arrived three days early, which was actually four days late. No one gave it any thought."

Excellent! To hell with being mature. Aunt Gina would love the extra dirt for teasing her sister and Jessica couldn't wait to be the one to tickle her aunt's funny bone.

~

It had been another long morning of assisting the Judge—always with a capital J. Monday through Friday, six a.m. to ten, Greg Slater helped his father. At first it had been something that Greg did to help out, but he'd come to like the simple routines and structure to his mornings.

"Ready?" he called back to the kitchen as he did every day. There was no real need to ask. The big old clock hung high on the wall said it was exactly six a.m. and the Judge was a very punctual man.

But Greg looked for the solemn nod before moving out into the diner and flicking on the fluorescents, "The Puffin Diner" sign, and the porch lights. There wasn't much need for the last, sunrise was twenty minutes ago, but the sun itself wouldn't clear the Coast Range ridge until at least six-thirty. For now, Beach Way, the town's main street, was mostly cool shadows and darkened buildings.

The bell mounted on the back of the door rang almost right away as Cal Mason Jr. came in. Greg had already set a mug of coffee on the counter for him. Cal ran the Blackbird Bakery and was hours into his day. Five days a week he was as punctual as the Judge. Cal Sr. wouldn't be in for a few hours yet.

"Your standard, Cal?"

"Double," though Greg knew that was a joke. Cal was one of the few men in town big enough that he could have eaten two of the Judge's generous portions. Six-two and as powerful as a bull-dozer; his hands dwarfed the coffee mug.

Because Cal sat at the six-stool wooden counter, the Judge was less than five feet away through the broad service window that connected the dining room with the kitchen, but he waited for Greg to fill out the order slip and clip it to the spinner.

It was Greg's own damn fault. The diner's service had been a bone of contention, or rather "lengthy negotiation" just as most things were with the Judge.

"They can pick up their own damn plates at the window. Coffee pot is right there behind the counter where anyone who wants a refill can get their own."

Greg had won that round by subterfuge. He'd numbered the tables and then only put the numbers on the order slips, making it impossible for the Judge to boom out with "Veronica, your order is up." Customers had slowly adapted to not having to leave their tables for every little thing.

At least Greg thought he'd won, until a full three weeks later his father had winked at him while sliding across a short stack with bacon and hash browns for Karen Thompson, "Like I don't know who orders what on a Thursday."

Now the Judge wouldn't cook a thing without a proper ticket. Well, he'd cook it, but he wouldn't serve it no matter how busy or harried Greg was.

Cal's plate came up less than thirty seconds after Greg hung the ticket just as it did every morning: western omelet, hash browns, farm sausage, and English muffin. The last was about the only kind of bread that Cal didn't bake.

"Gotta have something that I can order out for and enjoy without baking it myself."

Greg moved the plate across to the counter and refilled Cal's half-drained mug of coffee.

There wasn't much call for a judge in a town the size of Eagle Cove. Semi-retired for the last five years, he no longer spent three days a week in Newport to sit on the bench as he had throughout Greg's childhood. Instead he'd set up a small court-room in town. He mainly handled family matters like marriages and estates, and fines for drunk and disorderly tourists who soon learned that Judge Slater was a fierce protector of the town. There was only the occasional speeding ticket—no matter how hard Martin the cop tried to catch someone. The town was perched against the Pacific Ocean at the dead end of a winding two-lane that had left the coastal highway a dozen miles back; it had enough "Sharp Curves Ahead" signs to quell even the most lead-footed of souls.

So, "for something to keep me busy," the Judge held office hours only in the afternoons because his weekday mornings were all spent working as a short-order cook. And ever since Greg's return to Eagle Cove three years ago, he'd been his father's front-of-house man: waiter, cashier, and busboy.

The Puffin Diner had been a near derelict before his dad had bought and reopened it. It was a classic small town place built to serve the early morning fishermen, especially those returning from a long night's work on the offshore shoals; it was little changed over the last ninety years.

The clapboard building stood high enough on a heavy stone foundation that even the Christmas storm flood of 1964 had crested two steps below the front entry. It was one of the only structures on the town's main street that didn't have a street-level entry. All of the other businesses that had existed then had high-water lines drawn halfway or more up their walls. The Grouse Hardware store, the lowest spot in town close beside the docks, had a small wooden plaque of a fish screwed in just above the main door lintel. It was bright yellow with "Dec 22, 1964" painted on it in tropical blue—it was generally considered to be a little boastful, but old man Jaspar refused to tone down the color scheme that he'd painted on that fish in his youth.

The interior of the diner was so retro that it would have been ironic-modern if it wasn't quite so authentic. The steel-edged tables of blue Formica were scuffed nearly colorless by the thousands of plates and silverware settings that had been slid across their surfaces over the years. The chairs' red leather was sun-faded and the old chrome had pitted with rust from the salt air, making them uncomfortable to the touch without quite being painful. The linoleum floor had been replaced...back in the 1980s when mauve and hunter green had been trendy colors. The six round stools bolted to the floor at the counter squealed every time someone spun on or off them. The kitchen was authentic right down to the large service window, the steel spinner rack for order slips dangling in one corner, and the big grill and burners in the back. The scents of eggs, hash browns, and frying bacon filled the main street each morning enticing all passersby to come and find comfort food.

Ralph Baxter and Manny McCall came in and took their usual spot by the corner window. They'd have tourists out fishing off their boats within the hour and were both after black coffee and tall stacks.

At first Greg had resented serving the Judge's fare—it was as invariable as his father. Scrambles, omelets, pancakes—no waffles because the iron had broken the same day Mom had died and he couldn't seem to fix it and wouldn't let Greg try. The pancakes were big and fluffy. The very crispy hash browns were not an option; they were on every single plate, even with the pancakes. Farm fresh sausage or bacon was the other staple on every plate—not that it was a choice. Everyone received whichever Carl Parker had delivered the day before along with the eggs.

All of Greg's efforts to vary the oatmeal recipe, served with bacon or sausage and hash browns of course, had been in vain. The Judge served only rolled oats—not steel cut—with sliced, not diced, dried apricots and diced, not sliced, fresh apple. Whether brown sugar or maple syrup was used to sweeten it was wholly up to the customer; local honey was also available.

Omelets were the Judge's real specialty and by six-thirty there were already a dozen slips up for them. Omelets were the only dish where variations were allowed. He offered them with cheese, mushrooms, or smoked salmon fillings. Never all three of course, because there were limits to what was proper.

The Puffin Diner mostly served coffee. Greg's sole triumph at adjusting the menu had been when he managed to switch from Dad's "fresh ground" granules purchased in large plastic tubs to fresh-ground French roast. Tea or hot chocolate were the only other options, but asking for marshmallows with the latter was frowned upon unless you were a kid—the whipped cream came out of a spray can.

They'd fought royally over the Judge's inflexibility, but of course fighting over things was a tradition in the Slater household. Not that voices were ever raised, because that would never do. The few times Greg had tried that tactic he'd been ruled "Out of Order" and banished from the dinner table: the sole forum for Slater "discussions." With Ma gone to cancer three years before—Greg's original reason for returning to Eagle Cove—he didn't have the heart to "force" the Judge into driving him from the table after that first time. When he'd been remanded to the kitchen two weeks after Mom's funeral, he'd made the mistake of glancing back as he'd moved off to finish his meal. His father had looked old, sad, and impossibly alone.

Greg hadn't been able to face living in the big old house out on the beach, so he'd moved into the guest house. Once he finally understood that no number of cogent debates were going to sway the Judge, Greg had let the menu go. It had been unchanged in either content or price in the last decade—other than the wavy black line of magic marker through the "Waffles (with blueberries when in season)."

Greg had been on the verge of leaving town when the Judge sat him down at the big house's dining room table. Ma Slater had been in the ground for a month. Greg knew he didn't really have anywhere to go, he'd learned all he was going to from the banquet chef at the Sorrento Hotel in Seattle and there weren't any top positions open for an untested executive chef wanting to make his mark. He didn't have the capital to make his own splash, not in the insanely competitive restaurant markets in the big cities. But he'd find something.

"Been watching you, son. Been tasting your food," the Judge had tapped a fork on his dinner plate. Greg had roasted a pair of fresh-caught trout in hazelnut butter with a dressing of spring greens and homemade basil vinegar. Though Greg had cooked half the meals since Ma's funeral—"fair is fair" the Judge had declared—it was the first time his father had spoken of it.

"Uh-huh," Greg had gone for a neutral acknowledgement. He knew the Judge hated such prevarications, but Greg didn't know where this was heading and went for caution.

"This is good. Damn good."

Greg hadn't been able to offer even a neutral grunt over his surprise at the Judge's remark.

"Still needs some work, though."

Before Greg could snap at him about what did a man who scrambled eggs and ruled on law know about fine cuisine, the Judge continued.

"You need more seasoning," and he aimed a fork at Greg's chest, "and I'm not talking about salt. Your technique is the best I've ever seen, but I don't taste anything special. There's nothing here that isn't in any other fine restaurant. You need time to find your own voice, not some other chef's."

"My own voice?" But he didn't need to ask, he'd heard it a thousand times growing up.

The Judge looked down at the trout, one of the only times he'd ever said anything without looking at whoever he was addressing straight in the eye, "Your mother taught me that."

Ma had been a painter, a good one. Her seascapes had sold in galleries up and down the coast. Tillamook, Newport, Gold Beach, they all snapped up as much as she could produce and was willing to let go of—Grosbeak Gallery in town had always gotten first pick though. She'd often talked about finding your voice in your art so that it didn't look like everyone else's.

"So, here is the deal I'm offering you."

Greg knew that it wouldn't be open to negotiation; no one negotiated one of Judge Slater's "deals."

"The diner is mine on weekdays from six to ten every morning. I'd like you to stay as my assistant because you're good at it. That pays rent here at the house, a small salary, and we split the tips. What you do with the diner for the rest of the time, that's up to you."

And for three years, Greg had stayed in Eagle Cove and searched for his own voice. In the first year, he'd never cooked for anyone but himself and his father—who never again spoke about the food itself. Then one night Greg had invited a couple of buddies from high school who were still in town to the diner, as a test audience. Word got out about how good it was and folks had started asking when he'd do it again.

He'd eventually started "Irregular Friday Dinners at The Puffin." He only opened when he had a new meal to test. It was all *prix fixe*, fixed price—a twenty in the jar—and a set menu. After two years of those he felt almost ready to take his cooking out into the world; maybe spend a while as a pop-up restaurant —there and gone—rather than a full launch. He'd been saving his half of every morning tip and every goddamned cent for when he went back to the cities. At first he'd simply been trying to be better by the time he left Eagle Cove, but he'd become obsessed with finding and perfecting his "chef's voice." He wanted it to be so clear that it was undeniable. When he went back to Seattle, no one would label him the protégé of Charlene at Maximilien's or Angelo at The Tuscan Hearth. He'd be his own—

The old brass bell screwed into the top of the diner's front door rang like a small ship was coming into port. Morning service peaked as usual around eight and had now tapered off to just a few lingering diners.

Greg glanced at the big-face clock above the cash register— 9:57—and suppressed a groan. Judge's rule was that if you were in the door by ten, you could take as long as you wanted. If it was ten sharp plus a second, you were turned away—"Fair is fair." Maybe they'd be quick; he'd had an idea for a savory roulade that he wanted to try out.

Greg turned back and had to blink, then blink again. The morning sunlight shone through the front window and silhou-etted two dazzling blondes, their hair practically set afire by the sunlight streaming in from behind them.

Then his eyes adapted as they moved farther into the room.

Mrs. Baxter who was soon to be Mrs. Baxter once again.

And a woman he hadn't seen since the day she'd left for college, but he'd know anywhere.

Jessica matched his own five-ten and her hair, instead of being the waist-long waterfall he'd remembered, now floated about her shoulders in choppy wisps that framed a face of high cheekbones, full lips, and eyes that sparkled with mischief.

Halfway across the old linoleum floor, she stopped and looked at him.

"Greggie's gaping, Mom."

And he couldn't do a thing about it.

Available at fine retailers everywhere
Return to Eagle Cove

Other works by M. L. Buchman:

SIGN UP FOR M. L. BUCHMAN'S
NEWSLETTER TODAY

and receive:
Release News
Free Short Stories
a Free Book

Do it today. Do it now.
www.mlbuchman.com/newsletter

60915945R00151

Made in the USA
Middletown, DE
05 January 2018